PRAISE FOR TIN

For *One Step Too Far*

'A haunting psychological thriller . . . believable yet shocking with a great twist, this is well worth a read.'

The Sun

'A whip-smart thriller that keeps you guessing right up until the final shocking twist.'

Mirror

'Intriguing . . . dreamily tense . . . a really absorbing read.'

USA Today

For *When We Were Friends*

'Clever, intriguing, chilling – and utterly impossible to put down. Tina Seskis is proving herself to be master of the twist.'

Grazia UK

'One of the world's leading experts at pulling the wool over readers' eyes until the very end.'

Sophie Hannah

For *The Honeymoon*

'Everyone's going to be talking about the twists and turns of *The Honeymoon*.'

Good Housekeeping

'Endlessly gripping . . . It's a stomach-flipping humdinger of a thriller.'

Heat

'Will keep you on the edge of your seat.'

Prima

HOPE
CLOSE

ALSO BY TINA SESKIS

One Step Too Far
When We Were Friends
The Honeymoon
Home Truths

HOPE
CLOSE

TINA SESKIS

LAKE UNION
PUBLISHING

Text copyright © 2020 by Tina Seskis
All rights reserved.

Published by Lake Union Publishing, Seattle

www.apub.com

Amazon, the Amazon logo, and Lake Union Publishing are trademarks of Amazon.com, Inc., or its affiliates.

ISBN-13: 9781542093606
ISBN-10: 1542093600

Cover design by The Brewster Project

Printed in the United States of America

For Connie

PART ONE

AUGUST/SEPTEMBER

Chapter 1

I end the call to my solicitor, hand the phone to the waiting attendant, and gaze out across the pink-tinged Malagan hills. It's done. I've done it. I've bought somewhere to live. Whether it will prove to be the right place, the right thing to have done, is anybody's guess – but I have to do something, go somewhere. It seems it's time for me to officially begin the starting again. At last.

It feels so strange having bought a house, and especially this one. For a start I've only ever been shown around it via FaceTime, without even having had a chance to view it. It's ugly, but I don't care. The opportunity arose, and I've taken it. My solicitor tried to dissuade me, but he doesn't understand my reasonings, of course, and so once I'd decided, that was it. It's amazing how quickly things can get done when the right lawyers and enough cash are involved. And besides, I'd wanted somewhere quiet, and private, and although the house itself isn't perfect by any means, it will do. And what's perfection anyway, after such devastation? It was too extraordinary an opportunity to pass over. Perhaps it won't be for forever, but it feels like the right decision, for now. Hiding in plain sight, isn't that the term?

I lean back against my poolside sun lounger, my mind threatening overload suddenly, soft tendrils of panic beginning to seep out, as if permeating like smoke through a grille in my chest cavity.

As I force myself to remain still, eyes fixed on the scenery beyond, the late summer sun starts to soothe me. There's something about this part of Spain that touches me, heals me, and I'm glad now that I agreed to come here. During the day the hills are a dusty green, barren and parched-looking, but at sunset they come alive, and the way the light is shimmering on them now feels almost as if they are inching towards me, threatening to engulf me in a tide of rose-coloured rock. Entomb me perhaps.

I'm finding rehab a strange place. From the road the house itself looks like any other, and even its name, Villa Rosa, belies the fact that its occupants are most certainly not on holiday. (There are all types in here, but the one thing we have in common is that we have money. Fees of twenty thousand pounds a week ensure that much.) For a start, almost no one is allowed out, me included. But at least I'm in Stage Two of my recovery now, meaning I get to wander around the wonderful gardens, sit by the pool – although at night I still have to sleep in my austere single room, devoid of TV or electronic devices, with a nurse sitting discreetly in the corridor. I still have to rise at five every morning, to meditate in the pavilion by the carp pond, and then spend the day doing chores, or endlessly talking about my feelings, via both group and individual therapy, and sometimes even with a horse, for Christ's sake. Even after dinner there's still no respite, seeing as I'm forced to sit through a supposedly mind-expanding lecture, and then end the day with one last meditation session that never finishes before nine o'clock. Afterwards I fall into bed far too exhausted for any potential vices, which is one way to get clean, I suppose. And on the plus side this is a safe, warm prison, womb-like almost, infinitely preferable to the real thing. The only difference is that in here even my thoughts are under siege. It's both exhausting and confusing. Am I meant to forget? Or move on? And is there a difference?

I haul myself to my feet, walk down the sloping garden towards the giant cacti that have been planted beyond the lawn, my leg twinging even after all this time. I can feel eyes on me from behind, or maybe I'm imagining it, but I'm determined not to turn around and give them the satisfaction of seeing me check. When I reach the cactus garden, I clamber up on to an artistically arranged cluster of boulders and look out across the tree-swamped valley towards the now-greying hills. The wire fences are discreet, but they're there, a hundred feet or so away. Real prison had felt more honest in a way. In there it had been merely about raw survival. Nothing had been dressed up, sanitised. In there they'd all known what I'd done. They'd despised me, of course, but at least the disgust had been genuine.

I hear his voice, crying, begging me to stop. See the fear in his little face as I turn and laugh at him. The scene is as vivid as ever. It comes whenever I threaten to forgive myself. It comes to punish me.

I turn abruptly, and head back across the grass towards the villa. When I reach the pool, I stretch my arms above my head, my hands in prayer position, sit down on my lounger again. I wonder what these people would make of me if they knew who I am. It feels odd not being recognised, and in some ways I even miss it. Not the notoriety, of course; just the feeling of being unique, singular. Special. It was the most addictive drug I'd ever experienced. But according to one of the books I read in jail everyone thinks they're special, and maybe we all are, in our own way. No one thinks they're evil, though. No. Apparently even the most depraved perpetrators of the most heinous crimes refuse to believe they're evil, and it seems self-delusion is an integral, perhaps necessary, part of the human condition.

I sigh and the air feels dry and vacant as I breathe it out, stare towards the mute, knowing hills. Beyond the valley there's no one. No roads, no houses. Not even a bird can be seen in the sky. It's as if there's part of the canvas missing, as if my focus is too narrow, blinkered, and it causes a rapier-sharp zing in my heart. For all the world I might as well be alone, entirely alone. Once I get out of here it will be time to go back to England permanently; move on, try to forge a new life for myself. Try to forgive myself for my past mistakes. Maybe it's an insane idea, but I'm praying that Hope Close will be the place. I just have to play it slowly, take things step by step. I just have to give it time. After all, apart from money, time is all I have left.

Chapter 2

Layla

Layla kissed him goodbye for the final time, and then she turned around and left him, although she knew he was still standing there, watching her go. Her heart filled up, and then it just kept on going, overflowing with dark viscous agony, the pressure in her head extraordinary – and she knew that if she turned he would see her tears, and that just wouldn't be fair on him. She felt like a part of her was being detached, like an amputation, or a death, and although she'd known it would be difficult, she hadn't realised it would be quite like this. Charles was walking beside her, his arm around her shoulders in an outwardly supportive way, but really he was transporting her, literally propelling her, away from her son, giving her no choice. And, of course, that was where she was wrong. She did have a choice, and yet she had chosen passivity, and her complicity in this abomination was disgraceful and an insult to her label as mother. She was no mother. She was a monster.

Charles and Layla walked down the main staircase, left the building and crossed the car park to reach his latest Mercedes. As he clicked open the central locking, the clunk felt like an aural marker between then, and now. At last Layla risked a look backwards, but of course Henry wasn't there, swallowed as he'd been into the hungry belly of an institution that sucked in innocents, and spewed them out years later tough and damaged and unreachable. Charles had always told her that she was worrying unnecessarily whenever she tried to explain how she felt, and somehow she'd let her own opinions be subsumed by his family's traditions, and Charles's own will, and she was a coward.

The journey home was quiet and purring. Charles drove with that utter assurance that Layla used to find attractive. Now she found it psychopathic. She no longer knew how to reach her husband, and yet she needed to – he was all of Henry she had left. When she turned to look at Charles's profile she saw Henry's nose, yet older, her son's soft curves alcohol- and stress-hardened in his father. Layla couldn't think what to say, so she said nothing. She looked out of the window as the trees rushed by and on impulse tried to say hello to each one, like she had as a little girl, and when she was inevitably too slow and missed one she felt so sad for the tree, and she worried for her emotional state – as if her heart might be about to break, or else was moving into lockdown. Charles flicked on the radio, and there was a programme where people were talking earnestly about Brexit, but Layla didn't care, and she wished he would turn it off. He suggested they stop off for lunch at their local country pub, and she didn't like to tell him that she'd hate it there now, that the swings and the slide would taunt her that she had a child, yet did not have a child. That wouldn't even have occurred to Charles, of course, which only made her sadder. She kept wondering just how much she had let Henry down, and she could hardly bear to think what might happen that night if he cried for her or, God help him, wet the bed. She wasn't allowed to even ring him for two weeks. Cold turkey was their recommended approach, even though Henry was still only eight. He still liked her to tuck him in, rub his back before he went off to sleep. Her baby.

Charles sounded irritated, and Layla didn't know why. She stopped looking out at the countryside and gazed down at the knees of his suit trousers, which were a very finely woven midnight blue. She preferred staring at his legs to having to look at his face, see her son in him.

'I *said*, do you want to go to lunch?' The 'or not?' was left unspoken.

'Yes, fine, darling,' Layla said. She found sickly compliance the best way to deal with her husband when she was hating his guts, like now. Her segue from apathy into rage was yet another surprise to her. As if there was no telling what mood she might switch into. What words might yet come out of her mouth.

Charles put his foot down, making the car growl around the corners, like a low-slung panther, and the atmosphere was thick with the unspoken – and sometimes Layla wondered how they had ever made it to this point. She remembered how happy she'd once felt, when she and Charles had first been married and he'd been doting and relaxed still. It was only once she'd fallen pregnant that things had changed somehow. Layla had always imagined that their unborn baby would represent them, Charles and her, entwined in each other forever, and yet it seemed her husband hadn't felt like that. Even when Henry had been born, and he'd been the most beautiful baby ever (and although she knew that all mothers say that, in Henry's case it had been true), Charles hadn't seemed as enamoured with their son as he might have been.

And now? Now Layla didn't have a clue what Charles thought about anything. Sometimes she felt as if she were married to a stranger, and he frightened her in a way, and she found it so odd that they were here together, in this car, when once they hadn't even known each other. When once she hadn't known anything about him. Ten years ago she hadn't even met him. Henry had been nothing. No one. An explosion of cells still waiting to happen.

She and Charles had led totally separate lives that had somehow concertinaed into each other's, when they so easily might not have done. 'Turn A Different Corner', wasn't that the song? It could have been written for them.

Layla gazed sightlessly out of the window again, recalling the day she and Charles had met, trying to remember how she'd felt, but it was as if she were looking down from a great height at a different person, in a different life. Her stress levels had been sky-high, she remembered that much. She'd been running late for a meeting, due to a combination of polite failure on her part to cut short her eternally verbose boss, followed by a rare, anxiety-induced inefficiency in getting her presentation uploaded on to a memory stick. And so when she'd jumped out of a cab somewhere in the City, amidst an armada of shiny new buildings that seemed to be invading the sky, dominating the old, taking a wrecking ball to history, she'd been panicking at how late she was running. And that was surely why it was only once her meeting was over, when the receptionist presented her with a business card with a hand-written message on it, that Layla realised her purse was missing, and that she must have dropped it as she'd got out of the cab. She'd met the business card's owner outside a nearby café just a few minutes later, and as he'd handed over the purse, she'd blushed as she'd noticed that his eyes were as grey as the hair at his temples. She'd gabbled a thank you, and Charles had said that it was his pleasure, and then their eyes had locked again – and that had been the start of it.

Layla stared at her hands now and tried to recall the day, just a few months later, when he'd put the ring on her finger, and she willed herself to remember how it had been, but that day felt like dying time now. It was as if her hands were dead. She told her brain to tell her fingers to wiggle, and it did, and they did, and her engagement ring flicked its vapid light at her, and it looked belligerent almost, as if it despised her.

Charles swung his beast of a car into the pub car park, which was nearly full. The Mercedes was so large and shiny it looked out of place there, amongst the dusty Fords and French cars, as if it should have been chauffeur-driven by someone in a smart uniform and a peaked cap. When they entered the main bar Layla was embarrassed by Charles's manner, his innate expectation not to be kept waiting, and she smiled apologetically at the pig-tailed young barmaid, whose round wide face had switched from friendly to perplexed when Charles was so short with her. Layla yearned to feel the pressure lift from the top of her scalp, but the further away from Henry she felt, the more impossible it seemed. She wondered what her son was doing now, *right now*. She was glad that she'd been allowed to settle him into his dormitory, help him unpack, lay out his favourite teddies. One of the other boys had been sobbing as they'd left, ensconced in the matron's lap, restrained as well as comforted, and at least she hadn't had to witness Henry like that. Perhaps Henry and the other boys had already gone for lunch, would soon be doing the register for afternoon lessons – and as Layla felt the fear rising again, she forced herself to remember that little boys of that age wouldn't even recognise Henry's name, let alone remotely understand its significance. Charles had told Layla not to panic, and so panic she must not. Charles was in charge. He was the boss now, at least as far as Henry was concerned. Gone were the days when Charles would be late home from the office, and the atmosphere would be relaxed and casual, and she and Henry could curl up on the couch and watch TV, or play whatever games they wanted and read stories together. Now those evening hours waiting for Charles to come home would be spent alone. Layla apathetically wondered what she would do. She couldn't seem to broach the prospect of the gapingness of those future times right now. All she could think of was the impact the separation would have on her son. Now, and in his future, too. How might he cope with his very

11

identity, without her there to explain it? And what would boarding school do to him as a person? To his ability to love and be loved? Maybe it would ruin him.

'Sorry,' she said, when she realised that Charles had asked her what she was drinking. He looked merely surprised when she asked for a glass of white wine, large, and when he squeezed her hand, that surprised her in return. Already they were surprising each other in this new, child-free world they inhabited. Maybe Charles knew how she felt after all; thought she just needed time to get used to it – and perhaps he was right. Otherwise he wouldn't have insisted on it, surely. Why would he have wanted to hurt anyone? And Charles had definitely been thinking about her too, not purely what, in his opinion, was best for Henry. Voluntary work had been mentioned, and tennis lessons, and building projects. He'd suggested extending over the garage, but why should they bother? The house was big enough as it was. A mansion compared to their old place. But her husband was looking out for her, as much as he could do, and for that she supposed she ought to be grateful.

When the barmaid haphazardly poured wine into a glass in front of her, it was that overly dark colour that looked faintly poisonous, but Layla took a valiant sip. It was an overpriced Chardonnay and it was vile – too sweet, too warm – but it did its job well enough, and as she felt the edge rub off her panic, somewhere within her ribcage, it felt like it might even be a solution. Charles had ordered a pint of bitter, and there was something about the way he held it that made him look older than his fifty-three years, reminded her of her father somehow. The comparison appalled her.

'What time have you got to be at work?' she asked, to break the silence.

'Oh, I think I'll work from home this afternoon,' he said, and Layla was sure he meant for her to be grateful, but she wasn't. Charles looked at his watch, although Layla could tell he was trying not to. They sat quietly, she and the man she was married to, the father of her son, at a corner table in a cosy country pub that bustled with conviviality, and the world felt as grotesque and ill-defined to her as a murder scene. Layla gazed at her husband helplessly, but he didn't react, and she wasn't sure whether it was deliberate, or that he just didn't know how to. She couldn't even explain how she felt, except to say that the further she moved away from that moment of saying goodbye to Henry, in his red-piped navy blazer and his charcoal shorts, his long woollen socks, his eyes wide, his little chin quivering so bravely, the more bereft she was becoming, and the more it felt that the rubber band of her emotions was being pulled tighter, and tighter – until eventually, one day, it might snap.

Chapter 3

NICOLE

Charles's car was still not back. Or maybe it had already been and gone, and Charles had simply dropped Layla home and gone to work. Perhaps Nicole just hadn't heard it. She didn't like to interfere, but equally she wanted Layla to know that she was there for her, if she needed her. Nicole took another peep from behind her bedroom curtains across to Layla's house, but it still looked empty and Nicole was worried. Layla had seemed so fragile when Nicole had seen her coaxing Henry into the car this morning, but she guessed that if *she'd* only had one child, and that child was about to be shipped off to boarding school at such a young age, surely she'd have felt the same way. It was a ripped-apart feeling that Nicole recognised, and although she'd spent years trying to bury the sensation, for some reason it seemed stronger than ever today. It was almost as if Hope Close had an air of foreboding hanging over it, as if Layla and Charles were making a terrible, dreadful mistake. But what could she do? Nothing. It was none of her business.

Nicole placed her hands on her face, hard, shut her eyes, tried to squash her thoughts. She moved away from the window, and the rustle of heavy raw silk falling back into place made her jump, as if Layla had heard it too, but of course that would have been impossible. And yet if Layla *were* back, she might have seen the curtains move, a thought that made Nicole feel a little ashamed, as if she were spying on her neighbour, which she most definitely wasn't. It was simply that she felt sorry for Layla. After all, Nicole understood. She was finding it hard enough herself since the last of her own kids had left home, so that now it was just her and Ted for the first time in well over two decades. It was taking a renegotiation, that was for sure. Sometimes Nicole secretly wondered how Layla had even allowed Henry to be sent away. *Tradition, my arse*, she'd thought when Layla had tried to explain it, but of course she hadn't said anything. And yet sometimes not saying something makes it worse for both parties, makes the issue larger than it is somehow, the withholding of the opinion rendering the air more ripe with reproach. Nicole wondered if Layla had noticed.

Nicole sighed, went downstairs, lingered in the hallway. She checked the time. Two o'clock. Should she walk the dog now, or wait until Ted was home, try to persuade him to come with her? Maybe they could even stop off for a drink at the pub on the way back, do the crossword together. Ted would probably think she was mad if she even suggested it. He'd be tired, expecting his tea.

The spattering of rain starting on the conservatory roof made Nicole's decision for her. The dog seemed to have judged her mood, and immediately went from looking alert and hopeful to curling up on his bed, resigned and mournful. 'Don't you hang that guilt trip on me, Stanley,' she said. 'It's raining!'

Nicole walked over to the mirror by the front door and studied herself. Maybe the fact that she was nearing fifty was what was making her feel like this. Half a century. About to enter her sixth decade. Spreading outwards, slowly, insidiously. Her bones sinking, thinning. Her body gradually starting to die, from the inside, whilst heat poured out of her, as if trying to hurry up the process. Peri-menopausal, that was the official title. It was the beginning of the twilight of her life, and it was a shock to her. The past few decades had been kind to her – happy-enough marriage, although not without its moments; three good kids successfully sent off into the world. There was still time. She could still do something with her life. It didn't have to be all about walking the dog and going to spin classes and doing the washing and having Botox and spying on the neighbours and trying to think of things to say to Ted. No. There was something else out there, there must be. *Someone else.*

Nicole stopped herself, dragged her mind away from the precipice. Maybe she could get a job again, or even set up her own business. But who would want her, at her age? What work could she do on her own? The question made Nicole think of her daughter in London, and she wondered how she was getting on. It still felt odd that Tasha was up there alone in the bright lights, working in a bar in Shoreditch, about to start art college, when it seemed like just yesterday that Nicole had been walking her to her first day of school. She prayed that her youngest child was being careful, and was comforted by the knowledge that Tasha was savvy and streetwise, had been more than ready to flee the nest. She'd sounded so happy the other night on the phone, even though she'd made it clear her mother wasn't to call every day. It was fair enough, Nicole supposed. When she'd been Tasha's age there hadn't even been a phone in her house-share, so her mam had had to rely on a weekly call, or, God forbid, a letter. Nicole was glad that Tasha was so independent, certainly compared to some of her friends' children, who seemed incapable of earning their own money or coping without speaking to their mothers four times a day. It had never been like that in Nicole's time, when the day you left home was the day you were gone, never to return again – and, in Nicole's case, thank goodness for that.

Just as Nicole was thinking about what to try to conjure up for dinner, Ted rang, saying he'd be home late, as he needed to do a quote on a new job a good hour away. He'd grab something out, he said, and although Nicole was glad that she was released from that duty, it only added to her lack of purpose. She needed to find something to fill the days, especially now the nights were starting to draw in. She couldn't risk depression sneaking into these new holes in her routine, making itself comfortable. No, black moods were to be batted off in Nicole's book, usually by means of action. Sensible, pragmatic action. But what was the right action here? Go to more yoga classes? Have her nails done? Get another puppy? From what Nicole could tell, that's what lots of women did at this stage of life. But she already had Stanley, even if he was getting on these days. The thought panicked her suddenly, that Stanley's old age and death would be yet another thing she'd have to deal with alone. Ted loved the dog, of course he did, but it wouldn't hit him like it would her when Stanley went. Ted didn't spend the whole day with Stan. Stan didn't know Ted's every move. Stanley was an expert on both Nicole's wardrobe choices and her beauty routine – whether or not she put on lipstick predicating his chances of a walk; the picking up of her yoga mat making him immediately sulk off to his bed, knowing that she'd be out for well over two hours. Sometimes Nicole felt like she was being watched, all of the time . . . and it triggered her need to check on Layla. Again. Almost involuntarily, she went to the corner of the window and looked diagonally across the road, but Layla's drive was empty still. The whole close felt so quiet. Now that the Warners had divorced and moved out, no one even lived in the house immediately opposite – and it loomed, dark and brooding, like an ignored person at a party. Nicole wondered when it would ever sell. A fear was nipping at her edges, like a fish after flesh. Ted was a good bloke, but she couldn't even begin to tell him how worried she was about everything. He'd think her concerns about Layla were madness, wouldn't remotely understand how it made her feel . . . and anyway he was far too busy building extensions for insanely rich people, and he'd done all right for himself doing that, so she couldn't begrudge him. How could she complain when she enjoyed the trappings of it all? And yet somehow it wasn't enough. At least not any more.

Nicole went downstairs and took out a calorie-controlled ready meal from the freezer for her dinner. Briefly she imagined herself like Nigella, sucking seductively on her finger and glugging wine as she conjured up sumptuously fattening feasts for her and Ted, and laughed ruefully. If only. Instead her thoughts continued to circle around the void, as though if she stopped they would fall into themselves, collapse into nothingness, as hollow as an empty womb. Maybe getting a job was the best option after all, although she and Ted didn't need the money. Perhaps she could even go back to nursing. There might be some kind of refresher course she could do, as wasn't the NHS crying out for staff these days? Or maybe she could suggest to Ted that she start helping him in his business, with the admin, say, seeing as he was always so stretched. But he was a terrible delegator, and besides, they'd probably end up killing each other.

As Nicole put the kettle on, the house felt so empty. It had used to be such a sociable place, her kids and the Warners' kids always in and out of each other's houses. The detritus of family life was still here, but all the people were gone, and it reminded Nicole of that bride who got stood up on her wedding day – what was her name? *Miss Havisham.* Nicole had assumed she'd have one of her sons back home by now – but Jason had moved in with his girlfriend in Chertsey, and Sean was still up in Manchester, trying to get his break into TV. Nicole didn't have the heart to tell Sean how hard it was, without the right connections. And anyway, it was Sean's life; he'd always made that clear. There was no way Sean would ever have been bullied into going to boarding school – he'd have run away in a heartbeat.

Nicole halted her thoughts, reminded herself that it was none of her business what Layla and Charles did. Plus, she knew as well as anybody how alone Layla must be feeling right now, so the least she could do was support her friend instead of being all judgemental about it. Nicole was convinced that people could always tell what you thought about them, even if it was from across the other side of the road and through a total of twelve inches of brickwork. Her thoughts needed to stay kind, so they didn't seep down and poison her heart – or Layla's, for that matter. She needed to remember that no one was perfect, least of all her.

Nicole put a teabag into her outdated 'Keep calm, you're only forty' mug, and poured boiling water over it. She fished a teaspoon out of the cutlery drawer and squashed the bag against the side of the mug, watched it ooze blackly. As she plopped the spent bag into the food recycling bin she realised what her mini-project could be for now, and it made her feel better. *She'd make sure she was there for Layla*, over the next few weeks at least. Before this she and Layla had shared the odd neighbourly coffee together, but Nicole had been way more friendly with Marion Warner . . . until she'd found out what the Warners were really like. And yet despite everything, Nicole missed Marion, and it almost felt as if everyone was leaving Hope Close, like a mass exodus . . .

Nicole tossed her head, attempted to shake the maudlin thoughts out. At least Layla was still here, she told herself. Perhaps Layla would enjoy coming over for coffee now that she had more time on her hands, might even be happy to join the gym or walk the dog with her. It would be nice to have someone else to take Stan to the Common with, as Nicole still didn't like going there alone. In fact, maybe she and Layla could set up a little weekly routine that would help both of them through this period of adjustment.

At last Nicole heard the purr of Charles's car, the swoosh of the puddles. Almost as if she couldn't help herself, she dashed upstairs and watched from the corner of the bedroom window as Layla climbed out, and there was something about the set of her shoulders that made Nicole ache for the younger woman, made her want to cross the drive and beg her to come in, have a glass or two of wine and some crisps to take the edge off her misery. But of course, wine and crisps were fattening, and Nicole was so careful about what she put in her mouth that sometimes it exhausted her. And for what? To carry on looking good for Ted, who never noticed? Nicole knew she was still in good shape, but it wouldn't work forever. At what point did women like her have to admit that they couldn't hold back the tide any more, that the Botox and the dietary regime and the hours at the gym were pointless? At what point should she capitulate, and become *old*? When did that even happen? What happened to fading beauty queen gym bunnies like her? Should she *ever* give up? Or would she grow into one of those grotesques, with her features crooked and in the wrong places from one too many procedures? What was to become of her?

Nicole watched as Charles came around the car and helped Layla out, took her shoulders, and she couldn't work out whether the gesture was caring, or proprietorial. Layla glanced up suddenly and, as Nicole shrank back behind the curtains, she knew there was a very fine line between being a sympathetic neighbour and a stalker. And besides, it wasn't as if she and Layla had ever been close as such. There was the age gap, for a start. Plus, they came from different backgrounds. Different classes, if the truth be told.

The world felt fragile to Nicole suddenly, as if it were slipping away from her, and she felt so unbelievably lonely she wondered whether she ought to do something concrete about it. Perhaps it was simply everything mounting up. She continued watching as Charles and Layla went into the house, and even as their front door closed she could feel the silence pressing in on her. When she glanced across to the Warners' house, she thought how odd it was that houses gave off a sad vibe when they were empty, as though they too were lonely somehow, missed the people who had abandoned them. Hopefully a new family would buy it soon, help bring some life back into the close. Or maybe the house had a reputation now. Perhaps that was why it hadn't sold . . .

Nicole snapped her train of thought shut, tried to dissipate the images gathering behind her eyes. She tapped her fingers against the window ledge. Her throat felt constricted, as if there was something blocking it, stopping her breathing. The silence thumped in her ears, to the chaotic rhythm of her heartbeat. She felt the need to do something, before the scream escaped. She turned away from the window, glanced down at Stanley, who was shadowing her today, as if he were worried about her. He pricked his ears, cocked his head to one side, his eyes glowing black, ever hopeful, in his little tan-coloured face. He'd perfected the look, and it calmed her, that he was so pleading, so devoted. She knelt down beside him and buried her face into his silken ears, the back of his neck. He smelled very faintly doggy beneath the baby powder smell of his shampoo, and she wanted to stay there forever, never let him go . . .

At last, inevitably, it was Stanley who broke the deadlock. He gave a little strangled bark, stood up and sheepishly wagged his tail, and she knew she could deny him no longer. Besides, it would do her good, too. There was something about getting out in the air, even when the day was dismal, that made her feel better, less full of dread.

'Oh, Stanley,' Nicole sighed, only half-jokingly, as she let him lead her downstairs to the cloakroom. When she opened the door and took out the lead Stanley's tail started wagging so fast his whole back end was shaking. She pulled on her Ugg boots and her shiny cinched-in parka, put on Stanley's waterproof coat, attached his lead. Even though the rain was coming down hard now, they left through the side door, Stanley trotting along ahead of her, his tail as perky as ever. Just as he was leading her past the Warners' old house, a Lexus swung into the close from the lane, too fast, driven by a bald, arrogant-looking man she'd never seen before – and as he swept into the Warners' weed-infested ex-driveway, she scowled at him, before jumping sharply out of the way of the neat sheet of puddle water coming straight at her.

21

Chapter 4

Joan

The smell struck her before she actually made contact with its source, thank the Lord. Not again! It was *disgusting*. Joan Taylor hated cats at the best of times. She was a dog person, if she were ever forced to choose, although she wasn't especially keen on either. Pets were a waste of time and effort, in her opinion. She was particularly annoyed that she'd lived in this close for decades and it was the first time anyone had ever had cats. She didn't want to have to find cat excrement in the gravel, *again*. It made her feel sick. But after decades of stability it seemed to be all change in Hope Close, what with that loutish builder and his common wife having moved in a few years ago, and then those snobs Layla and Charles, and latterly all the scandal with the Warners meaning they'd practically done a midnight flit. The rumours about that pair had been utterly vile, and yet it seemed they were all true. Good grief, what was the world coming to? And on top of all that, Joan thought primly, instead of getting a nice new family into the close, some new blood, apparently another weirdo was moving in now. What was he even doing, with all the homeless people in the world, buying a house that size, with four bedrooms, no less? Joan had already made up her mind about him, although she hadn't even met him yet, convinced that he was probably a drug dealer (or a banker, which was almost as bad), what with how young he apparently was, according to Lionel, who'd heard it from Ted. It was all very strange. No one had ever seen the man, let alone spoken to him. Apparently, his solicitor had done the viewings. None of the estate agents seemed to know anything about the sale, from what Joan could tell. The situation gave her the willies, that was for sure.

Joan liked to think of herself as one of those pillar-of-the-community types. She went to church every Sunday, served on the local council, helped out in the Cancer Research shop on a Wednesday, dared to count the local MP as a friend. She knew most things about people round here, one way or another. And yet she still couldn't get anything on her new neighbour. Not even his name. Joan's husband had told her she should stop being so nosy, but Joan hadn't been the daughter of a local reporter for nothing. She had always been able to sniff out a story – and she was certain there was one to be found here.

Joan poked her handheld fork into her side beds and scowled. The bindweed was a disaster, really it was. No matter how many times she treated it she couldn't get rid of it. In normal circumstances she'd ask Ted to tackle it from his side, too, in case the roots had spread, but he didn't even acknowledge her now, relations between the two households having reached an all-time low. They'd originally fallen out over Ted's van, amongst other things, and it was still a major sticking point. But Joan simply didn't see why she had to put up with a builder's van in the driveway every single day, and she'd told Ted so. 'But it's not in your bloody driveway,' Ted had roared, and she'd said, tartly, that there was no need to shout at her, and that she didn't want to have to look at the cobalt-blue monstrosity. It was an eyesore that spoilt her view. She'd just about stopped short of opining that it lowered the tone, and that she hadn't moved into a secluded bungalow in the heart of the Surrey countryside to live next door to pikeys. But she'd complained repeatedly thereafter, of course, as well as getting her friends on the council involved, and yet no one had been able to do anything about it.

Humph, Joan thought now. It was like living in the Wild West around here. Five years down the line and she still hadn't got over the sight of Ted's van. There was plenty of room on his driveway. He could easily tuck the wretched thing around the corner, out of her sight, and Joan swore he parked it as close to her boundary as he could get away with now, purely out of spite, and she *hated* him for it. Her husband had told her to get over it, or just plant a hedge, and that you couldn't see the van anyway unless you were in the front garden, or else looking out of the drawing room window, and they hardly ever did either. But it was the principle, Joan had said, and you should never give up your principles. Lionel hadn't answered.

It was a cold, miserable day. Joan's knees felt stiff, and it was as if she could feel the winter approaching, the ground gradually hardening, preparing to shut up shop for the year. Lionel had suggested that now they were older they should think about getting a gardener, but Joan liked doing it herself. It gave her a sense of purpose, and it was good exercise to boot. As she continued scratching around in the soil, she noticed Layla start to open her front door across the way – and then suddenly the door shut again, as though Layla had changed her mind. Was it because she'd seen her, Joan wondered. Even she was an odd one, the older woman thought. Sending her son away, and then seeming so sad all the time, even when you tried to engage her in conversation. Joan had tried befriending Layla, had made her a chocolate cake when she'd first moved in, had even invited the boy in to help ice it, but Layla hadn't seemed remotely grateful. In fact, she seemed quite a self-absorbed type to Joan, even more so now Henry was off at boarding school. She still thought it was a strange decision in this day and age, and Layla was obviously completely devastated, especially as her husband never seemed to be there. He was probably having an affair, Joan thought, and decided that was one theory she wouldn't share with Lionel. He would just accuse her of being a gossip, and an unkind one at that.

Layla's cat slunk by. It was large and grey and luxuriantly furry, and it had big unblinking yellow eyes that it turned on Joan now. She scowled at it, but it just stared at her insolently, as if daring her to turn her complaints on to him now, causing Joan to feel such a sharp twinge of ire, it was as though she were in danger of revving up to full-throttle fury. The cat was trespassing. It did its business in her gravel. *She wished it were dead.* She thought of Lionel drowning the squirrels over the years, and although she found the thought unpleasant, wouldn't have done it herself, they *were* such pests, and at least it stopped all her pots being dug up. Perhaps Lionel could drown Aristotle while he was at it. What a ludicrous name for a cat, apart from anything else.

Joan stood up at last and, as she spotted that the holly bush had berries already, she felt a rare stab of regret. She wondered what she and Lionel would do for Christmas this year, as of course her sister wouldn't be coming. Joan thought of all the trouble poor Anne had endured over the years with her wayward, ultimately tragic son, and what a toll it must have taken on her health. Joan herself had actually adored her nephew once, had thought of him almost like a son, but perhaps how Peter had turned out had been inevitable. On the one hand Anne had failed to ever discipline the boy, and on the other he'd had a brute for a father. Joan tried to summon up a feeling of grief, and yet still she couldn't. Initially it must have been due to the shock, according to her doctor, blunting her natural responses – but surely four months later some sort of emotion should have flooded in. After all, Peter was dead, and now so was her only sister.

Joan startled as a sleek grey car pulled in off the lane. It was a brand she didn't recognise, of an indeterminate age, with a personalised number plate and blacked-out windows, but as the car straightened up, she caught the driver's eye through the windscreen. His gaze flickered, and his mouth turned down at the edges a fraction, although otherwise he ignored her. She shivered as she wondered if that was the new owner, and was determined to find out. After all, you never knew who you were living next door to these days (the Warners being concrete proof of that!) and there was Henry to think of too, at least in the holidays. You couldn't be too careful.

Joan stood and watched as the man got out of his car and went into the house, but she only saw the back of his dark suit, the sheen of his bald head before the dusty dark blue front door firmly shut, as if the man knew he was being watched and wanted to make it clear such interest was unwelcome. He didn't seem young to Joan at all, as Ted had apparently claimed. In fact, he was distinctly middle-aged and rather evil-looking – and as usual it seemed her next-door neighbour had been talking rubbish.

It was getting late, but Joan had one more job to do before she tidied up for the day. At least it would enable her to hang around in the front garden for a bit longer, try to get a better look at her new neighbour as he left. She marched quickly down the side of her bungalow, along the once-grassy path that was nothing more than moss at this time of the year, a horticultural mirage, through the wooden gate and into the back garden. The water splashed icily at her as she filled her watering can from the tap by the back door. Then she walked briskly, her bones frigid and brittle-feeling, to the shed at the end of the garden and opened it, searched along the eye-height shelf where she kept her impressive range of gardening products. She found what she was looking for almost immediately. She returned to her watering can and measured out the weedkiller precisely, before adding a bit more for good measure. They never told you to make it strong enough.

As Joan picked up the can it felt as if her arm was being pulled out of its bony socket. It was a long way to the front of the house, and she cursed that Lionel had never had a tap installed there, despite her telling him to do it. When she finally reached the front garden again, the car at the house opposite was gone. She swore softly under her breath, thought about what she would say to Lionel about it, what punishment to mete out to him, even though she knew this particular situation wasn't really his fault.

Finally, Joan turned her attention back to the bindweed. It was impossible to keep control of it just by pulling it up. This should do it. She untangled and unwound all the creeping, stealthy strands from the now-scrawny roses, as diligently as if she were going back to correct a mistake in her knitting, and laid them out on the bare hard earth, being careful to keep the stems attached to the roots. As she poured the contents of the watering can over the defiantly lush stems, the liquid pooled in a couple of places, and then she poured some more, just to make sure.

Afterwards Joan returned to the tap and rinsed the watering can thoroughly. The afternoon was drawing in, and she could feel the threat of the cold seeping, ever seeping, into the earth. Darkness was coming, as relentless and inevitable as death. At last she went inside through the garage door, took off her wellington boots and washed her hands at the sink in the utility room. She'd done quite enough in the garden for one day. It was time to start dinner.

Chapter 5

My solicitor can be such a jerk sometimes. He is the only person in the world that I trust, but only because I pay him enough. He's in his fifties, bald, in that way that must be eminently disappointing to him, and what is left of his monk's head hair is shaved close in an attempt to make it less obvious. His ears are large but so neatly aligned to his head I swear they have been pinned back, and yet I would never ask him, purely because I don't care enough about the answer. His eyes turn down, like sad smiles, and carry a depth of sorrow and self-disgust that I recognise in men of his age, of his class, and I wonder what might have happened to him once . . . and yet, of course, I don't ask him that either. But anyway. He is a man who clearly hates himself, and they are the ones you need. They are the ones who will do anything for money. As if money is the route out of the purgatory they find themselves in. My solicitor is a Success. A hired hand. A corrupt soul. Like me. He and I walk hand in hand towards the abyss, and he attempts to save me, but who tries to save him? I don't care. I'm past caring.

I've worked hard to prepare for my return to the country of my birth. For my repatriation into normal society, whatever 'normal' is. And yet everything seems too intense, too bright for me now. Even the journey itself – my first not taken under the cover of darkness – is a sensory onslaught, like staring into the sun. I've been around throngs of people in prison, of course, but the airport might as well be an alien planet in comparison. The presence of women and children, for a start. The noise. The colour. The glaring lighting. The queues. The feeling of anonymity amongst the crowds, which is both a curse and a comfort. And so it's a relief to make it into the airport lounge, into the curious atmosphere of hushed, upmarket tones – although soon enough I feel uneasy in here too. In prison, in rehab, I'd been labelled: someone with a known defect that was a part of me, of my history. But now it seems no one knows who I am, what I've done. I don't know how to act. How to behave. The simple act of observing a woman sitting directly opposite me feels confronting, as if she's too vivid, too alive for my liking, as if she can see into my burnout eyes and spot the truth of my wickedness. The woman is wearing tight scarlet trousers, towering heels and the most wonderful long red and black coat, covered in sequins and embroidered golden birds, and she has on red bat-wing glasses, and her skin is lustrously inky, and her hair is geometric perfection, the tiny cornrows so painstakingly neat they must have taken hours. She's gloriously, peacockishly decorated, and I haven't seen such beauty and colour in a person in too many years. And yet at the same time I can see inside of her too, and I know that along her veins and arteries red blood is pumping, and one day those veins might burst, and that heart might smash, gushing blood and pulp . . . and she has no idea of the impact she's having on me. Even now. Even still. I find my hand is shaking as I bring my coffee cup to my lips, and when she catches me staring at her she looks alarmed, scared almost, as if I'm dangerous perhaps. Unhinged. I admire her perspicacity.

The rest of the journey is uneventful. It seems the clinic has prepared me well. Only the faint memory of a whisky in my hand as the plane soars over the bumps and lumps of the air flows is like an imprint from my old life. An itch. Faint, but ever-present. A low-level need to drink. A low-level fear of flying. And now a new sensation: a low-level fear of everything.

But at last here I am, in a cab on my way to a cottage in Surrey, which – it has been decided, by someone – will be the best place for the next stage of my recovery. It's like a halfway house, it seems: a picturesque, thatch-roofed haven of peace and tranquillity, with prescription drugs and shrinks on tap, my final induction before I return to the real world.

The car drives slowly, as I have requested. The route is straightforward, mostly motorway, which I can deal with. When I arrive, the place, quite improbably, is as secluded and picture-book pretty as its sales material promises, and I'm greeted as if I'm a long-lost relative, which almost feels good, although I know it's not for real. These people are merely paid to be nice to me, and even if they don't know the truth of who I am, my new persona's backstory is pathetic enough for them to pity me. When I'm taken to my bedroom, it has dark timber rafters and I immediately think how easy it would be for someone to hang themselves in here, until I notice that the towelling robe they provide doesn't have a cord. And then I remind myself that I am officially In Recovery, and that I shouldn't even be thinking like this.

And so. As I unpack my few possessions I consider how, right this minute, my new house, which is only a few miles away, is being prepared for me. My solicitor has employed a local builder to install a comprehensive new security system, undertake some basic redecoration. He is sorting out the furniture himself. (He even asked if I wanted a Dobermann, and although in other circumstances that might be quite nice, I'm barely ready to look after myself, let alone a dog. I declined politely.) In the meantime I will be treated here in this cottage-asylum, and then in two or three weeks I will be moving into my very own house, in the heart of the glorious Surrey countryside. As soon as I'm ready for it. As soon as it's ready for me.

Chapter 6

LAYLA

Never had there been more of a misnomer than Hope Close, Layla thought, as she stared morosely out of her bedroom window. The once-vibrant leaves on the trees were drab now, seemingly desperate for the chance to turn, and the front lawns were visibly sodden from all the recent rain, and the flower borders had faded, and the absence of any colours other than green and brown and grey was dispiriting somehow. It was as if everyone was waiting for something to happen, even nature: summer not yet quite over, but too soon for the showy opulence of autumn. Layla pictured the bright red leaves of the near future, the dazzling blue skies, and yearned for their coming. It had been eleven days since Henry had left, and the time was passing too slowly. This very place moved too slowly at the best of times, but now the pace seemed funereal. Layla missed the speed and hum of London, where people had a sense of purpose, and largely minded their own business. She missed her old friends, the easy, messy play dates their kids had enjoyed while the mothers had shared a bottle or two of wine and moaned about their husbands. She liked this house, but she found living in a dead-end (God, even the name was depressing) invasive, almost as if she were being monitored. It didn't help that Hope Close was so isolated that, before the advent of satnav, no one could ever find it. There were only four properties: a handsome manor house, which was where she and Charles lived; and then in the sixties some of the land had been sold off and three further houses had been built. It was an odd set-up, and not ideal, but that was how Layla and Charles had been able to afford such a house so close to London – and to be fair, the location was spectacular. The Taylors' bungalow was directly opposite, and had been built in that ugly faux-chalet style beloved of the period, with white-painted wooden slat cladding. Nicole and Ted's house was adjacent to the Taylors' and had originally been identical to it, but over the years had had so many extensions that now it was twice the size and, as Joan Taylor had often remarked, the height of vulgarity. Finally, next door to Layla's, was the Warners' old house, which had once been owned by an architect, and who'd attached a cuboid concrete box to the rear of it, like a carbuncle.

And so, perversely, although Layla's house itself had the most privacy of all those in the close, tucked away as it was in the furthest corner, the opposite was true in terms of her movements. Everyone could see when she came and went. In fact, sometimes she almost felt as if she were being stalked. She wished she didn't have to drive everywhere, announce her journeys to the neighbours, but stealth just wasn't possible in a Range Rover Evoque – and walking was even more exposing.

Charles didn't appear worried by any of these issues, of course. He seemed quite happy swinging out of their semi-circular drive each morning, purring past the other houses and into the lane, heading off for his schedule of meetings and away-days and formal dinners. He didn't have to stay in the house for hours, hearing its silence ring in his ears, the high ceilings and grand open spaces all the better to echo his solitariness back at him. Charles didn't have time to feel lonely, to miss their son. Layla swore her husband was too busy being important to notice that she was sad or, more shockingly, that Henry was even gone. More times than not he'd used to arrive home after his son's bedtime anyway. Nothing was all that different for Charles in this new scenario. He'd said that boarding school would be good for Henry, would give him backbone, confidence, access to the right connections. It hadn't done *him* any harm, Charles had insisted, but now Layla wasn't so sure. It seemed that since Henry was temporarily out of the reckoning, she'd been able to see her marriage more dispassionately, and she didn't know what to make of it – as if the disparate swirls and flourishes were definitely building to something, but the picture still wasn't clear. 'Can you tell what it is yet, kids?' Rolf Harris had used to say, before his words had taken on a more sinister meaning. Layla blanched. Abuse still happened. What if that was what Henry—

No. She was being neurotic. Times had changed. There were safeguards nowadays. A much greater threat to Henry was being bullied about his name, what people might think about his father – and Charles had told her enough times not to worry about that. The staff were aware of the issue. Henry would be fine. There was nothing they could do about it anyway, Charles had said – but Charles was wrong. Henry could easily have taken her surname instead, but Charles had refused to allow it. She still wasn't sure whether she resented him for that, or not.

Layla turned away from the window, left the bedroom, drifted along the landing, down the stairs, past the black-and-white portrait of the three of them at a wedding, when Henry had been just a few weeks old. She and Charles had been captured laughing in hapless new parenthood, their son in her arms, bawling. Layla studied the picture now, gazed into the depths of her husband's eyes, searching for something. Yes. It had been there then, definitely. Love. He'd loved her. He'd even loved their son. But there'd been something else too, of course. Fear. Or sadness. Or regret. Or self-hate. Or infamy, deserved or not. Or all of those things, tainting the love for her and their child . . . and maybe *that* was why Henry had been crying. Even then, Henry had instinctively known that his father would never be able to overcome his past, give his infant son the love he needed . . .

As Layla stood still, halfway up the stairs, she could feel her head becoming light, ever more unsettled, dizzy almost. She wanted to call her husband, hear him reassure her that everything was OK, but she didn't dare. Relations between them seemed so different now from when they'd first met, when the unlikeliness of their union had given it a sparkling edge, a sense of adventure, even. He'd have been happy to hear from her back then. *Love at first sight.* Was that what it had been? He'd reminded her of her favourite movie star, and perhaps that was why it had almost felt as if she'd known him. But what had been going on in Charles's mind? Why hadn't he just handed her purse into reception, instead of going to all the trouble of leaving his business card? Had he not trusted the purse would reach her? Or had he witnessed her dropping it, and deliberately engineered their meeting?

Layla unwrapped her ivory silk dressing gown, took it off and draped it over the portrait, very, very gently. As she stood there naked, her limbs long and coffee-coloured, her belly softly rounded, there was something about the picture that bothered her, that she couldn't stand to see today. Perhaps it was the suspicion that Charles's life with her, Layla, might be satisfying enough for him after all. He had his glamorous young wife, their beautiful little boy safely ensconced in the most prestigious of schools, the job, the house, all the trappings. Yet what did she and Henry have? Was this set-up *really* the best one for an eight-year-old?

How had she allowed it?

Layla turned on her heel and went back upstairs to their bedroom. She half-heartedly messed up the bed a little, which made her feel better. She preferred the covers creased and askew these days. It didn't seem right for things to look perfect any more. She was becoming aware that there was something lacking in all this. Her son, of course, but something else, too, always fingers' length out of reach and indefinable. How had she ever thought that meeting Charles would have fixed it? But hadn't that been the dream she'd been fed, from the fairy tales and the movies and the love songs, and even the lessons she'd learnt at school? Wasn't love meant to be the answer to everything? Weren't all little girls promised that, even now? *What a load of rubbish*, she thought. And besides, she'd hardly snared the archetypal prince – she was pretty sure Prince Charmings weren't meant to be old enough to be your father and on to their third wife already. She snorted at the absurdity of it.

When Layla heard the doorbell, she was tempted to not answer it. It might be Joan from next door, come to complain about the cat, again. Her heart shrank, pulled away from its veins and arteries. Her breathing shallowed. But then it occurred to her that it might be the postman, with something from Henry – and so she rushed downstairs, grabbing her dressing gown from the picture as she passed it. She shrugged herself into the robe as she crossed the polished oak of the hallway, still doing it up, just about decent – and opened the gleaming front door three inches.

'Hi, Layla,' said Nicole. She was smiling, her nose crinkling. Her skin was deeply tanned, at odds with the weather, surely fake. Her hair was jet black, as lustrously long as a teenager's. Her figure looked unnaturally voluptuous in skin-tight designer gym gear. Her trainers were those mesh ones that Layla knew were expensive because Henry had wanted a pair and Charles had said no, telling him he'd grow out of them before he knew it and that it would be a waste of money. Henry had tried every single boarding-school-related guilt trip, and Layla might even have succumbed, under the circumstances, but Charles had not been for turning.

'Oh. Hi, Nicole,' Layla said, opening the door a little further but standing her ground, although Nicole was clearly expecting to be asked in. It seemed Nicole was on another mission to Cheer Up Layla, whether Layla liked it or not.

'Hi, love. I just thought I'd come and say hello, see how you're doing.'

'Oh . . . thanks. Well, I'm fine.' She smiled, hopefully convincingly, as Nicole continued to stand there, unbudging. 'Er, d'you want to come in?' she said, at last. 'I'm sorry I'm not dressed.'

'That's OK,' said Nicole. As Layla opened the door a little further, the older woman sailed past her, through the hallway and into the kitchen, where she started filling the kettle at the tap.

'You making me tea, Nicole?' said Layla, half-raising an eyebrow.

'Well, you look like you could do with a cup, love.'

Layla smiled, despite herself. Nicole was brazen, she'd give her that, but it was attractive in a way. After all, Layla could be just as forward herself when it suited her, and she was reminded of the time she'd suggested to Charles that they book a London hotel on only their second date. At the time Layla had been living in a cramped studenty flat-share and Charles's house had been out of town, but her presumptuousness at asking him had still shocked her. She'd made it absolutely clear that nothing of a sexual nature would happen, had negotiated strict terms in advance involving oversized T-shirts and pillows down the middle of the bed, and he'd been resolutely compliant. She'd still been embarrassed checking in with him though, worried at how it must have looked, spotting the sardonic glint in the receptionist's eye – and it was only once she and Charles had reached their room that she'd allowed herself to relax. She'd felt safe, cocooned, enthralled by a man who even then she'd somehow known would make an impact on her life. And after just a few more dates it had seemed as if she and Charles were simply meant to be, that they'd been inordinately lucky to have found each other . . .

And now? Now, ten years down the track, it was hard for Layla to know what was the truth in the tight tangled centre of her newly childless marriage. Nothing felt like it once had done, and she wondered if she and Charles had ever truly recovered from the crisis that had consumed them so soon after Henry was born. She still had no idea how Charles felt about it, as he'd refused to ever discuss it . . . but since those days she had felt her husband separating from her, the emotional ties loosening, sagging, like worn-out lingerie. Time would tell, she supposed.

Layla realised that Nicole was staring at her, and she could feel her cheeks starting to redden, as if she were a teenager that owed her mother an explanation about where she'd been last night. Layla was still surprised at how much she missed her mother, but maybe the absence of a child was made yet worse when your parents were gone, too. 'Oh, Normandy isn't far, darling,' her mother had breezed, but the sad fact was that she no longer lived near enough to pop round for lunch, or when Layla was having another meltdown, or to help out babysitting a child that Layla *didn't have any more* – and so what difference did it make anyway? But at least her mother was happy at last, Layla thought. After all, happiness didn't throw itself at you, like love did. It was merely there for the taking, and Layla's mother and her dashing young husband had certainly grabbed at it. Layla could still picture them now as they'd set off like a pair of overexcited teenagers in Barney's customised Land Rover, en route to their converted barn project. It was odd that Barney was a mere seven years older than Layla, and Layla's mother a mere six years older than Charles, the family's ages a veritable mathematical cat's cradle. Furthermore, Barney had the name of a toddler, and the face of a cherub, and was it really so wrong that Layla found him a teeny bit attractive? She giggled suddenly. Maybe it was just as well her mother and step-father had relocated to France.

'Ha,' said Nicole, hands on sheeny hips. 'What's so funny?'

Layla stopped smirking. 'Just thinking about my mother. How she's married a toy boy, and I married a sugar daddy.'

'Oh,' said Nicole. She took two teabags and put them into mugs. 'What *is* the age gap between you and Charles?'

'Seventeen years,' Layla said. 'It's not actually as much as it sounds.'

'No,' Nicole said. 'And after all, don't they say age is just a number?'

Except when you're eight, Layla thought. She didn't say anything more as they waited for the water to boil, but she felt the angst there again, pushing gently at somewhere inside the fleshy part of her stomach, jabbing to get out.

'By the way, have you heard that next door's been sold?' Nicole said, perhaps deliberately changing the subject.

'No!' Now this was interesting. 'Are you sure?'

'Well, Ted heard it from another builder, so as sure as you can ever be. It's just one bloke, according to Ted. Young. Single. Now why would someone like that want to move in round here, on his own?' Nicole had that look on her face, as though she'd got some good gossip. 'Apparently he's having gates fitted.'

'Well, hold the front page!' Layla said.

'But can you imagine what the Taylors will do? Joan will be down the council complaining like a shot.'

'Hmm. I think you can build gates if you want to, as long as they're not too high and it's not an open-plan development, which this isn't.' Layla used to be an architect once, in an old life, but she didn't really talk about it any more.

'It's a bit unfriendly, though,' Nicole persisted, as she went over to Layla's fridge and took out the milk. 'Don't you think?'

'It's OK. How d'you know, anyway?'

'Ted's mate's doing it. The new owner's having all the fences reinforced, too.' As Nicole spoke Layla spotted the Liverpudlian twang, so faint you'd almost miss it. It was a friendly voice, one that enabled Nicole to get away with saying things she shouldn't. Maybe Layla should start saying things *she* shouldn't. It might help unfreeze the feelings that seemed to be solidifying inside her, like a lead-edged lump.

'Wow, that seems like overkill,' said Layla. 'But at least it's sold at last, I suppose.' She paused, took a tentative sip of the tea Nicole had passed her, which surprisingly was just as she liked it. 'It must be a relief for the chandelier-swingers.'

Nicole's eyes widened for a moment, and then she cackled. 'You are *wicked,* Layla. You look so innocent, and then you say things like that.' Her tone turned more serious. 'How's Henry doing?'

'He's OK – I assume. We're still not allowed to speak to him.'

'Who says?'

'The school.'

'What does Charles think about it?'

'Oh, he's fine with it. After all, he went through it himself, thinks it's character building. Plus he's got loads on at work at the moment, anyway.'

'Hmm,' said Nicole, and Layla knew not to ask what she meant. Nicole and Charles were about as different as two people could be. It didn't help that Charles could seem so dour these days, especially to people who didn't know him. Layla debated whether she should even start calling him Charlie again, whether he approved or not, as Charles-the-name seemed to have impacted Charles-the-man. Was that possible? That a name could affect a person's whole character? That her husband seemed like somebody completely different to her now? To how he used to be when she met him?

'And how are *you*, Layla?' Nicole asked, and Layla couldn't work out whether the hint of a tremor in Nicole's voice was genuine concern or just well-disguised nosiness.

'Oh, I'm fine,' Layla said. 'I've just got to get through these first couple of weeks.' She felt mortified as she heard the faint crack in her own voice now, but not as much as she did when a single tear started rolling down her cheek.

'Oh, Layla, it's OK, love. Henry'll be *sound*. He's probably loving it.' Nicole moved towards Layla and put an arm on hers, and although the gesture was kindly, somehow it reminded Layla of when a dog does that with his paw, to show he has the upper hand. Nicole smelled fragrant and expensive, although Layla couldn't identify the perfume. She liked the feeling, for an instant – and then she really didn't. She felt unnerved suddenly, and she wasn't sure whether it was the prospect of a new neighbour moving in at last, or the fact that she was crying in front of Nicole. It felt disloyal to Charles somehow.

'Well, no news is good news and all that,' Nicole said, her tone determinedly chirpy, and it was clear to Layla now that Nicole secretly thought that what they'd done with Henry was barbaric, and she longed to tell Nicole that she *agreed* with her, that she wished she could get in the car and just go and get him – and sod what Charles, or the school, or her in-laws thought about any of it.

Layla swilled her tea in her cup, daring it to spill. Why *couldn't* she do that? Why *didn't* she do that? For God's sake, Henry was her child, too. Her head was thudding with clashing sensations, her husband's belief in such institutions wrestling with her own fear of them. Her own fear of everything. An invisible weight started settling on her head, pressing her neck forward, making her back stoop a little, like a crone.

'Are you OK, Layla?' Nicole said. 'You've gone a bit pale, love. Here, sit down.' As Layla let her neighbour guide her into a chair, the rush in her head was overwhelming. She put her arms on the table and rested her head on them, tried to breathe. A picture forced its way into her mind, of Henry looking bereft, perched on the end of his bed with his favourite teddy in his hands, sobbing . . . And now Layla saw a different boy, one who was snapping a squirrel's neck with a deft twist of his hands, as if he were breaking open a bread roll . . . And now that boy was morphing into Henry, and next into Charles . . . For a moment Layla thought she might actually faint, and she didn't know why this fear was starting all over again. She could only assume it was her heightened concerns for her son, now that he was away from her. And all the while Nicole was sitting beside her, rubbing her back, until at last the feeling passed. It might have been twenty seconds or two hundred; Layla had no idea. When she finally sat up, wordless still, she was so grateful for the sympathy in the older woman's face. But, of course – Nicole was a mother too, and it seemed she understood, wasn't judging Layla's decision after all. Yet there was another nuance to Nicole's look, too: a hunger, as if there was something she wanted from Layla. Perhaps it was simply that Nicole was also lonely, missed her own kids. Maybe that was all it was.

As the two women stared at each other, the Swiss railway clock on the wall ticked relentlessly, and the noise seemed louder than it should be, cutting into the silence. Layla felt so overwrought she was half-tempted to ask Nicole about Ted's ongoing feud with the Taylors, purely to change the subject, but somehow she knew not to go there. The Taylors seemed like a vindictive pair to Layla, and Ted was a hothead. Anything could have happened.

'Have you got any plans, Layla?' Nicole asked now.

'For what?'

'For how you're going to fill your days?'

'I haven't decided yet.'

'Me neither. It's tough, isn't it?'

Layla hesitated. It felt good in a way, though, to share the burden with someone else. 'I was thinking about looking for a job,' she said, 'but I haven't worked in nine years. And I'd need all the school holidays off.'

'Well, I'm sure you'd get something easily enough if you put your mind to it. It might do you good. What did you do anyway?'

Layla found it odd that they'd never asked each other what they used to do, as if their lives before Hope Close and motherhood were irrelevant somehow.

'I was an architect.'

'An architect?' Nicole sat up straight, like someone had poked her. 'I need an architect.'

'What for?'

'I want my kitchen redone.'

'But your kitchen's fine. Didn't you do it when you moved in?'

'Yes, but I don't like it any more.' Nicole drained her mug and grimaced. 'Ugh. Bloody rooibos. Why can't you buy normal tea?'

'Well, please feel free to bring your own teabags next time you barge your way in,' Layla said. She smiled, to show she was joking. 'What don't you like about it?'

'Oh, I don't know. It's a bit dated, plus I want it extended, so I've got room for a sofa. Ted suggested it. I think he's trying to keep me busy.'

At just that moment the cat came sauntering in, and although Nicole went to make a showy fuss of him, Aristotle proceeded to eye her disdainfully and instead wandered over to his basket, where he curled up and stared at Nicole as if he hated her, although he looked at most people like that. That was one of the things Layla liked about him.

'Well, it's late, I'd better get on,' Nicole said. She stood up, went over to the sink, rinsed her mug and put it on the draining board, being ultra-careful with her nails, which were long and sharp and aubergine-coloured. 'Have a think about my kitchen anyway, and let me know if you're interested.'

'Will do,' Layla said, escorting Nicole to the door. 'Bye.'

After Nicole had left, Layla went upstairs, pulled off her silk robe and threw on underwear, jeans and a jumper without bothering to shower. No one would know, and besides, it was getting on for midday, and failing to be dressed by the afternoon crossed the invisible line into bona fide sluttery that she *must not* cross. How could she still be in her dressing gown when Henry was probably already having his lunch? She had a sudden image of him, forlorn, with no one to sit next to, the other boys whispering about him, spreading it around the lunchroom who Henry's father was.

Layla's throat felt scratchy. *Her son needed her.* She snatched up her phone, as if to call the school, check he was all right, ask to speak to him, but she knew it would be for her benefit rather than his, and so she didn't. It was important she keep her resolve. Instead she tried to reach Charles, but he was probably in a meeting, of course, and he simply replied with one of those formal auto-texts – *Sorry, I can't talk right now* – which she'd used to find insultingly impersonal, before she'd realised the phone wrote them.

Grrr, Layla thought. How come Charles appeared so oblivious to how she felt, when Nicole seemed to sense her moods from across the neatly clipped gardens? Perhaps it was because she and Nicole were both abandoned mothers, albeit in totally different circumstances – and although Layla was fully aware that Nicole cultivated their friendship as much for her own benefit as for Layla's, maybe her designing Nicole's kitchen might be the distraction they both needed. Perhaps it was simply that the universe provided in myriad unexpected ways.

Layla's phone rang. 'Hi, darling,' said Charles. His voice had that rich textured tone to it that she'd noticed the first time she'd heard him speak. 'Did you call? Are you OK?'

'Yes, I'm fine, thanks.'

'Look, I'm sorry, but I've got to work late this evening.'

Layla paused. 'Oh. I thought you said you'd make a special effort to get home earlier at the moment.'

'Yes, well, I know, but something's come up. I'll call you later, OK?'

'OK.' She was too annoyed to say any more. There was no point continuing the conversation when Charles was in the office, when he couldn't speak openly, when who knew might be listening.

'Bye, love you.'

'Bye,' Layla said.

As she came off the phone the world was essentially the same, and yet it felt bleaker now, more unstable. Not only did she have an absent son that she couldn't stop worrying about, she also had a husband who, despite his promises, still put his work ahead of her. He was so unbelievably *selfish* sometimes. Couldn't he see it? What was wrong with him? And why the hell did she put up with it?

Layla stood up, walked over to the window and stared out into the close. The air was pressing down on her, as if it were filled with sand and she was caught in a desert storm and would end up buried soon, unable to breathe, the pain becoming ever more physical. *She had to do something*. Without thinking it through she grabbed her mobile, waited for it to ring, prayed it would be answered.

'Hi, Nicole,' she said. There was no need for her to discuss it with Charles. Why should she? She could do whatever she liked. 'If you're serious about your kitchen, I'm happy to come over and take a look.'

Chapter 7

Joan

As she put on her pink gingham pinafore to start making dinner, Joan could feel one of her headaches coming on, and it was as if she could still hear the banging and the drilling, feel the ground shaking, although in truth the noise of next door's building work had been completed years ago. It had affected her nerves, and she still resented Ted and Nicole for coming in and shattering her peace, virtually taking the roof off the house and rebuilding it, only to make it look worse. The stress hadn't been good for Lionel's health, either. The whole reason they'd chosen this bungalow was because it was in a quiet little cul-de-sac, off the beaten track . . . but then that lot had turned up, with their wayward children and not two, not three, but *four* vehicles, including two vans, no less, and the close had been turned into both a building site and a car park overnight. Ted and Nicole had seemed friendly enough at first, had even invited Joan and Lionel in for a drink, which had seemed like a nice neighbourly thing to do – until it soon transpired, over a far-too-strong gin and tonic, that all they'd wanted to do was butter her and Lionel up about their building works. And as if that weren't bad enough, Ted had then proceeded to ask them outright, with absolutely no decorum, to cut down the maple tree that sat on the border between the two back gardens, about two-thirds of the way down. Joan still felt aggrieved about it now – about the vans, the building works, the faux friendliness, the tree, the ulterior motives. And besides which, she thought again now, it was *her* tree. There was no way she was ever going to agree to cut it down, no matter how hard Ted and Nicole tried to persuade her. Too bad if it spoilt their view. They'd bought the house with it there, so trying to pressure her and Lionel just wouldn't wash, especially after all the disruption they'd caused. Some people were just so unbelievably selfish.

Joan was a quiet woman, in some ways averse to confrontation. Instead her tactics were often ones of stealth, so she'd stopped having the tree pruned, making it a problem that was getting bigger, quite literally, with each passing year, and Joan quite liked it that way. She glanced out of the window and saw its silhouette, ghostly against the rain-loaded sky, and she smiled. She ripped the skin off the chicken breasts, the flesh gleaming pinkly at her. The red of the tomatoes as she pulled open the tin lid and they oozed at her made her feel curiously satisfied. And then her moment of quiet reverence was spoilt by her husband wandering in to the kitchen, tea mug in hand, clattering it into the sink. He annoyed her. He got in the way.

'Fancy a cup of tea, Joan?'

Joan turned and looked witheringly at Lionel. 'Since when did I drink tea at this time of the day?'

'Sorry, love.' Lionel moved away from the sink, chastened, and sat down at the kitchen table. It was oblong and oak, yellowed by the sun. A pair of stainless steel salt and pepper pots sat in the middle, next to an old-fashioned serviette holder, one of those ones with a hinged metal spring, containing just a few dog-eared checked paper napkins that she didn't allow Lionel to use.

'Have you found out any more about our new neighbour?' Lionel said.

'No. Why?'

'Just wondering.'

Joan raised an eyebrow. 'What's that supposed to mean?'

'Just what I've heard.'

She turned sharply. 'Just what *have* you heard?'

'Only that his building work starts next week.'

'No!' said Joan. She sloshed the tomatoes out of the tin and into the pan, causing red juice to spatter against the pale grey tiles. 'Not again. I don't think I can stand it.'

'It's across the road, love. It won't affect us as much as Ted's house did. Apparently, it's only gates. The rest is internal.'

'Gates? What gates? Who told you that?'

'Ted.'

'Ted! What have you been doing talking to him?'

'Well, he is our neighbour,' said Lionel, but he seemed to regret having spoken now, as if he'd said the wrong thing, as usual.

Joan picked up the knife and glared at her husband. She could see the sudden fear in his face, and it made her feel better.

'How big are these gates?' she said.

'I'm not sure. Security gates, I think.'

'I'm going to be talking to the council about this,' Joan said.

'You do that, love,' Lionel replied.

Joan surveyed her husband, wondering whether he was trying to placate her, or was being smart. In the end she gave him the benefit of the doubt and continued with her cooking, but her heart was no longer in it. As soon as she'd got the dish on to simmer, she left the kitchen and went into the sitting room, where the computer was. It was old and took an age to fire up, but eventually she managed to get online to research what was going on at Number Three Hope Close. And yet she couldn't find out who had bought the house, how much had been paid, or even which estate agent had sold it. She couldn't find any applications put into the planning department, either. There was definitely something odd about the whole situation. After all, one minute the house was still for sale, and now apparently gates were about to be erected – next week, if Lionel were to be believed. It was absurd.

Joan looked at the time. Five fifteen. If she called now, she might just catch someone. As she keyed in the number, she pressed the phone's screen harder than was strictly necessary, irritation nipping at her, making her feel unsettled. She was determined to find out what was going on and put a stop to it, though. She'd had quite enough of the disruption in this close.

Unfortunately, the planning officer Joan managed to get through to gave her short shrift, much to her disgruntlement. He didn't appear to care one iota that Joan knew Anna Carmichael, MP. Fitting gates on your own property was completely legal, he said, and as for any plans the new owner might or might not have to extend out the back, seeing as Joan wouldn't even be able to see any such theoretical alterations from her house, what difference would it make to her?

'But what about all the building noise and disruption?' Joan said. 'My husband has a heart condition.'

'Well, madam, if we had to take those kinds of issues into account, nothing would get built at all. I'm afraid that's just the way the process works.'

'Well, I'm going to write to the papers,' Joan said.

'That's up to you, madam,' said the planning officer, 'but I think the best thing for you to do would be to put in a formal objection about the gates to the planning department.'

'Which will count for nothing?'

The man sounded slightly alarmed now. 'Well, yes,' he conceded.

'Well, that's the most ridiculous thing I've ever heard,' Joan said, and hung up. She scrolled through her phone, looking to see who else she could complain to, but even in her heightened state she knew she had to be careful, that there was no point doing anything hasty. Normally she might have called her sister to have a moan, and all over again the pain resurrected itself, like one of those pop-up tents that you can't ever get back into its original bag. She and Anne had had their moments over the years, but Anne had been her best, perhaps only, friend. And so Joan almost took it personally that she'd died, as though everyone was deserting her, that the gods were against her. She had a sudden dread of the situation in Hope Close, that Ted might even have won the building contract himself and would be working there every day, with his sweary, common ways, the crack of his fat, hairy backside on show. Good grief. She simply wouldn't be able to stand it.

Joan went out into the front garden, ostensibly to check on her borders, see whether the weedkiller was doing any visible damage to her bindweed yet, but really to take a closer look at the house opposite. She contemplated walking up its unkempt driveway, peering through the unwashed windows, trying to see what was going on inside, but Nicole or Layla might spot her, and she knew it would look peculiar. As she stood on her neatly mowed lawn, surveying the house diagonally opposite hers, she tried to imagine what the gates would be like. She wondered if they would have bars, like a prison, or be solid, so there would be no way to see through them. Either way, they would look frightful, she knew that much. They would spoil the open, country feel of the close.

Joan stared at the house with a new-found venom, convinced that it was cursed. First that architect's son had ended up in a psychiatric ward, disturbed child that he'd been . . . and then the Warners had got up to all sorts in there . . . and now there was *this*. She almost thought that maybe she and Lionel *should* call it a day after all, perhaps move to one of those retirement places and be done with it. But then she imagined how pleased Ted and Nicole would be if she were to leave, how the neighbours would probably have a street party to celebrate – and she resolved that no one would bully her out of her own home, especially seeing as she'd been here first. Yes, Joan decided, as she stalked back towards her bungalow, her grey bush of hair blowing in the wind like witches' dust – she knew the history of Hope Close, and it was her home. She would end her days here, even if it killed her.

Chapter 8

Everything's done, at last, and I've moved in. While I've been cooped up for the past few weeks in my pseudo-fairy-tale cottage in the countryside, supposedly putting the final kibosh on my demons, my solicitor has managed to sort out everything. When I arrived I had a made-up bed. A couch. A giant TV. Internet access. I'm impressed.

Being here in Hope Close is more bearable than I might have imagined. The house itself is nothing more than passable – a few rooms newly painted, blandly and sparsely furnished – but the location is nice. Not just nice. Magnificent, in fact. The cure for my extreme level of isolation is more isolation, this time of the bucolic kind. The garden sweeps and swoops towards the Surrey Hills and they are green and lush – not dry and pink like Spain – and they remind me of how life could have been, if it hadn't been for all the craziness.

And so, perhaps surprisingly, living alone here feels manageable, and for that I am grateful. I have arranged a weekly Ocado shop. I have opened a Deliveroo account. I have even organised an exercise regime. There is no need for me to talk to anyone, except my new therapist. For now, I will keep myself to myself and take stock.

But really. Those gates. As I've said before, my solicitor is a fool. The gates he's had built looked monstrous enough in the pictures, but in the flesh they're hideous, and no wonder the neighbours tried to stop them – and they must hate me almost as much as they would do if they knew who I truly am. But I don't care. It's a price worth paying not to be spied on. I have only seen one fellow resident, a woman, as we passed each other in our cars on the close a few days after I moved in. She was young. Good-looking. Unknown to me. She nodded. I nodded in return. It was a transaction. I managed it.

And so at last I have a home. A basc. Privacy. Security. Perhaps future salvation, here in this very close . . . although of course no one but me knows that yet, and I have absolutely no idea whether I'll ever let on. Who knows whether my instincts will prove correct, or where they will take me, but for now at least I have some hope again – and that, I suppose, is all that I can ask for.

Chapter 9

LAYLA

These days, whenever the doorbell chimed ostentatiously through the silence at some time in the middle of the morning, Layla was pretty sure who it would be, and would be dressed and ready, prepared for the invasion. In fact, she and Nicole seemed to have seen each other more in the past few weeks, almost entirely at Nicole's instigation, than they had in the whole of the previous year.

Today, unusually, Nicole didn't attempt to come in. Instead she loitered casually on the doorstep and adopted an overly chummy tone, which didn't remotely fool Layla.

'Hi, love. I'm going to hot yoga later. Wanna come?'

'Ugh, no way.' Layla screwed up her face in mock disgust. 'It sounds like absolute hell.'

'Well, what else are you going to do today? What time will Charles be home?'

'Early – he's taking me out.'

'Well, you've still got the whole day to get through. Hanging your head between your legs while feeling dizzy will be just the thing.'

'I admire your sales skills, Nicole, but no. I'm busy.'

'Busy doing what?'

Layla paused, unable to think of anything even slightly plausible.

'I'll knock for you at a quarter to two,' Nicole said. 'You'll need a towel and lots of water.' She smirked. 'There'll be nearly-naked men there. See you later.'

Layla couldn't help but smile as she shut the door. She was grateful to Nicole for making the effort with her, and yet it felt a little odd, too. There was the age gap, for a start, plus the two women didn't have a great deal in common. Layla wasn't the type to spend hours in the gym or having her hair or nails done. She didn't wear designer Lycra. But Nicole was funny and fun, had helped pull Layla out of herself, and that was surely a good thing. Layla was still undecided about Nicole's kitchen project, though. This was a very small close, and Layla didn't want to risk falling out with anyone. Relations between the Taylors and Nicole and Ted were awkward enough as it was – and although privately Layla didn't like Joan either, she didn't want to appear to be taking sides. No, it was probably better not to get too involved. And yet Nicole could be very insistent, so Layla needed to be careful that she didn't get sucked into anything she'd rather avoid.

Like hot yoga.

Layla shook her head, tried to gain some perspective. All she'd done was arrange to go to an exercise class with a neighbour. She hadn't signed a contract for anything. Who knew, she might actually enjoy it. And even if she didn't, it was something to do, a distraction – and besides, the exercise would do her good.

The room came at Layla, as if it were moving towards her, rather than the other way round, and the gush of heat reminded her of when aeroplane doors used to open on to a tropical location, before there were air-conditioned tunnels taking weary passengers straight into the terminal, from one artificial atmosphere to another. The memories were so enveloping Layla almost forgot that she was in a yoga studio, surrounded by lithe self-contained men and women who all appeared to have a sense of purpose, a mission, an inner landscape that, no matter how hard she tried, it seemed she couldn't access.

'Grab a mat,' Nicole hissed. 'Before all the spaces have gone.' She pushed Layla into the room and ushered her towards the instructor, who although friendly made Layla uneasy, and she wasn't sure whether it was her own feeling of inadequacy, or something else. The instructor's name was Rain and she had a tattoo of some kind, perhaps a Sanskrit phrase, encircling her upper arm, and myriad bangles and a tiny stud in her nose. And although the look suited Rain, she was almost too calm, too serene, too hip somehow – so much so that Layla imagined her going straight out the back after class and smoking a Marlboro Light, and that her real name was Tracy. Layla stifled a giggle. The entire front wall of the room was mirrored, and as she moved reluctantly towards it, all she could see were her three-quarter-length leggings, her baggy black T-shirt that she wore to bed sometimes, and she wished she didn't have to look at herself. She'd always thought yoga was meant to be internally focused, not a fashion parade like this place seemed to be. A woman was already lying prone on the mat next to the one Nicole had directed Layla to, and she was wearing black Lycra shorts, gym knicker-sized, and a designer sports top that exposed her teak-coloured midriff. Her bleached hair was cropped close to her head. Her pout was cartoon-like, definitely enhanced. And although she was probably nearing fifty, she had the body of a Russian athlete.

'Lie down, Layla,' stage-whispered Nicole.

Layla seriously debated whether she should make a run for it, before the class started, but people were streaming in now, lying down or sitting with their legs crossed and their eyes closed, their hands resting on their knees, both forefingers and thumbs joined in the shape of what Nicole had told Layla was called the Om mudra. To exit now, Layla would have to pick her way through the bodies with as much grim purpose as if fleeing a battlefield. She regretted allowing herself to be coaxed into such a situation when she hadn't wanted to come, and it reminded her of what had happened with Henry, and how she was too weak to say no sometimes – and all she could think of was how to escape.

'I'm sorry, can you budge over, love?' said a lilting voice, and as Layla opened her eyes she saw a young man in nothing other than tiny red running shorts who was trying to unroll his mat between her and the pouty athlete-woman. His skin was black and oiled, his chest smooth and muscly. When he lay down – far too close to her – he was so unlike Charles, who had a pale slack body and wore old man's boxer shorts, that the odd feverish feeling this stranger was creating near her hipbones evolved into an almost physical urge to push him away. Layla kneeled up and shuffled her mat towards Nicole, who had such a wide grin on her face it just made Layla go even more red, and, *really*, Nicole was too old to behave like a schoolgirl and, yes, the man might be Adonis-like but she was married, and he'd never be interested anyway, and Nicole should definitely know better.

When the class finally started it was far more brutal than Layla had imagined. Even the standing poses, where all she had to do was push her hands out in front of her and rotate her wrists, made her feel dizzy from the furnace-heat. Her body had broken out in an all-over sweat that felt oppressive, as though someone was trying to hold a pillow over her face. When she nearly keeled over as she came up from an attempt to touch her toes, that was it – she'd had enough. She lay down on her back and closed her eyes, which was what she'd been instructed to do if she felt at all unwell. *Stay in the room,* she'd been told. *Don't quit.* Her heart was pounding, and it felt as if she were sinking through the floor, as if there were a great weight on her, pushing her down . . . And now the room appeared to be tipping, tilting, lifting Layla up, and up, and as she opened her eyes the room was hot and heaving and the floor had settled at a crazy angle, as if she might fall off. On the next mat the man's sweat-beaded thigh, his scarlet-clad groin, were mere inches from Layla's face . . . and so she snapped her head to the other side. And although she didn't trust herself to not stagger, or perhaps barrel into someone's perfect downward dog on the way out, it was just too bad – she was leaving. She stood up and made a dash for it, almost made it – before she stumbled over a man at the very back, closest to the door. As he opened his eyes her own eyes widened. Surely not?

Layla mumbled an apology and fled to the changing rooms. She showered and dressed, and then she sat outside on the wooden bench seat and waited for Nicole. As she watched the people coming out at the end of the class, she didn't see the man she'd trodden on again – and so she was never quite sure whether it had been her new neighbour. Or not.

Chapter 10

JOAN

Joan had felt a familiar stab of jealousy as she'd seen Nicole get into Layla's Range Rover and had watched the two women drive off together. It was that constant feeling of being left out, as if she was never included in anything. It had permeated her entire life. And even though the last thing she would ever want to do was dress up in that ghastly Lycra Nicole always wore and go to an exercise class, it was the principle of the thing. Why didn't *she* ever get invited in for coffee at Layla's? And why did Layla seem to ignore her too now? What pack of lies had Nicole told Layla about Joan's ongoing feud with Ted? The whole situation was getting Joan down, in truth, and along with her indignation at the sudden, disruptive arrival of their mysterious new neighbour, it was compounding her grief that her sister was dead, and Lionel was getting on her nerves more than ever, and Layla's wretched cat was still doing its business in her garden, and she hadn't had her letter objecting to the proposed new off-licence in the village published in the local paper . . . and Joan felt as if she were reaching the limits of what she could endure. It was as if something needed to give, and soon, and she wasn't sure where to channel her wrath, what home to give it, on whom to take out her ever-increasing pique.

Joan let out a strangled kind of a growl as she stood up from having treated the bindweed to another shot of poison, and it wasn't just because her knees were creaking. She surveyed the close now as if it were enemy territory. She glowered at the brand-new gates that she'd been unable to prevent, despite her council connections, and it irked her all over again that they looked so alien, so out of place, but also that she couldn't see anything beyond them any more, had no idea what was going on at Number Three. The whole situation seemed creepy to her, as if there was something not right about it. Queer, her mother would have called it.

Well, Joan thought, she might not be able to see what her neighbour was up to, but at least she knew his name at last. When she'd spotted the postman coming up her driveway the other day, she'd rushed to open the door, claiming she was expecting a new credit card, although of course she wasn't. She'd asked the postman if he was *sure* there wasn't anything for her from her bank, and in the process had managed to snatch a look over his fleshy forearms to see a letter from Ocado for a Mr Andy Meyer. Joan had been cock-a-hoop about it, as it had only taken a total of four fake conversations over the past several days, and even if the once-ebullient postman never seemed happy to see her any more, she didn't care. Her strategy had paid off.

Sadly Joan's glee had been short-lived. It hadn't given her a single clue as to her neighbour's identity, and he'd have been hard pressed to have a more common name if he'd tried. Joan was determined to keep looking, though, keep trawling the Internet, as surely there must be something on there about him. Everyone had some kind of digital footprint these days – but, in truth, Andy Meyer's appeared to be very faint indeed. It only stirred her interest further.

Joan cast her beady glance around the rest of the close. Charles's Mercedes was absent, as was Ted's ghastly van. She'd just seen Layla and Nicole leave. Now was her chance. She put up the hood of her anorak, walked swiftly past Lionel's burgundy Volkswagen Passat, left her driveway and crossed the road. Up close the gates were even more unsightly and out of keeping than they appeared from her garden. On the adjacent pillar there was a chrome plate that contained a keypad and a small black screen; a single shiny button that Joan itched to press. She started to peer into the screen, and then it occurred to her that the owner might be able to see her, so she backed away and stood scowling at the gates. She felt tempted to pick up a stone and pelt them, but that would be childish. As she stood watching, her hands on her scrawny hips, her pointy chin jutting out, there was a sudden faint rumbling sound and the gates started to slide open. Joan was so shocked that she tried to turn around too quickly, stumbled on the damp sappy grass, only just managed to catch herself . . . and before she knew it the car had swept out of the driveway and driven away down the lane, as the gates slowly closed again.

Chapter 11

LAYLA

The car phone rang on the way home. Layla had offered to drive, mainly because Nicole was such a self-confessed terrible driver that Layla preferred to be in control of any potential near-death situations. She still had damp hair from the shower and her jeans were undone under her coat, as she hadn't realised how much the heat made your body swell up, and how hard it would be to get them on afterwards.

'Hi, Charles,' Layla said, and then added, pointedly, 'I'm on speakerphone.'

'I'm sorry, darling, I can't make tonight after all. We need to take a client from the US out to dinner and the chairman's coming, and, well, they're expecting me . . . Hello? Layla? Are you all right?'

'Yes, I'm fine,' she said. She made her tone as off as it could be with Nicole in the car, without Charles having a go at her about it later.

'I'm sorry, really I am.'

'I know you are.'

'Any news from the school?'

'No.'

'Well, no news is good news . . .' Even Charles seemed to realise how trite that sounded. 'Look, I won't be late, darling. Midnight at the very latest. See you later, bye.'

Layla tried to keep her face neutral as she pressed the button on the dash to end the call, which cut out slightly too late for them both to avoid hearing him say, 'It's OK, Lou, you can let Mike know I've got out of it,' and maybe it was because Nicole remained silent, surely trying to be tactful, that Layla reacted.

'You think he neglects me, don't you?' she said, as she turned off the lane and swung the car into the close, as aggressively as she could manage without crashing. It was so out of character of her to confront something, but she relished the feeling of exposure. What was there to hide? Her anguish was there for all to see, in her son-lost eyes. Why was she bothering to pretend she was OK about everything? Who was she pretending for anyway? The gravel on her driveway half-grumbled, half-squealed beneath the Evoque's tyres as Layla pulled to a halt. As she pressed the button that activated the handbrake she mourned her old car, its ability to have its lever yanked upwards, make a statement through stopping.

'You what?' said Nicole. She pushed her glossy black hair behind her ears. 'No, not at all. He's obviously got a lot on.'

Layla turned in the driver's seat and glared at Nicole. 'Go on, admit it. You think it's terrible what we've done with Henry, don't you?'

Despite Nicole's face being still a little red from the yoga, Layla could see her neighbour flush at the hairline, and she knew she was being unfair. Briefly she wondered whether there was a direct correlation between Henry leaving and her turning into a bitch. A bitter, bereft bitch. Let's see if she could pass on her pain, like it was a hot potato, or a bomb. *You asked for it, Nicole.*

'Layla, calm down, love,' Nicole said. 'Yoga's meant to destress you, not the opposite. I don't think anything. It's none of my business.'

'Well, that's a joke,' said Layla. 'Everything's *everyone's* business round here. Where I go shopping. What I do all day. Just what the Warners got up to in their spare time. Where they've moved to. Why the Taylors haven't replaced their car this summer, when for the past twenty years, apparently, they've had a brand-new Volkswagen *every* single year. Where Ted parks his stupid van. Who the new guy opposite is. How he can afford that place on his own, when he doesn't even seem to work. Why my cat insists on shitting in the Taylors' front garden. It's driving me crazy.'

Nicole got out of the car, looking as if she'd been punched. 'Layla, I'm sorry, love. I didn't know you felt that way. I was just trying to help.' She hauled her gym bag on to her bony shoulder. 'Listen, I won't have a coffee after all, thanks. I, er, need to get a couple of emails to the kids done. I'll see you later.'

As Layla watched Nicole walk across the road to her house, she looked frail suddenly, and too, too thin. She fumbled in her coat pockets for her keys, and then searched through her bag, seemingly increasingly desperately, and as she unlocked her front door, even from this distance it was clear to Layla that Nicole's hands were shaking. How could she, Layla, have been so *rude*? Why had she taken out her anger on her neighbour? It wasn't Nicole's fault. She'd just been being nice. *What was wrong with her?*

Layla clambered out of her car and stood on the running board to look out across the top of it.

'Nicole,' she yelled, not caring who might hear her. 'I'm so sorry.'

Chapter 12

Well, I need to find a new yoga studio. There is no way I'm going there again, if my beautiful neighbour attends. The look of shock on her face was gut-wrenching, and I wasn't sure whether she recognised *old* me, as I used to be, or *new* me, as I am now: the mysterious new neighbour she once passed in her car in the lane. I'm praying it's the latter. Even now it strikes me that maybe, all these years later, I'm still a version of the boy I once was, an identifiable one, and that people can spot me, know what I've done, and that's why they give me a look which is so nuanced, so complex, I'm not sure there's one single word for it. Curious disgust. That's the closest I can come to describing it. But hopefully I'm simply imagining the looks – merely dredging up the expressions from the sewer of my memories of twelve years ago – and people now are not looking at me like that at all, because they don't know who I am. How would they know? I'm unrecognisable. I have to remember the advice I've been given.

My official diagnosis is paranoid personality disorder. Everyone is out to get me, and I can't remember whether I always felt like that, or whether it has been made worse by who I became, what I did. But the end result is that, for now at least, I need to keep everyone at arm's length before they can hurt me or, perhaps more to the point, I can hurt them. The treatment I've had, both in prison and since I left, has allegedly had a positive effect, but the recommendation is that I need to steer clear of relationships for now, re-enter life gently, as if I'm coming up from deep water slowly, so as to avoid the bends. Hence my need for the gates. The gates that people will hate – and therefore hate me. I don't care. It's preferable to them despising me because they know the truth.

In the gym car park I start up my top-of-the-range Tesla. It has every last gadget, every last safety feature, but it appears unassuming to those who don't know about cars. I breathe deeply and hold my breath, count to twenty, as I've been taught, to control my impulses. I'd thought that a yoga class would be OK. I'd booked online, arrived late, slipped into the back, spoken to nobody. I'd assumed no one would notice me, that I would be able to relax, but I'd felt way too tense. For a start, the journey here had been terrible. I'd panicked when I'd seen someone, a woman I think, lurking just outside my gates as they'd opened, and although her hood had been up and I hadn't seen her face, I hadn't been prepared to see *anyone*, and my desire to flee had been so overwhelming I'd put my foot down, too hard – although fortunately I'd managed to keep control. But who was she? And what had she been doing? Had she simply been prying – or does she know something?

But these two events, these two unintentional encounters today, have made me realise that there are consequences to being out in the world. To being here in Hope Close. I have become a neighbour. I have neighbours. Short of living in a cabin in the woods, I will have to come into contact with other people at some point. Interact with them, in time. I knew that, of course. I wanted it, even. After all, I moved to this specific close for a reason. But not now, not yet . . . I'm not ready. And if that means that I can't go to hot yoga or head out in my car for fear of being spied upon, I will simply stay home, order takeout, and that will have to do for now.

Chapter 13

Nicole

Spin classes were like a form of torture, but Nicole felt as if she deserved it today. It was as if her sense of loss at the last of her children having left home had blown her wide apart, had made her doubt and regret every last decision she'd ever made. She couldn't pinpoint exactly what was wrong with her, but no matter how much she tried to concentrate, her mind was slipping way off course, leading her down futile alleyways and into hopeless dead ends, even if the bike itself remained fixed. It had been a week or so since Layla's tirade following their yoga class, and although Nicole had accepted her apology, what she'd said had hit home – had made Nicole wonder what she'd become. At least five times a week she drove to the gym in her fancy four-by-four with its personalised number plate, and she pedalled like hell to nowhere until her legs were sap-soft and her head was ready to fall off, and she tried to think about anything to take her mind away from the pain, but in the end the pain always won – and maybe that's why she did it. It seemed that the only thing that her mind could focus on right now was the agony.

After her class today Nicole showered as usual, got dressed, dried her hair, did her make-up, as usual, and then she got back into her big shiny car and drove home. When she unlocked her front door, Stanley was there, waiting for her, as delighted to see her as ever, and she dropped to her knees and buried her head in his furry shoulder. Once she finally stopped hugging him she realised her eyes were wet, and it was a surprise to her all over again how lonely she'd become since Tasha had gone. Thank God she still had Stanley, at least. She loved him and he loved her, and it was nothing more complicated than that. She put her arms around him again, breathed in his comforting doggy smell. She'd read somewhere that dogs don't like being hugged, but she didn't believe it. Stanley liked it.

At last Nicole stood up and headed into the kitchen, poured herself a glass of iced water from her American-style fridge dispenser and, as the cold scraped at her throat, she wondered who she was trying to punish here. The anger still burnt, almost as much as the water, and she tried to push the thoughts out of her mind. Yet it wasn't simply an ancient rage from the past any more, or her more recent resentment at the inattentiveness of her husband. There was new indignation, too, at her children, for daring to grow up, daring to dispense with her services. God, she missed them – and was it so wrong of her to wish one of them home? Almost even to yearn for their failure, their inability to manage in the big bad world? Was that so selfish? Or did that just make her a mother?

Nicole sank on to a chair at the kitchen table, put her head in her hands. These slow autumn days were perplexing her. Before this year it had always felt like a relief to get the kids back to school, get some peace and quiet after the mayhem of the summer, but this new level of entirely child-free calm was unsettling. She was barely sleeping from hot sweats and cold dark thoughts, and Ted was working so much at the moment he was hardly home, either – and although Nicole knew he had too much on, whenever she tried to say something he shut her down. Barked at her, almost.

He always took it as a criticism, couldn't see that she was only try-ing to help. Ted was a self-made man, and they were more than comfortable now, but he enjoyed his work, and good for him. It wasn't his fault how she felt. She'd thought she'd be glad to have some time to herself after all these years. She hadn't expected to become so needy. She'd tried not to let Ted hear the plea in her voice when she'd rung him to ask what time he'd be home. She'd never had much of a problem with the thought of being alone before. In fact, when Tasha had first headed off to London so full of optimism, Nicole had even breathed a sigh of relief, that she'd done it. That she'd managed to navigate her children through the minefield of school and friends and exams and college applica-tions, and that they'd made it out the other side apparently free of antidepressants or eating disorders or drug habits, unlike too many kids these days. Tasha seemed to have settled into her new life as easily as if she'd always lived away from home, and so what if she survived on soda bread and peanut butter, from what Nicole could gather – at least she was eating. Sean was fine in Manchester too, and Jason was set to become as successful as his father had been, if he carried on the way he was going.

And yet it seemed these new gaps in Nicole's daily life were raising doubts in her mind about who she was, what she had done, what her marriage meant to her. It was as if there was a hole open-ing up in her very psyche that she'd never realised was there before, one that she couldn't discuss with Ted – and what could he do about it, anyway? He couldn't fix it. No one could.

Stanley sauntered into the kitchen, and he had that look about him, as if he couldn't decide whether to be naughty, just for the fun of it, or whether he should try looking cute, to see if that got him a snack. He cocked his head as Nicole talked to him, and even after all these years it melted her heart, and as she got up from her chair and went to the cupboard to get him a Schmacko she remembered that Tasha always called them Crackos, as a reference to the treats' level of potency as far as Stanley was concerned. It made Nicole miss her daughter's funny little wisecracks, and somehow it was those tiny moments that were the hardest. The unexpected ones. The ones she always used to take for granted.

After a great deal of procrastination Nicole looked in the larder to see what she could make for tea. There were potatoes, and she had some mince in the fridge, but she couldn't be bothered to make a shepherd's pie, although she'd used to enjoy making big family-sized ones. Even the thought was exhausting now. She had a frozen lasagne from M&S in the freezer. Perhaps that would do for Ted, and she could have a salad. Nicole briefly wondered what was going on over the road from a culinary point of view. She and Layla might be in the same familial boat now, but Nicole would be prepared to put a bet on it that Layla didn't feed Charles ready meals.

Poor Layla, she thought, yet again. At least her three had flown the nest naturally, when they'd been ready. *Poor Henry.* Nicole had hated seeing the way his little body had drooped under the weight of the knowledge that he was leaving, and that his mother hadn't wanted him to go, and it had been painful to watch the three of them get in the car on that first day, as if they were heading off to purgatory. Henry was a smashing little boy – in one way old for his age, with precociously grown-up manners, and in another a baby still. It wasn't right. Nicole couldn't say anything, of course. Layla was so prickly about it, and it wasn't Nicole's place to do so, anyway.

Nicole's phone made the weird *ding-dong* trill of an incoming email. Tasha.

Hi Mum, Nicole read. *How are you? Not missing me too much I hope, lol. Job is good, but looking forward to starting college at last and getting some rest (joke!!). Out to a party tonight so must dash. Love you, Txxxx*

Nicole smiled. It was so nice to get an email like that. Tasha sounded so bright, so alive, that Nicole was tempted to press dial, call her daughter, but she knew she needed to give her some space. She mustn't encroach into Tasha's life, just because their respective iPhones meant they were never really away from each other. It had been so different when Nicole had first moved to London, in the days before everyone had instant connectivity. *She'd* had to grow up fast, way too fast in fact, but that was simply the way it had been back then. She'd survived. Just about.

Nicole went upstairs to deposit her gym bag, and as she entered her and Ted's bedroom it instantly brightened her mood. She loved the thick white carpet, the mirrored dressing table, the huge high bed with the satin cover at its foot, the thick silk curtains that swept the floor like a bridal train. It was just like a movie star's room, with its marble bathroom and walk-in wardrobe, and so what if people thought it was tacky. It was what she'd wanted.

Nicole padded over to the window and looked out, as if she couldn't help herself. The close looked as mismatched and incongruous as ever. There was the sweep of Layla and Charles's drive, the expanse of their lawn, the tasteful understated elegance of the house that had been there before all the others. She looked to the side, and there was the Taylors' prim neat bungalow, which still looked as if it had simply been plonked there, with its doll's house-like chalet roof lines and prissy window dressings. In fact, from up here it almost seemed as if the house was in miniature. Nicole disliked its tidy borders and twee hanging baskets, its air of coy menace, as though it were merely pretending to be welcoming, and she wondered if houses were just like their owners. Whether they chose each other. Grew into each other. The thought was disquieting.

The last house, with its brand-new black solid gates, had an unmistakeable 'keep out' vibe to it now. In some ways Nicole preferred that to the cutesy insincerity of the Taylors' house. This unfriendliness was unequivocal. Again, Nicole wondered at the house's new occupant. He seemed to have bought it very quickly, and she wondered whether, what with the house's history and how long it had been on the market, he'd got himself a bargain, and perhaps that was why he'd done it. As an investment or something. For a second Nicole almost found herself wishing the Warners still lived there . . . but that was what divorce did to families. It ripped them apart.

Oh, God. Nicole gave a little ineffectual stamp of her foot, cushioned as it was by the lushness of the carpet. She was turning into a curtain-twitcher, like that old boot next door. Why couldn't it have been the Taylors who'd moved, rather than the Warners? The Warners had been fun, far too much fun in retrospect, and the situation was comical almost. Nicole was still in shock at the revelations. The Warners really hadn't looked the type – but there again, maybe they never do.

Nicole went back downstairs, still in her leggings and vest top, and she was grateful that being dressed as if you were going to the gym was the fashion these days. Stanley followed her, still hopeful of a snack or, even better, some kind of sign that a walk might be on the cards. The postman came, and Stanley went predictably bananas, but there was nothing except a bill for Ted and a sale notice from Sweaty Betty, and Nicole was momentarily disappointed that no one wrote letters any more. She thought of the letter she'd written a million times in her head, but had never actually put down on paper . . . and perhaps *that* was the real problem. Maybe now was the time to confront it.

Guilt pulled at Nicole, toyed with her. It wasn't just what she'd done, but the fact that she'd never admitted it to anyone. Surely that was the real betrayal. She and Ted had had a whole lifetime together and yet she'd kept something so fundamental from him that to tell him the truth now felt almost impossible.

Nicole was restless. Her brain wouldn't stop for a break. How many times could she go up and down the stairs, look out of the window, see what was going on? *Nothing was going on.* Being alone with her thoughts was sending her mad. Eventually, she went into her marble bathroom, filled the oval standalone bath, even though she'd had a shower at the gym. She didn't even think consciously as she did it, and it was only when it was full, and the exquisitely scented bubbles were foaming luxuriously that she knew she wouldn't get in it. Have a bath in the middle of the afternoon? What kind of decadence was that? She was from Toxteth.

Nicole had had hundreds of days to herself before, of course, when the children had been at school – and yet now she didn't know how to fill them, how to stop unwelcome thoughts invading her brain. Maybe she'd walk into the village, go to the butcher's and get some really good steaks for dinner. That would impress Ted. Or perhaps she could go over to Layla's . . . but Nicole wasn't at all sure she'd be welcome, and the thought saddened her.

Stanley appeared at the bedroom door now, sniffing, looking ever-hopeful. Nicole told him to sit, and then she patted his big solid head, noticed the greying eyelashes around his adoring dark eyes. Maybe the steady pace of taking the dog down the lane would calm her. Perhaps she'd even be brave enough to head on to the Common for once, and it was funny how time passing dulled the fear. Besides, even if the killer had never been caught, it had been a one-off, an aberration, Nicole was sure of it – murders simply didn't happen in this part of Surrey. Despite it having been years ago, Nicole could still recall the shock, the sense of disbelief – especially when she'd found out that the victim had been the mother of one of Tasha's friends in primary school. Nicole had racked her brains, but she hadn't remembered the woman, and the disappointment she'd felt had been shameful. *She could have known a murder victim, if she'd helped out more at cake sales.*

Nicole sat down on the floor next to Stanley, for lack of anything better to do. She could still picture the young woman's face, which had been splashed all over the press for months, catapulting their little corner of the Home Counties into the forensic spotlight of notoriety. The woman had been laughing and carefree, and now she was dead – and Nicole decided she wouldn't go to the Common after all. There was a feeling in the air today that was unnerving her. Maybe she should call for Layla after all, ask her if she fancied coming with her. She could even suggest they share a glass or two of wine afterwards. Yes, that sounded like a plan.

A squeal of tyres took Nicole back to the window. She peered down, and saw it was Ted's van, the big cobalt-blue one, the one that annoyed Joan Taylor the most. She'd told Ted to stop baiting Joan, that it wasn't worth the aggro, but Ted was his own man and always had been. The dog started barking madly, and dashed down the stairs joyfully, making Nicole smile at his ability to recognise vehicles by their sound alone.

And yet even over the racket Stanley was making, Nicole could hear Ted shouting now. He was outside still, sounding absolutely outraged, and she needed to find out what was going on. She started to head downstairs, but had only made it as far as the half-landing when Ted burst through the front door, ranting, blood pouring from a ragged gash on his cheek.

'That is *it*!' he yelled. 'That fucking woman. I swear to God I'm going to kill her.'

Chapter 14

The sirens are a wailing banshee that send shockwaves through my very being, all over again. I hear them from afar, as if I'm attuned to them, and I try to convince myself that they will pass by, continue up the lane, but dismayingly, horrendously, they don't. Instead they get louder, more high-pitched, and when I run upstairs, peer out of the window, panic patrolling my body, poking me from the inside, there is a police car pulling up outside, and my worst fears are confirmed.

They are coming to get me. I'm surprised it took them so long. Inevitability is a form of defence, I suppose. There's no point trying to make the outcome any different, and I should have known not to have bothered. I am the hunted. As I continue watching proceedings from the front bedroom, I can feel my guts melting, liquifying, as I wonder which of the neighbours has reported me. I am too horrified to look away, too appalled to run.

And yet now the narrative is veering off-piste – and instead of the police tramping their way to my gates, I see them rush to the big house next door. It's confusing me, and I can only assume they've got my address wrong. But when they go inside and don't come out again, I start to question whether they've come for me after all. I begin to wonder what has happened next door, whether the husband has murdered the wife, perhaps. While I'm still processing that hypothesis, an ambulance rips around the corner and roars into the close, and two men in dark green uniforms jump out and rush inside the house too. It seems there really is something serious going on in there – and that it's definitely nothing to do with me. The relief is like that moment when you wake up to find the nightmare you're embroiled in, have been living through, experiencing via every cell of your overwrought body, is just that. Except when it's not.

I keep my vigil at the window. After another few minutes I see the two police officers leave, cross the close and knock on the door of the blingy house opposite, the one with the van. Someone answers and the police go inside and the door shuts. Soon after that I see an old woman being taken out of the first house in a wheelchair, the dark-skinned beautiful woman I saw at the yoga studio by her side. The injured woman is pinched-looking and ugly, with a shock of horrible hair, and I don't know if it's from pain or whether her face always looks like that. As she gets loaded into the waiting ambulance, I still have no idea what's going on. Why are the police at two houses now? Might they still be coming to call at mine next? The prospect sends my pulse racing again. The uncertainty is freaking me out.

At long last the police and the ambulance leave – without visiting me, thank God – and the close is quiet once more. I feel so shaken I head downstairs to my living room, which still smells of paint. Now that this room has been stripped bare it feels like a sunken white box, with bright sharp stairs leading down from the hallway and plate-glass windows that give a great green vista out towards the surrounding hills. I sit on my grey corner sofa and gaze out at the swaying green trees, the drifting blue-and-white sky, trying to feel grateful, but I fail. How can I be *grateful*? For what?

And now my mind flips and beats and it seems I can't help it. I have to do it. I have to punish myself. I take out my new laptop and go online, google myself, search out my past, unveil my secret history . . . and as I see the images in all their dread vibrancy, I revile myself, feel that physical tug of self-disgust. *I hear him crying, telling me to stop, but I'm oblivious, there in that oh-so-beautiful moment.*

I breathe deeply, commune with the memory, try to make peace with it. Finally, when I'm mentally drained from the pictures served up to me, of uncorrupted youth, guileless innocence, I clear the computer's history, lie down on the hard wooden floor, stare up at the blank bare ceiling and concentrate on the dragging pain in my bones, the gaping wound in my heart, the slack hopelessness in the very depths of myself.

And then I close my eyes and wish the world away.

Chapter 15

JOAN

The emergency services had taken an age to turn up, which in Joan's opinion was a disgraceful dereliction of duty – Ted could have murdered her by then for all anyone cared. It was shocking what a thug her neighbour was, and Joan knew she'd been right about him all along. You couldn't disguise trash, and Ted and his common-as-muck wife were the biggest trash of all. All she, Joan, had done when Ted had come roaring round the corner in his hideous van and pulled to a stone-flinging halt in the middle of his driveway was go over and ask him, really quite politely, all things considered, if he could move it round to the side of his house, where there was plenty of room, but he had point-blank refused.

'You know what, Joan,' Ted had said, in his coarse, overloud voice. 'You need to understand that this is *my* house,' and he'd jabbed at his chest like some kind of Neanderthal. Next he'd gestured towards the other houses, one by one. 'And that is *Layla and Charles's* house. And that is *the new fella's* house, and those are *the new fella's* gates. We can all do whatever we like on our own properties. What *you* think about any of it matters not a toss. Why can't you ever understand that, and just mind your own fucking business for once in your pathetic little life?'

'Don't you dare speak to me in that way,' she'd said.

'I'll talk to you how the fuck I want,' Ted had continued, fully revving up now. 'You make my life absolute hell. You moan about *everything*. My van. Smoke from my barbecue blowing on your washing. Weeds. Stuff being mysteriously put in your bins! *We've got our own bloody bins.* We don't *need* your bins. And all the while you let that fucking tree at the back grow, ruin our view and you *enjoy* it. You enjoy making other people's lives a *misery*.' Ted had paused then, raised his voice even louder. 'You know what? Everyone round here *hates* you, and it's no bloody wonder.'

Joan had advanced towards him at that point, not even consciously, and so what if she'd been holding a pair of secateurs. What on earth did he think she was going to do with them?

'Don't you aim those fucking things at me, you stupid bitch,' Ted had yelled. 'Why don't you just fuck off out of here, go to an old people's home or something. Even your own husband bloody hates you!'

Something had snapped in Joan then, and it was hard to remember the details of what had happened next. But suddenly she'd been down on the ground and there'd been a searing pain in her knee, and she'd started screeching for Lionel, but in typical useless fashion he'd just left for Camera Club. And then Ted had stormed into his house and slammed the door and Joan had been left there, injured and all alone. It was Layla, of all people, who'd come out to see if she was OK, and Layla, under Joan's instructions, who had called 999. After that she'd helped Joan stand up and hobble over to her house while they'd waited for the emergency services to come – and even in her shocked, injured state Joan had noticed how grand Layla's house was, and it had made her feel peeved all over again that she'd never been invited over the threshold before, not even once. To give Layla her due, though, she'd been attentive enough. She'd sat Joan down in the luxurious front room and propped up her leg with cushions. She'd fetched a bag of frozen peas to put on the alarming lump that had appeared through Joan's tights. She'd brought Joan a mug of hot sweet tea, and had asked her continually if she was all right. And she'd seemed genuinely shocked when Joan had told her how Ted had verbally assaulted her, and then pushed her over. Joan was hopeful that this episode might even break up the budding friendship between Layla and Nicole, despite the fact that she could tell that Layla was one of those types who never liked to take sides, wanted to keep in with everyone. She was wishy-washy, in Joan's opinion, had no backbone, which was probably why she'd allowed the boy to be packed off to school, almost certainly against her wishes. And yet, still, Joan wanted Layla to like her. There was something about Layla that drew people to her. She seemed vulnerable, weak even, but there was a side to her that was unknown. Unknowable. She intrigued Joan.

Joan sighed. She was lying in a hospital bed in a curtained-off cubicle in A&E, being ignored, which appeared to be par for the course. Layla had ended up coming in the ambulance with her, mainly because the ambulance crew (who'd acted like they were some kind of comedy double act, which Joan had found entirely inappropriate and had told them so) had assumed that she was Joan's daughter. As Joan had seen the look of horror that had whipped across Layla's face at the mistake, gone as soon as it had come, it had made her all the more determined to make Layla accompany her. And anyway, who else could she have called on? Lionel hadn't taken his phone out with him, as usual, and Anne had been the only other person who'd be there in such an emergency, and she was dead.

Joan took a breath. Her knee was agony, and she hadn't even had it X-rayed yet. Plus her waste of space of a husband still hadn't turned up, and neither had the police. The police officers she'd briefly spoken to at Layla's – who'd been very nice, to be fair – had suggested she get off to the hospital to have her knee seen to first, and that they'd come to take her statement there, once they'd finished interviewing Ted. At the time Joan had been OK with the suggestion, but now she regretted it. It wasn't fair that Ted was getting to give his side of the story first. Who knew what he would say? And although Layla was still here with her, having promised that she'd stay until Lionel turned up, it was clear that she was desperate to leave. The whole situation was a shambles, Joan thought – and she was mortified to discover she was near to tears.

A friendly woman in a blue uniform poked her head around the curtain. 'Would you like some tea and a sandwich from the trolley, love?' she said.

'No, I would not,' Joan snapped. 'What I would like is to know what on earth is going on!'

When Joan saw the apologetic look that Layla gave the hospital worker, it merely made her more furious. Perhaps unfortunately, it was at exactly that point that the police arrived, looking bulky in their black uniforms, and thoroughly out of place in the spick white of a hospital.

'Well, about time!' Joan said.

'Mrs Taylor,' one of the police officers said, and she was noticeably less friendly than she'd been earlier. 'We need to find out exactly what happened between you and your neighbour. Are you OK with doing that now?'

Joan let out a disgruntled huff. 'Of course,' she said. 'Why wouldn't I be?'

The police officer turned and looked at Layla, appeared uncomfortable.

'It's all right, you can say it in front of *her*,' Joan said.

'Because,' the police officer said at last, 'I'm afraid your neighbour wants to press charges against you.'

Chapter 16

Layla

Layla thought Henry might look as if he'd grown in the three weeks since she'd deposited him at boarding school, but if anything he appeared to have shrunk – become diminished in both stature and soul. She'd felt inordinately excited as she and Charles and all the other parents had waited in the school's main hall for their children to burst through the door, so they could be taken for their very first weekend home. Layla had longed to see her son, regain some normality to her life, especially as Hope Close had felt like a car crash of late. First there'd been Joan's strident, ultimately fruitless campaigning about Number Three's new gates, where she'd even knocked on Layla's door and tried to lobby her to add her name to a petition to the council. Layla had done her best to explain to Joan that it would make no difference, but Joan had stomped off as though she herself, rather than her sad little petition, had been rejected by Layla. And then when the builders had eventually turned up to fit the gates, Joan had proceeded to harangue them so rudely that they'd finally told her to just go away, loudly enough for Layla to have heard it from inside her house. When Layla had looked out of the window she'd almost thought Joan was about to lie down in front of the lorry, and it would have been funny if

Layla hadn't felt sorry for her. People seemed to always take a dislike to Joan, from what Layla could tell, and no one deserved that. Everyone had some redeeming features.

Unfortunately, though, things in the close had taken an even more unpleasant turn lately. Layla was glad that she hadn't actually seen what had happened between Ted and Joan, so still had no idea who to believe. All she knew for sure was that Ted had sustained a nasty gash to his cheek and Joan had ended up on the ground, badly spraining her knee in the process. It seemed absurd for two adults to behave like that over where a van was parked, and Layla wondered what was going to happen next. It appeared that Ted was trying to press charges, but seeing as there were no witnesses, how would anyone know who was telling the truth, who had attacked who first? It seemed like a waste of everybody's time and energy. Layla wished Ted and Joan would just make up and reside next to each other civilly. Life was too short for such feuds, and Layla had never known anything like it. No one had behaved like this in London. Maybe it was simply that there was nothing better to do in Hope Close than worry about what everyone else was up to. It was sad. She was so glad to be having Henry home for the weekend at last, so she wouldn't have time to think about the neighbours.

Layla had imagined today's scene at the school a thousand times, had pictured Henry running to her, rude of health and chatty, the reunion between mother and son joyful and reassuring to them both. Yet instead Henry had skulked into the hall looking pale and out of sorts, and she'd swooped down and buried her face in his raven hair so he couldn't see her instant, involuntary tears. He'd tried to shrug her off, but fortunately she still very much had the size advantage. The pain was like a poisoned jab through her heart, transferring the anguish, his suffering becoming hers, too – the agony being enough for the both of them. What made it worse was that all the other boys seemed to be laughing and chattering, introducing their new friends to their parents, while Henry seemed woefully, painfully alone. Even nine-year-old Jacob, who had been Henry's mentor and had solemnly shaken Henry's hand in welcome when they'd arrived on that first bewildering day, blanked Henry as he passed by in the melee. Layla couldn't stand to see it, and she wished they were being mean to *her*, rather than to her son. As she and Charles swiftly made their exit and ushered Henry to the car they spoke to no one, waved goodbye to no one. And now, on the drive home, Henry was monosyllabic, and she knew that she'd been right all along, that one day he would resent her for this.

'Looking forward to getting home, sweetheart?' she said, her tone as bright as she could manage.

'I guess.'

'Is Matron nice?'

'She's OK.'

'What are the other boys like, darling?'

'All right.'

'What are the names of the boys you like most?'

'I can't remember.'

'Well, you must be able to remember some names, sweetie. Who do you sit next to in class?'

'I dunno.'

And at that Charles had leant over and squeezed her knee, as if to warn her not to harass their son. Layla was bewildered by Henry. Where was her sweet, relaxed boy, with his easy, friendly manner, the ebullient closeness they'd used to share? It was gone, perhaps forever. She hated Charles suddenly, that he'd done this to their family.

'What, am I not even allowed to talk to my son now?' she said. She couldn't see Henry's face in the seat behind her, didn't care that he'd heard, and her unfettered childishness was a shock to her. Usually she and Charles didn't argue in front of Henry. Normally they managed to be the grown-ups, and yet maybe, Layla realised now, that was part of the problem – that she hadn't ever been honest about her emotions, and so her son had no idea how she really felt about him going away to school. Perhaps he even thought that she'd *wanted* to get rid of him.

'Shush, Layla,' Charles said. 'Of course not.'

'Don't you "shush" me!' She glared at him, her eyes black with rage.

Henry started to cry now, and the sound was different to anything Layla had heard before. His weeping wasn't lusty or raucous or indignant, like it used to be. This was the quiet whimper of the defeated. The closed confines of the car only made the atmosphere more fraught, more fragile, as if they were all steering off course, towards a cliff edge perhaps.

'Layla, be quiet,' said Charles now. His voice had a rare note of sternness – usually his will prevailed in less overt ways. 'We'll discuss this when we get home, when we can all be calm about it.'

'Calm about it? I've *been* calm about it and look where it's got us all. I'm not going to be calm any more!' Layla was yelling now.

Charles squeezed on the brakes, pulled off the road into a lay-by, glared at Layla. Her eyes flashed at him in return, and for a moment she thought he might strike her. Instead he let out a low, growling, 'For God's sake,' and leapt out of the car, slamming the door as he went. Then he stormed round to Henry's seat, undid his son's seatbelt and hauled him out.

'It's all right, little man,' Layla heard her husband say, as he pulled open the passenger door now. 'Mummy's just a little bit upset. Why don't you have a cuddle with her?' And then Charles gently placed Henry on Layla's lap, and as she held her little boy to her, she realised that this was typical of Charles – that just when she hated him most, he would do something like this. Was he saint, or arch manipulator? Layla could never tell.

'I'm so sorry, darling,' she murmured into Henry's hair.

Henry sniffed and pulled away. 'That's OK,' he said, in the manner of someone who didn't mean it.

'I'll make it up to you, I promise.'

Henry brightened at this, spotting an opportunity.

'How?'

'Oh, I don't know, sweetheart. We'll think of something.'

Henry didn't miss a beat.

'Can I get a drone?' he said.

Chapter 17

I have a new activity, one that I haven't discussed with my latest therapist, as I'm pretty sure he wouldn't approve. But it's harder than I thought being completely on my own. I flick sideways. And then I flick again. And again. I flick and flick and flick and still no one interests me. One girl looks cute, but beneath the hair and the make-up I can see the deadness in her eyes. And yet maybe that's what I need. I swipe right, and the impact on me is almost immediate. *Relief.* I have something to look forward to now. A response. A chance of a response. The impulse to keep checking my phone, just in case I've missed something. The anticipation at the prospect of her swiping me back, of what she might say if she does, which doesn't even matter. I won't meet her. What matters is the *chance* of being noticed. It's like casting a stone out into a pond and watching the ripples grow, until potentially at last they reach back to you, make an impact, instead of simply fizzling out into calm again.

I'm sitting on my drab grey sofa in my bright white lounge. The giant TV is on, broadcasting an inane procession of terrible daytime programming, but I have the sound off. It's company, of a sort. The sun is shining, and the room feels glaring and shiny, almost like being in a heavenly dream, or else an asylum. The windows still unnerve me, but I've checked from the outside, in all kinds of weather conditions, and the glass the previous owners had fitted is definitely one hundred per cent mirrored. So even if some-one did manage to get through my security fences, prowl around out in the garden, there's no way anyone would be able to see me. I can look out, butt-naked if I want, yet no one can look in. No one can get to me. Not any longer. And at night I pull the heavy blackout curtains to obliterate every trace of the outside world, as if it no longer exists.

I'm still unsure of my state of mind. I'm lonely, that's for sure, but I've been told I need this period of self-imposed reclusion while I continue adjusting to being a free man. My therapist says I need to take it slowly. After all, it's hard to start all over again. But on the plus side it's as if I've been given a second chance. A blank slate. And although I'd thought that solitude would be a blessed relief, I miss the process of connecting with the world, at least rudimen-tarily. I find I miss how I used to look once – my strong jaw, my mussy blond hair, my exuberant, don't-give-a-fuck youthfulness. Being dark suits me well enough, and the beard is trendy, allegedly, but it doesn't feel like *me*. I don't mind my new profile, though, and who knew a basic nose job could make so much difference? My multi-skilled lawyer has drawn up a watertight contract with the surgeon, so I won't need to worry on that front. In fact, I'm almost certain I'll never be discovered – I'm as separate from who I used to be as only a decade in jail could make me.

Ahh, prison. I almost miss it. The regime, the hierarchy, the fact that you have to stay strong as fuck to survive. Stay impassive. Follow the rules. I even miss the fact that in prison there were people everywhere, and even if you couldn't see them, you could still hear the drumbeat thrum of a thousand flawed hearts aching for some kind of release. Here the sound is of silence.

And thus, as I rattle about this house, it's about as different from an eight-by-six prison cell as it could get. But did being locked up make me who I am today? And, if so, how ashamed should I be?

Do I despise myself, or merely what I have done? It's a philosophical question that years of prison study still hasn't answered.

When my phone pings it is an alien noise. I snatch it up from the hard-edged glass coffee table that I need to get rid of. I don't like it. It is cold and the angles are sharp, and it feels too fragile, a bit like the world I inhabit now. When I look at the screen I see that Dead Eyes has swiped me back. *She's interested.*

Should I meet her? Will I meet her? What the hell else am I going to do? I'm still only in my thirties. I can't live like a monk forever. She won't ever know who I am – I'm a different person now, quite literally. And I can't go back, make the bad stuff be undone, however much I might want to. Death is death is death. And casual sex is just that. Casual.

And so. As I start to type out my message, I try to convince myself that I've done my time. I've paid my penance. I won't hurt her. I won't tell her, either, of course. What more, on God's earth, can I do? At long last I press send, and when I hear the message swoosh its way through the ether, to her, to where she is, the relief I feel is painful in its sweetness.

Chapter 18

LAYLA

Layla thought Henry's new drone, bought the next day in Guildford, was a very bad idea, and told her husband and son so.

'Joan will go mad,' she said mildly, as Charles and Henry were in the kitchen opening up the drone's box, as excited as little boys at Christmas, unveiling squeaky polystyrene packaging that set Layla's teeth on edge, her reaction further delighting Henry. The drone itself seemed a flimsy, ugly-looking thing, certainly not worth the three hundred pounds that Charles had allegedly spent on it.

'There's enough grief amongst the neighbours as there is at the moment,' Layla said. 'Plus the new guy will think we're spying on him.'

'Well, maybe that's my intention,' Charles replied.

Layla turned sharply and stared at her husband, and then realised he was joking. He was surprising her lately, in ways that she was unsure about.

'So why *have* you bought it?'

'Oh, I don't know, Layla.' There was a note of weariness in Charles's voice now. 'Because Henry wanted it. Because it's his first weekend home. Because he was upset. Is that OK with you? Or do I have to ask your permission?'

'Well, that's rich,' Layla said, her voice flaring a little. She tried to communicate the rest of her thoughts through the look she threw at him, over the top of Henry's head: *You've made all the decisions about our son, to the extent he doesn't even bloody well live with us. I have no say at all.*

And now Layla and Charles were glaring at each other, the mood erratic, combustible, unprecedented. It was Layla who capitulated first. She dropped her gaze, stared instead at the cool hard surface of the oversized kitchen island. As she surveyed the deep vein of the marble, she thought about how much she disliked it, how the pattern reminded her of the backs of old people's hands, or stinky blue cheese. Unfortunately, she couldn't blame her husband for the worktop. That particular decision had been made by the previous owners, and they'd presumably been convinced, by someone, that the marble would be a 'statement' – even though it showed every mark, so you couldn't even risk cutting a lemon on it, and was so big it reminded Layla of a slab at a morgue. The thought made her shudder. And then she realised she was as much to blame as her predecessors were, for buying their stupid house in the first place. For agreeing to move to the country at all.

'Henry, will you go and find my toolbox and fetch a screwdriver, little man?' Charles was saying now, even though he didn't need one.

Henry, being both resourceful and obedient, duly trotted off to the cellar.

'Is that how you really feel, Layla?' Charles said, as soon as Henry was out of earshot. His voice was soft now, tinged with sadness.

Layla took a breath. 'I just don't know if boarding school's right for Henry, Charles. He doesn't look well, and he's such a timid little boy, and what with his—' Layla stopped, as if sensing she shouldn't mention her other concerns, that it wouldn't help anything. 'Perhaps there's just too much stress on him.'

Charles came over to her, put his arms around her, from behind. At first she liked the feeling . . . but as she felt herself slipping into acceptance, which is surely what he wanted, she extricated herself, went over to the glass sliding doors that gave on to the terrace, and which seemed too far away from the island, as if the kitchen had been supersized, rendering the distances all wrong. This was a two-way decision. She was Henry's mother. She had rights, too.

'Just give it a chance, darling,' Charles said now. 'Let's review how it's going at Christmas.'

Layla gazed out to the garden and the countryside beyond as she pondered her husband's suggestion. Clouds scudded in the wide, whirling sky above a smorgasbord of greens. It was the world on time-lapse, the clouds in a hurry to split and form, dip and dive, flee the wind, chase the sun. Already autumn had started robbing the trees of their leaves, and soon the scene would be curiously blank, bereft. Like her. Layla pictured the drone flying up there, above the branches, amongst the clouds, swooping over the four houses, pitching, diving, searching for secrets, unearthing something. It still felt implausible, that Charles would have bought such a thing for Henry, from Argos of all places, but most events that happened in Layla's world felt implausible these days. She hadn't expected Joan and Ted's feud to have descended into an unedifying physical fight that had left Joan in hospital. She hadn't bargained on Nicole trying so hard to befriend her, or for a handsome mystery man to have suddenly moved into the house next door.

'What do you mean, Charles?' Layla said, at last. 'You really would be prepared to take Henry out of boarding school?'

'Of course I would,' Charles said. 'I don't want him to be miserable any more than you do. But it's done now. He's there, and we need to give him time.'

As Layla was deciding how to reply, her son appeared at the kitchen door, a choice of flat-headed and Phillips screwdrivers in his hands, and she admired his ability to hedge his bets. Like his father. She was relieved to see that his face had started to regain a bit of colour and his eyes seemed alive again, as though there was stuff burning beneath the surface, illuminating him, animating him. But why hadn't he been like that at school? Had it been due to homesickness, or bullying, or not eating enough . . . or something else yet more sinister? Charles always insisted that none of that stuff went on any more, and that Layla was imagining things. Maybe she should just ask Henry outright, yet it felt like the wrong way to approach it. And weren't abusers notoriously good at making their victims unwilling to tell? But she didn't have a clue what the right way to broach it was, either.

As Layla watched Henry and Charles tinker with the machine, she tried to convince herself that she was overreacting. Henry's behaviour appeared completely normal now, and it seemed the drone hadn't been such a bad idea after all. In fact, it could even prove useful. Maybe Charles and Henry could spy on the neighbours for her – check out Joan's shed, deliberately fly over Number Three's garden, breach the new guy's defences, find out just what mystery he was hiding behind those black forbidding gates. There was something untoward about him, Layla was sure of it – some untold story behind him moving here. Maybe she could even ask Joan what she'd found out about him during her campaign to Stop The Gates. If anyone was ever going to get to the bottom of a story, it was Joan. And at least talking to her neighbour would give Layla something to do, something else to think about, other than relentlessly worrying about her son.

Chapter 19

There are times when I question why I haven't chosen the crowded-ness, the anonymity that London affords, even wonder whether I have made a monumental mistake coming here. One answer is that London was the place of my myriad sins, and so it feels impossible to go back – it holds too many bad memories for me. My reasoning for a move to the country was that it would afford me peace, privacy, a sense of protection; would enable me to hole up behind a full security system, complete with entry-phones and a suite of surveillance cameras; would allow me time to adapt, in my own private prison.

And yet moving here was irresistible for another reason too, of course – not that I've admitted it to anyone, not even my admirably amoral solicitor, who, given the amount I'm paying him, I know I could trust to remain tight-lipped. But I didn't want to tell *anybody* about my link to Hope Close, and who knows whether I will ever reveal it – or even one day be discovered. It's unlikely, but it's a possibility. What will be will be. It adds a frisson. I almost like it.

The other unexpected thing about living here is that, despite all four properties having large rear gardens, the houses themselves are near to each other, like sheep huddled together for warmth in a giant field. It makes the close feel overly intimate, and I hadn't bargained on the impact of living in a cul-de-sac. It hadn't occurred to me that whenever my smooth automatic gates are in operation, it might be noted by one or other of the neighbours. It's a major strategic flaw, one I'd failed to consider. I'm tempted to blame my solicitor, as he physically visited the house, should have spotted the issue, but I guess there's no use hanging everything on him. It's done.

As I pull through the gates into my driveway and hear them rumble shut behind me, the ambivalence I feel about being here surprises me all over again. I get out of my car, unlock the front door, make my way to my living room, sit down on the sofa, gaze out at the garden . . . but I find that I'm shaking now, and it's happening again . . . and it's a guttural kind of shudder that resonates through my spine, amplifying its impact . . .

And now I can feel that familiar deep need for escape, from the very bones of myself. Tiny bubbles start to form in the furthest depths of my lungs, and I can feel them pop and fizz, fizz and pop, slowly build to a crescendo of horror and self-loathing so debilitating I can hardly breathe. *Suddenly I can see Sian's face, there in my mind's eye, twisted and full of hate.* She was my best friend once and we grew up together, and yet now I despise her – although it's too simplistic to blame her for my downfall, as I know that I'm just as culpable. I wish with all my heart I'd said no to her, had never ever got involved . . .

And still my throat is tightening, ever tightening, holding back the primal roar of hopelessness, and I need help, relief of some kind, but I have relinquished my old form of decamping from myself, and there is no respite, and it is agony . . . and so although the next thought is inevitable, part of the doom-laden cycle, it very nearly destroys me all over again.

I miss my family. But what can I do about that? It's too late. They're dead.

When at last the panic starts to pass, I'm almost proud of myself, that I'm through it. That my coping techniques are working. I lean back on the couch and my arms and legs are so heavy they feel like they may never work again, but I know that they will. The body is a machine like no other. You have to fight harder than you might imagine to destroy it, and I should know. I concentrate on gradually slowing down my breathing, bringing myself back from the edge, of what, of where, I don't even know. I can feel the throb in my leg now, pulsing through the scar tissue, reminding me of the dismal past. And then, amidst the still-swirling flurry of disturbing images and relentlessly futile memories, the intercom buzzer goes – and it feels so jarring, so violent, I might as well have been shot.

Chapter 20

Layla

Despite Layla's misgivings, the drone was proving to be an undeniable success, and it was down to more than simply Henry's delight with it. There was something oddly attractive about small boys and their fathers playing with remote-controlled objects that moved or, better still, flew. Layla herself couldn't see the point of launching a flimsy, arachnoid piece of plastic into the sky, merely to take uninteresting footage that no one would ever look at, but she'd found her heart softening as she'd watched Henry and Charles assembling the drone, poring over the instructions, working out how to make it fly, and she couldn't decide whether father or son was more thrilled at the prospect. She was so delighted to have Henry home, and yet the situation felt fraught, too, seeing as they would soon have to go through the separation all over again – although Layla tried to reassure herself that it couldn't possibly be as bad as the first time. She was fully aware that Henry would be picking up on her own distress, so she determined to convince herself that her son was OK. That all three of them were OK. Surely, she told herself, if you believe it so, you can make it so.

Layla pulled up the hood on her sweatshirt and hunched her shoulders against the cold. She was out in the back garden, ready to witness the inaugural flight, which was taking so long she debated whether she should go in and get her duffel coat. As she waited for her husband and son, she found herself swept away all over again by the beauty of the views – and agreeing with Charles that this house was special. Beyond their boundary, lollipop trees clustered around patchwork fields where the odd horse grazed. A church spire nestled bucolically, before the hills rose again in the far distance, fragile like mist. Perhaps everything would work out, Layla thought. Henry would be home every few weekends, as well as for all the holidays, and now that he'd got through the official settling-in period she'd be allowed to go and watch him play sports during the week. And anyway, maybe it was time for her to start focusing on other things aside from being a mother to Henry, seeing as he was destined to grow up one day, whether he went away to boarding school or not. He wouldn't be a child forever, and Layla didn't want to end up like Nicole, approaching middle age with no rhythm or purpose to life now that her kids were gone. Maybe taking on Nicole's kitchen project would be good for her, assuming Nicole was serious about it. She knew it could be awkward working with friends, especially ones who lived across the road from you – but on the other hand it would give her something to do, a way back into her career even. Briefly she thought about discussing it with Charles, and then she decided to keep her counsel for now – not because she was afraid of what he would say, of course, but because she wanted to be surer of how she felt about it herself.

'You ready, Henry?' Charles said now.

'Yes, Daddy.'

'I'll get it into the air, and then you can have a go, OK?'

'Ohhhh.' The little boy stuck out his bottom lip, turned to his mother for support. 'I wanna do it.'

'No, sweetie.' Layla smiled at her son, lowered her voice to a mock whisper. 'Let Daddy have a go first, so we can laugh at him when he crashes it.'

Henry looked unimpressed. 'No! He'll break it.'

'No, he won't, and it will make him feel important. You know how much Daddy loves to drive.' She winked.

Henry hesitated, crinkled his nose, and then decided to play along.

'You ready, Henry?' Charles said.

'I suppose so,' Henry said, pretend-sulkily, flashing a conspiratorial grin at his mother.

'You do the countdown, then,' Charles said.

'Five, four, three, two, one, lift-off!'

Even Layla felt her heart stall, as if waiting for something, as the drone lifted vertically into the air. Just a few inches up it wobbled a little, like a bumblebee trying to land on a flower it was too heavy for, and for a moment it threatened to nosedive straight into the grass . . . but at last the machine righted itself and soared away in a haphazardly upward fashion, increasingly resembling an angry, drunk hornet, with a single unblinking eye. Charles seemed like an excited little boy himself as he pushed the buttons on the controller, trying to work out how to manoeuvre the drone, a thrum of concentration writing lines along his forehead. And all the while Henry was screaming, 'Me, me, me, my turn!' as he tried to grab the controls from his father.

'Let him have a go now, Charles,' Layla said. 'You did buy it for him, remember.'

Reluctantly, Charles handed over the remote and Henry took over. Weirdly, he was instantly way more proficient than Charles had been, and it seemed to Layla that the kids of today had innate skills that their parents just did not possess – and that must be what spending hours on the PlayStation did to you.

'Send it over towards the village, Henry,' Charles said now.

Henry ignored his father and directed the drone in completely the other direction, towards the open fields, throwing in an expertly executed barrel roll while he was at it.

'Have you done this before, Henry?' said Charles, clearly suspicious, and surely a little put out.

'No,' said Henry. 'But it's easy.' His eyes were shining with delight, and Layla rarely remembered him looking so happy. *He was fine. He was going to be fine.*

'Where are you going, Henry?' Charles said. 'There's nothing over there.'

'Don't you dare even *think* about dive-bombing the horses, Henry,' Layla said, twigging what her son might be planning. Henry grinned and ignored her.

'Henry, bring it back!' Charles yelled. 'You'll go out of range.' He lunged at his son, tried to grab the remote controls off him, but Henry skipped away, seemingly enjoying winding up his father almost as much as flying his drone.

'Henry . . .' said Charles, warningly. At last Henry capitulated and turned the machine in the sky, started to bring it back towards the houses . . . but the wind was against it and it didn't seem to be making much progress, despite Charles's exasperated proclamations for Henry to hurry up.

Just as the drone finally reached the sky above Hope Close, it appeared to stall, hang in the air for a second . . . and then, before any of them had time to do anything about it, it started plummeting towards the ground . . . before crashing, plumb in the centre of their new neighbour's back garden.

◆ ◆ ◆

The neighbour had refused to answer his buzzer – even though Layla was pretty sure he'd been there, having seen his car through a crack in the gates. And now it was hours later, and Layla and Charles were holed up in their bedroom, the door closed, and Layla was nearing hysteria, although trying to contain it. She spoke in a loud, insistent whisper. 'I'm telling you, Charles. That reaction is *not normal*.'

'He was just having a tantrum, Layla. He's playing you.'

'He is not playing me! I've never seen him behave like that before, ever. It was as if he were *possessed*. And now he's fast asleep, in the afternoon, and he hasn't done that since he was three!'

'Well, he's probably tired. Look, it's a tricky time for him.' Charles paused, as if debating what to say. 'I remember feeling like that at first.'

'At first when?'

'When I went away to school.'

'Oh, so *now* you're telling me!' Layla said. 'Bloody hell, Charles. You insisted that boarding school was the making of you, that you loved every last minute of it.' Her voice began to rise. 'I knew I shouldn't have agreed to this.'

'Shush, Layla,' Charles said. 'Henry will hear.'

'Well, maybe I want him to hear!' Layla ran over to the bed, picked up one of the plush silk cushions, debated whether she should throw it at her husband's head. There was a fury inside her that she felt barely able to contain, but her sentences were being spoken sufficiently quietly so as not to be overheard by their son. 'Maybe he needs to know that I've got his back,' she continued. 'That someone has.'

Charles was pleading now. 'Come on, Layla. Seriously, let's just give it a bit longer, and then we can take stock.'

'Take stock of what?'

'What's best for Henry.'

'What's best for you, you mean.'

'Look, Layla, if you were this unhappy about it, why didn't you say something before?'

'I did. You just didn't listen.' But even as she said it, Layla knew Charles was right. She had complied. Boarding school was a tradition in Charles's family, and Henry had been expected to go, right from before he'd even been born. Layla had always known that one day Henry would be sent away to the school that Charles had attended. She'd willingly agreed to their move here, so they would be nearer to their son when the time came. She'd agreed to it all. It was her fault as much as anyone's.

'Aargh!' she shrieked. She pulled her arm back and flung the cushion, not at her husband but at the window, as hard as she could, and it gave off enough of a soft thud to at least take the edge off her despair.

'Layla!' said Charles. The note of surprise in his voice was what jolted her.

'Jesus, sorry,' she said.

Charles came over to her then, put his arms around her, and although she stood stiffly, refused to reciprocate, she let him. Suddenly she felt utterly depleted, and she wanted to go to Henry, climb into his bed, lie with him so that she could breathe in his sweet childish smell, ruffle his midnight hair. But he was eight now. At boarding school. He might hate it.

'Why don't you have a lie-down, Layla,' Charles said. His voice was coaxing, not quite insistent, and it was always thus, she realised. Charles never overtly dictated anything. He managed to bend her to his will by a strange kind of osmosis, as though him simply saying something was true made it so. She felt extraordinarily tired.

'Have a sleep, Layla,' Charles said. 'Just for an hour. I've got some work to do anyway, and then we can all go out for dinner. Henry would like that.'

Layla glared at her husband. 'Don't you think he'd like to be at *home*, on his weekend *home*?'

Charles looked alarmed then, as if he'd made a wrong move. 'Of course,' he said. 'I'll cook dinner.'

'Fine,' she said.

Chapter 21

The intercom buzzer goes yet again, more demandingly this time – rudely in fact, if I were going to pass judgement. I try to block out the noise, but it continues loud and insistently, pulsing like blood. I have no idea who it is, and I'm determined to ignore it . . . but the caller clearly has no intention of being ignored. When at last I go to the door to take a look into the video screen, just in case it's someone innocuous, like the postman, I nearly gag when for a moment I think it's *him*. But of course, it can't be. He appears to be alone. It seems I have no choice but to answer.

'Hello,' I say. I can feel my breath catching in my mouth, sticking like mud, while my heart is working on overload, almost as if it's in its death throes, like when you run over a rabbit – legs going crazy, yet about to stop for good.

'Can I get my drone?'

'Your what?'

'My drone.'

'Who are you?'

'My name's Henry. I live next door.'

This is weird. I am ninety-nine per cent sure that the people next door don't have kids. Sometimes I sit at my bedroom window and watch the comings and goings of Hope Close, for lack of anything better to do. Over the past week or so I have seen a few people. A brassy-looking woman in skin-tight Lycra. A matinee-idol type getting into his Mercedes, wearing a handmade suit. The builder, with a sizeable plaster on his face. Never before have I seen this child.

'Where did you say you live?'

'Next door.' There is a hint of irritation from the boy that he needs to repeat himself, and in my day I might have got a whack for that attitude.

'Where are your parents?'

'They told me to come and ask.'

Now, that's even weirder. Why wouldn't they come with him? I'm not convinced. My pulse is still all over the place: briefly elevated one minute, low the next. Fitful.

'Well,' I say, at last, 'tell them to come back with you and then I'll let you in.'

'Pleeease,' says the boy, his little lip quivering so violently it's visible even over the video screen. His eyes appear huge in his head, but it's probably just the camera angle. 'I'll only be five minutes. I think I saw where it landed.'

Fortunately, I'm managing to pull myself together now. I find I'm back in control of my impulses, bodily or otherwise. I can handle this.

'Why can't you just fly it out?' I say.

'The battery's dead.'

What to do. I find myself feeling sorry for the kid. I still have no idea who he is, and I'm not sure whether to believe that he lives next door. He might be a runaway for all I know. It seems the best thing to do would be to call the police and have someone come fetch him, but the thought makes me pale. It's too risky. And besides that, there's something about the boy, the age he is, the way he looks, that touches me. I find myself almost wanting to meet him, see him in the flesh, see what he's really like . . . and then I pull myself up, warn myself not to go there, that that would be a very bad idea.

'Sorry, I can't help you,' I say.

I put down the receiver, but the buzzer goes non-stop now, and the boy is persistent, I'll give him that. I feel like the noise is getting inside my head, swirling up the bad stuff. I have to do something about it. I have to do something about him. At last I press the button that opens the gate.

'All right,' I say, over the intercom. 'You can come in and get it – but hurry the hell up about it.'

Chapter 22

Layla

When Layla awoke she didn't know what day it was, let alone what time it was. Where was Charles? *Where was Henry?* She grabbed her phone from the bedside table, and it said 17.08 – that must make it teatime, on Saturday afternoon. Her head pounded, and that was even before the memories of the drone debacle set in. She jumped up from the bed, hurried along the corridor to Henry's room, where she found his bed crumpled, empty, cold to the touch. Reassuringly, his teddies were still lined neatly along the wall, but his enormous box of Lego had been tipped out on to the floor, although perhaps not played with. All was still. Too still.

'Henry!' Layla called. Where the hell was he? When she'd first retreated into her bedroom, Henry had been flaked out in his own room, so it had seemed OK to have a quick lie-down herself, try to regain her composure, get rid of the monumental headache that had set in. The whole weekend had felt ruined, which was perhaps unsurprising. After all, the event itself had represented virgin territory, and Layla had been out of sorts anyway, worried sick about her son from the moment she'd seen him drag himself into the school hall to meet them. Things had only felt all right, joyful even, in those few brief minutes when Henry had been in the garden, flying his drone. But once it had crash-landed into the next-door property and the neighbour hadn't answered the intercom, presumably deliberately, Henry had had such a meltdown outside on the close, Layla had never seen anything like it. At one point she'd thought her son might even need restraining, in case he physically hurt himself – until finally, tumultuously, he'd turned and thrown up, there on the grass verge, and it had been heartrending to see. It hadn't seemed normal, in truth, and not for the first time, Layla had secretly wondered what might be wrong with her son, and whose fault it would be. Hers? Or Charles's?

After his tantrum, Henry had been depleted, compliant even. Layla and Charles had taken him home to his bed, where he'd cried himself to sleep, his breathing ragged, his thumb quivering in his mouth, Layla's palm stroking his forehead as if in apology. She'd even debated whether, if they couldn't get the drone back, they should simply go out and buy Henry another one, although she knew that would be a cop-out – as if now Henry didn't live at home they should compensate him in other, material, ways. No, she'd decided. She wouldn't play that game. She would put her foot down on that decision at least. And besides, life was full of loss – she had to teach Henry how to deal with it.

'Henry,' Layla called, but there was no reply. She checked the other bedrooms, and then went downstairs and searched the living room, the kitchen, the TV room . . . but apart from Aristotle, who was asleep in the very corner of the sofa, looking to all intents and purposes like a cushion, the room was empty. The only other place was Charles's study. Henry never went in there, although he wasn't strictly banned – but maybe he'd gone in today. Perhaps father and son were playing some kind of game quietly together – chess even, seeing as Charles had taught Henry once. The whole mood of the house felt off-kilter, as if anything might have happened. Layla needed to quell it. She ran upstairs and barged into the study, although normally she would have knocked. Her husband visibly startled, hastily turned off his screen, a look of surprised perturbation on his face.

'What's up?' he said.

'Where's Henry?'

'What d'you mean? Isn't he asleep?'

'No. His bed's empty. He's not in the house.'

Charles jumped up and followed Layla out on to the landing. 'Are you sure?'

'Well, I've looked everywhere. I'm pretty sure he's not in the garden either.' Layla's throat felt tight, as if she could barely get the words out.

'Maybe he's hiding,' Charles said, calmly. 'To punish us.' But a look of pure panic passed over his face, which only succeeded in making Layla feel worse. And then he dashed past her, down the stairs, taking them two at a time and way faster than Layla had ever hitherto seen him move – before running out of the front door, through the garden, and on to Hope Close.

Chapter 23

Joan

'Lionel,' Joan said. 'Lionel! Come here.' She was standing at the front window, pulling back the cream velvet curtains, peering through a chink in the snowy-white nets.

'What?' said Lionel.

'Look over the road.'

'I can't see from here.' Lionel was prostrate in his favourite armchair, which was velour with a pseudo-faded green and pink floral pattern, and he had flipped the footrest up and was watching the end of *Final Score*. Anyone would think he was at the dentist's, the way he was sprawled back there, Joan thought crossly.

'Well, get up then!' Really, getting Lionel to do anything quickly was like trying to induce a tanker to do a three-point turn. It had been hard enough persuading him to come out to the super-market this afternoon, and now it seemed like he was spent for the day. She knew he didn't enjoy grocery shopping, but why should she do it all on her own?

'Do I have to?' Lionel said.

Joan gave him one of her looks, and that was enough for the inevitable capitulation. Lionel appeared to suppress a huff, but then he pushed down the footrest, lumbered to his feet and started making his way over to the window. His face was flushed bright red as if he'd just been for a run, or had drunk too much, or was embarrassed, but it was always like that. He had rosacea, which was a nervous complaint, apparently, although Joan didn't know what he had to be nervous about. His gait was one of those timorous ones that made him look like he was trying to avoid the school bullies, as if he were walking on tiptoes, hoping to sneak past them unnoticed, and it was annoying. He was hardly a man, in Joan's opinion; never had been, in truth. No wonder she had no respect for him.

'Hurry *up*, Lionel!'

'All right, Joan. I'm going as fast as I can.'

'Oh, for God's sake!' said Joan. She stared crossly at the gates as they were gradually closing, creeping ever closer to each other, unremitting, unstoppable . . . and now they were fully shut, and it was as if they'd never been opened. 'You've missed him.'

'Missed who?' said Lionel as he looked across the street, at nothing.

'I *told* you to hurry!' Joan's pulse was racing, and she wasn't sure what she was more angry about – her husband's eternal uselessness or the fact that she didn't know what was going on, as if the final curtain had come down on a play and she had no idea how it ended.

'What did you want me to see?'

'The boy's back.'

'What boy?'

'*Henry*, Lionel.' Really, he was so dense at times.

'That's nice,' said Lionel, clearly distracted by the football results (in fact, doing his best not to react to the news that Liverpool had grabbed a late goal), but Joan wasn't fooled. She glared at her husband, and then she glared at the TV. And then she walked over and turned it off at the socket.

'Oi,' said Lionel, mildly. 'There's no need for that.' He made a move as if to switch it back on again . . . and then he saw the look on her face and appeared to change his mind.

'It was definitely Henry,' Joan continued now. 'He must be back from school. I just saw him go into that weirdo's house. On his own.'

'Well, maybe Charles and Layla are already in there?'

Joan scowled. She hadn't thought of that. She pulled at the ends of her hair, enjoyed the sensation at the base of her skull. She was proud of her hair – even if it was grey and frizzy now. She was particularly pleased that she still had so much of it, unlike her poor sister, who'd been thinning terribly on top before she'd died. Not that Joan had said that, of course. Well, not to Anne, anyway. Perhaps subconsciously it had been one of the reasons she'd kept her own hair so long, though: a visual display of superiority over her sister, in that department, at least.

'I would have seen them go in,' she said, at last.

'Joan,' Lionel sighed. 'I know you're nosy, but you're not that nosy.'

'And what's that supposed to mean?' As Joan advanced towards Lionel, she enjoyed the fact that he visibly quailed. He was a drip. A lifelong disappointment, who'd never given her anything of value. She should never have married him.

'Nothing. It was a joke. It's just that we were out – and besides, since we've been home you've been in the kitchen. You haven't been looking out the front window the entire time.'

'What should I do?' Joan said now.

'About what?'

'About Henry.'

'Nothing. It's none of our business.'

'Well, maybe I should just check with Layla that she knows he's in there. We have no idea who that man is.'

'Joan,' said Lionel, his voice stern for a change. 'We have no idea *what's* going on. The new chap could be having a party, for all we know. I don't think we should interfere.'

'A party?' Joan said. 'Don't be ridiculous.' But her heart tightened as a tiny doubt entered her mind, that maybe her new neighbour was having some kind of Hope Close gathering, inside his house, behind his gates, and that, just like with the Warners, and the Kirks before them, she and Lionel were the outcasts, and hadn't been invited.

Chapter 24

In real life the boy is exquisite-looking, which makes his sudden appearance even more disconcerting. His eyes are huge in his head and his hair is black as death, the too-cute smattering of freckles on his nose a visual reminder of his age, his innocence. He reminds me so much of Bobby, I almost can't breathe, and I want to reach out and touch him, stroke his silky hair. He's wearing skinny chinos and a hoodie, bright pink trainers. It occurs to me that he is the first stranger I have had a proper conversation with ever since I left rehab. It's not the ideal scenario, of course, but I try to stay as cool as I can.

'Where do you think it went?' I say.

'Somewhere in the back garden,' he replies. When he speaks he has a very slight stammer, as if the words are piling up in his brain and he's not sure in what order they will come out. He has an air of sadness and I feel for him, wonder what his story is. Somehow, I can tell that he's like me. Needs a friend. I feel so drawn to him, and I almost want to ask him to come down to the lounge, sit on the sofa next to me, watch a movie. But of course that would be insane.

'Where do you live again?' I ask.

'There,' says the boy, using his thumb to indicate the house next door. 'Or at least I used to.'

'What do you mean?' I'm alarmed now, at where this kid has come from, if he doesn't actually live in the close after all. Has he been sent as a ruse? Is someone playing a trick on me?

'I'm at boarding school now,' he says.

'You're *what*?' He looks about six.

'At boarding school. My parents wanted me to go.'

'Oh.' I can't tell if the kid is lying or not, but I'm tempted to believe him. 'Why haven't your mum and dad come over here with you?'

'They said I could come on my own. That it's good for my resilience and independence.'

Hmm. Although that doesn't sound remotely plausible to me, I admire his vocabulary. It helps me pull myself back from the past, remind myself that this is now, that he is a different boy. Progress. If you can call it that.

'I'm sorry,' I say, doing my best to take an authoritative tone. 'But I can't let you in on your own. You'll have to come back later, with your parents.'

'OK,' the boy says, his shoulders slumping, more easily defeated than I'd anticipated. He gives me a wan, dejected look, and then he turns and starts walking slowly down my driveway towards the gates, and he looks so forlorn. So alone. A prick of genuine pity strikes behind my forehead, as if parts of my brain are firing up that I thought were long dead. I don't know what to think, how to feel, as I watch his sad little trudge, but I determine to keep an eye on him, make sure he really does go into the house next door, so I can be shot of him. Be shot of the worry.

Ha. Sucked in.

It seems the boy is a wily little fucker, as well as a potential future champion rugby player. When he gets halfway to the gates, he suddenly turns and starts sprinting back in my direction . . . and before I can even try to stop him, he swerves expertly past me, and scarpers around the side of the house.

Chapter 25

NICOLE

The phone cut through the air with all the shrillness of a dying cat. Nicole was watching *Pointless Celebrities*, which was one of her favourite shows. She loved its quiet humour, its calming tones, even its educational value, and it was a part of the ritual of an autumnal Saturday night. At around five o'clock she would have a bath, put on her towelling robe and slippers, apply a face mask, and then go downstairs to watch TV while she was waiting for the mask to harden. She always found it odd that the celebrities she would expect to do well often did badly, and yet the ones that she'd assumed were as daft as her would frequently triumph. It was proof, as far as Nicole was concerned, that you never could tell what was going on beneath the surface of people. That everyone had the capacity to surprise you.

The next part of Nicole's routine was that, as soon as the show ended, she would press pause on the TV, go upstairs to her porn-star bathroom (as Ted called it), take off her face mask, apply the night cream that cost more than Ted would ever know, and then head back down to watch *Strictly*. At around this point Ted would usually come in to the lounge, huffing and moaning and pretending not to be watching, and they would share a bottle of red wine and get a Chinese takeaway, and the fire would be lit and the TV would be alive with dancing and spangles, and the world would seem as hectic and colourful and full of life as it ever had. Saturday nights were still Nicole's favourite part of the week, despite no longer having Tasha as her *Strictly* viewing companion. Ted was a definite poor second on that front.

But now, right in the middle of Nicole's regimen, the phone was ringing. No one tended to call at this time of the week. Tasha would be getting ready to go to work, and Nicole only ever spoke to Sean on Saturday mornings – unless it was a bona fide emergency – and she hardly ever heard from Jason.

This call, though, was from Layla – and there was still something about her that made Nicole feel special, chosen almost, whenever the younger woman gave her any attention. It was a strange feeling, and Nicole knew Ted had clocked it, but he never said anything. Nicole pressed pause on the TV and snatched up the phone, smearing it with sticky white clay, not even caring.

'Hi, Layla. Everything OK?'

'No, it's not. Have you seen Henry?' Layla's words were rushed, the tone panicked.

'What d'you mean?'

'I can't find him. He's not in the house.'

'You what?' Nicole jumped up from the sofa and looked out of the window, but all she could see was gloom. She screwed up her ever-tightening face, gazed past Ted's van, towards Layla's house, across to the forbidding black void of her neighbour's gates. There was no small boy out there. Not one she could see, anyway, and the light was fading, and it would be dark soon.

'He's not with us,' Nicole said, and it made her feel guilty somehow, as though he should be, or at least that Nicole should know where he was, even if his mother didn't.

'Oh, my God,' said Layla, and hung up.

Chapter 26

I find the boy kneeling towards the back of my lawn, sobbing with all the energy you might expend on a dead kitten. He has found his drone, which clearly has two busted arms, and they are hanging off disconsolately, still just about attached to the body by the internal wires, like a broken puppet.

'Hey, buddy,' I say, as I approach, trying to sound as friendly as I can. 'It's OK. It can be fixed.' But it can't, and I don't know why I even said that. That's what we teach little kids, though: that things are always fixable. Except when they're not. I should know.

'But I only just got it,' the boy wails, and he seems so broken himself I'm tempted, so tempted, to take him inside the house and try to make everything better. It feels too weird that he's been brought to me, that he's the first person I've allowed, albeit reluctantly, over my threshold. And yet perversely I feel all right about it too. I find myself just wanting to make him feel better.

The boy is shivering now, as well as still bawling, and when he turns towards me I can't help myself. Touching him makes me feel alive and dead at the same time, and I realise I need to get rid of him. I can't bear this.

'I hate my dad,' Henry sobs now.

'No, you don't,' I say, as I rub his little back, trying to pacify him.

'I do. He doesn't love me.'

Jesus. What am I meant to say to that?

'You need to go home,' I say.

'I don't want to.'

For fuck's sake. What do I do now? It seems I'll just have to take him back myself, physically deliver him to his parents, although the thought of doing so is excruciating. It's far too soon for me to meet anyone. I haven't worked out my polite chit-chat. These are far from ideal circumstances. Plus, the boy's clinging to me now like I'm a human life raft, and it's making me feel so weird, and I don't know how to deal with it. And yet I can't just throw a wailing kid off my property. I need to hand him over to someone.

'Look, what's your name again?' I say, as I push him away, study his angelic little face, his button nose. Those lashes. The emotions rise again, tearing at me. Bobby. My Bobby.

'Henry,' the boy sniffs.

'Well, Henry,' I say, doing my best to sound composed. 'You're going to come with me and I'm going to take you back to your parents, OK?'

'I don't want to go. They're yelling at each other.'

'No, they're not,' I say, although I have no idea whether he's right or not, and I don't want to know, either. 'What are their names?'

'Layla Montague and Charlie Dolphin.'

What? What the fuck? Why would he say that? And now he's looking at me like he's taunting me, daring me to say something. But why has he brought an infamous *child murderer* into the conversation? Charlie Dolphin can't be his father. The kid is a freak. I need to get rid of him.

I take hold of Henry's arms, firmly, but hopefully not too firmly, and the warmth of his little body through the sleeves of his sweatshirt is yet another reminder of who I used to be. When I lift him to his feet, my leg is throbbing, the pain both physical and remembered, a ghastly vision of the past. The boy's knees are visibly wet and dark. He needs to get out of those clothes, get warm. I want to take him into the house, run him a bath, but I can't. I mustn't.

As Henry and I walk to the gates, I realise that this will be the first time I've been out in the close on foot, rather than in my tinted-screened car, and people will be able to get a good look at me, if they happen to be watching. It's a truly horrendous feeling. I stand as if I'm an actor in the wings of a stage, about to go on, my hand in a small boy's, and I feel as naked and exposed as I ever have. Do I do it? Or do I turn around and take him inside the house after all?

The boy looks up at me now, as if alarmed at my hesitation. I take a deep breath, try to calm my roiling senses. As I feel the warmth of Henry's hand in mine, it makes me feel better. Bobby might be dead, but this boy is alive, at least . . .

And now the whole world feels as though it's on edge, waiting for something. Waiting for me, to do the right thing. I screw up my eyes, try to suppress the ever-simmering panic. I place my finger on the gates' remote button, steel myself to press it, as if it's a trigger . . . *Come on*, I urge myself. *Do the right thing, for once.*

'I'm hungry,' Henry says, suddenly. 'Have you got any pizza?'

Chapter 27

NICOLE

Just as Nicole was staring open-mouthed out of the window, trying to process the fact that on Henry's very first weekend home he appeared to have gone missing, she saw her neighbour's gates widening, so slowly at first she thought she was imagining it. And then out of the dimness she saw the silhouette of a man, holding the hand of a small boy. Somehow, it reminded her of a terrible scene from the past, from the news perhaps, and it was one of such innocence and trust and—

No.

Nicole wasn't known for her decorum, and she could be as easily enraged as her husband at times. She didn't even think as she dashed to the front door, still in her fluffy dressing gown, and ran out into the close.

'What the fuck d'you think you're doing with Henry?' she yelled, her Liverpudlian twang more noticeable than usual, her face mask gleaming ghost-like in the half light.

The new neighbour (who, according to Layla, who'd been told by Joan, was called Andy) approached Nicole then, almost squared up to her, dragging Henry with him.

'What the hell d'you mean?' he said. 'I'm trying to find out who he is. Does he belong to *you*?'

Nicole watched as Henry gripped Andy's hand, shrank back towards him, grabbed around his left leg, and she was shocked at the inappropriateness of the gesture, the over-familiarity.

'No, that's Nicole,' she heard Henry whisper, quite perkily, to be fair. 'I live over *there*.' As he pointed at Layla's house, its front door almost magically opened and Charles came rushing out, closely followed by Layla.

'Henry!' Layla screamed.

'Mummy!' cried Henry, immediately bursting into tears as he ran towards his mother, throwing himself into her arms.

'He was fine a minute ago,' Andy said, and although Nicole had seen that with her own eyes, could vouch for the fact that Henry had seemed quite unharmed, Andy sounded riled, overly defensive. There was something strange going on, Nicole was sure of it. Layla might have only just realised Henry was missing, but she'd admitted she had no idea when he'd actually left the house. How long had Henry even been with the new neighbour?

Layla was crying too now, as she cradled her son in the middle of her driveway, while Charles hung back, looking helpless.

'Henry!' Layla said. 'Thank God. Where on earth have you been?'

'Now, look,' Andy cut in (aggressively, in Nicole's opinion – he wasn't going to make any new friends taking that tone with people). 'He turned up unannounced at my gates, and when I told him to go away, he refused. And then he ran round the back of the house to get his stupid drone, and I didn't know who he was, and so I thought I couldn't just leave him alone on the street and that I'd better check where he lived, and then deliver him home.'

Nicole stared at him. He might be obnoxious, but his explanation was convincing enough. Perhaps he'd simply had enough of all the drama and merely wanted to get rid of the kid, which would be perfectly understandable – especially as Joan's door had just opened too, and the old cow was on her way over to add her tuppence worth, and they might as well be having a street party.

'I saw Henry go in there *ages* ago,' Joan announced in her horrible, squeaky voice, as intermittently grating as a rusty door. 'Lionel told me not to interfere, Layla, and that you and Charles were probably already in there.'

'It wasn't *ages* ago,' Andy said, and he sounded like he was ready to explode now. He was looking at Joan with such disgust that even Nicole was shocked. She knew Joan was ugly, of course, but at least she didn't make her feelings quite so obvious.

'Well, when was it then?' Joan said.

Nicole could hear the suspicion in Joan's voice, but she supposed it was fair enough. You could never be too careful where children were concerned.

'Look,' Andy replied, as if he really was close to the limit of what he could tolerate. 'There was a call on my buzzer and I tried to ignore it, but it wouldn't bloody well stop, and then this little kid was peering into my video screen, and I was worried about who he was, out in the close on his own . . .' He stopped, pointed inanely at the pathetic, pulverised drone that Henry had dropped on the ground when he'd run crying to his mother. 'He was looking for that thing,' Andy continued, 'and he ran into my back garden, even though I told him not to, and then he became completely hysterical when he realised it was broken. And that was it. End of story.'

All three women were glaring at their new neighbour, and Nicole even started to feel a teeny bit sorry for him.

'So anyway,' Andy continued, 'here he is. Officially fucking deposited. I'm having no further part in it.' As he crossed his threshold, back on to his drive, set his hated gates in motion, Nicole could feel the ridiculousness of the situation, almost found it funny. It was one way for him to become acquainted with the neighbours, she supposed.

'Absolutely fucking delighted to meet you all,' Andy said, nearly took a bow – and then the gates swallowed him up, as if he didn't exist, and he was gone.

Chapter 28

Well, at least meeting all of my neighbours in such unfortunate circumstances appears to have got one thing out of the way. I did it. I've done it. I've actually talked to people, *even her*, out in the real world, and the world hasn't blown up in my face. She definitely had no idea who I was. None of them did. A victory, if you can call it that.

But still. There is a darker side to the encounter, of course. It's pretty clear what they all thought of me. What I thought of them. And so now there's further, non-gate-related antipathy between me and my new neighbours. There is a suspicion that has landed on me, albeit completely accidentally, and thus my supposed clean slate is tarnished already. I am the weird single guy who hangs out with small boys. Of course, I'd known how it had looked, what they were all up in arms about, but it's not my fault his parents can't keep bloody tabs on him. If I'd been a woman, no one would have batted an eyelid. But now they think I'm not to be trusted, and it is striking a nerve in me, like chewing on tin foil. It is making me jumpy, on edge. *Angry.*

I try my hardest to force my mind to change tack, and it sort of obliges, instead embarks on a critical appraisal of the three women I encountered last night. It was hard to tell what the first one on the scene even looked like, in her furry robe and face mask, but she'd sounded like a fishwife, that was for sure. The second one, Layla, I've seen before, of course. Up close she's extraordinarily beautiful, perhaps of Indian origin, her features so highly attuned to each other that nothing is quite perfect, and yet the imperfection was what struck me. There was only one word for her state of mind, though. Delicate. I can recognise it. A kindred spirit, perhaps?

And finally there was the late arrival, the gate-crasher, the old woman who was so keen to get in on the act she would have said anything to be relevant, even if it meant stitching me up. I'd seen her before, of course, being taken out of the big house in a wheel-chair that time, but I hadn't known who she was then. She's so seriously unpleasant-looking I'd been shocked. Repelled, in fact. Her hair had been pulled tight to her head, presumably in some kind of a ponytail, before exploding into a mass of grey frizz that appeared to sprout out of her neck and then cascade over both shoulders, like grizzly cobweb-fur. Her face is long and thin and manly. I'd taken an instant, unequivocal dislike to her. She has hardness in her heart, I could tell. She'd appalled me.

But now it's the next day, Sunday, and the late September morning is misty and ethereal, the far-off hills skimming in and out of view, as if teasing me, making me question their very existence. I stare out at them, continue trying to slow down my breathing, keep reminding myself that nothing that bad has happened. My guilt or otherwise is in other people's minds, after all.

When my phone pings, it feels like a bizarre interruption, especially once I see that it's Dead Eyes again. She says she has a day off tomorrow, suggests a lunchtime drink. Tinder didn't even exist before I went to prison, but suddenly it feels like the perfect practice ground for human interaction now. After all, there is no connection. We have no connection. My potential match knows nothing about me. Who I am. Where I live. What I've done. She is a mere rehearsal, but for what, for whom, I'm not sure. It doesn't matter. I need to do something. I've got nothing else on. I reply, saying yes, that sounds good.

◆ ◆ ◆

I wake up feeling nervous, scared, excited, angry, depressed . . . I almost cancel, but then I go anyway. It's only a drink, I tell myself. At lunchtime. I arrive early, find the furthest-flung table and sit with my back to the room, try to convince myself that the thud in my ears is normal. And yet I can't remember ever having felt quite like this before. It is virgin territory. I am a virgin at this game.

Sadly, when Dead Eyes arrives, she is as dull as anticipated, but in mitigation she looks nice. I smile at her and hope I don't look creepy. I've practised and practised my smile in the mirror, and yet still it doesn't feel right. Maybe I've just fallen out of the habit of smiling. Perhaps it's as simple as that.

'So, what d'you do, Carla?' I ask, once my date is settled in the chair opposite me, which is imitation bentwood with a plaid-covered seat. Huge lanterns with lamp post-thick candles dangle from the ceiling, but the candles are fake, and unlit anyway, which doesn't help with the atmosphere. A group of forty-something women are the only other customers, and they are loud and cackly, almost certainly office workers on their lunch break.

'I'm in administration,' my date says. She has taken off her coat and is wearing a silver top with spaghetti straps, which feels rather exposing for a Surrey lunchtime in late September. Her eyes bat up and down like a dolly's and I presume her eyelashes must be stuck on. Her eyebrows are fierce, Slavic. There is something else about her face, too, and I think it must be the lips, which are full and pink and labial, surely pumped full of collagen.

'Oh, really?' I say.

'Yes . . .' she says. 'Exciting, huh?' She laughs and the noise is tinkly, like a scary doll with one of those strings you pull from its chest. For a moment I doubt she's actually human.

'What kind of company is it?'

'It's a finance company.'

'Oh.'

The girl proffers nothing more. It's weird. I plough on, ask her where she's from (born and bred locally), what she does in her spare time (cinema, pubs, reality TV – watching rather than taking part, I hope) and then I stop speaking, and so does she. What do people *do* on Tinder dates? Maybe she's expecting me to suggest that we leave. Is that the underlying issue – that I'm not fulfilling my part in this ritual? It's impossible to tell. But I still have a nearly full glass of Coca-Cola, and she has approximately half a double vodka and tonic. It surprised me when she asked for a double, and something about it bothered me. Was it greed? Or alcoholism? Or is that simply the done thing, that girls ask their Tinder dates for doubles? Are they out for what they can get, as am I? As my confidence dips I feel my paranoia soaring, and it occurs to me that maybe I should have started my repatriation into society somewhere lower stakes. An art class, perhaps. It doesn't help that sex, with a girl, feels totally beyond me. I think what I really crave is a hug, especially after my recent encounter with Henry, but I wouldn't dream of asking her. She'd think I was strange.

'What do *you* do, Andy?' she says.

Now it's my turn to be stumped, not just by the question, but by hearing myself being called that. It feels jarring, an aural reminder of the road I have travelled. To hell and back. And then I remind myself that I am not the victim. I am the perpetrator. There is no place in my heart for self-pity. I need to remember that.

'Uh, not much at the moment,' I say.

'Oh.' I watch my date take another gulp of her vodka, and I can feel the nerves radiating down her body, through the table, over to me. *Can she tell somehow?* Fear flicks itself at me, like flames.

'D'you live alone?' I say, at last. The silences are pathetic, in the very literal sense of the word. Anyone watching us would feel pity. No one can hear us, though. The wine bar is busier now, and we are out of earshot of anyone, as long as we keep our voices down.

'No, I've got a flatmate.' She pauses. 'She's at work . . .'

I raise an eyebrow and I think it might make me look creepy. Or not. Dead Eyes shifts in her seat. 'Do you want to come back there?' she says.

'What? Now?'

'Yeah, why not? That's what usually . . .' That girly laugh again.

I should be tempted. A good-looking, albeit somewhat plastic young woman. On offer. Is this what dating in the real world is like now? Meeting in a public place first, checking each other out, making sure we look OK – as well as providing proof that we've been out together, just in case anything untoward happens? Just in case I rape or murder her? I look into Carla's eyes for the first time, searching for her true motivation, and I realise that their expression isn't dead at all. It is sad and lonely and desperate, and it's like looking in a mirror again, at long last. The memories pile in now, and they are of screaming girls and boys; the flash of cameras, persecuting me, outing me; disgrace and self-hatred. For a moment I picture Sian – my friend, my nemesis, my fellow fucked-up kid-from-a-troubled-background – her lips twisted in rage and contempt, her words inaudible, having no impact on me. A silent movie of shame. The only impact to be had on either of us is what we have done. Together. I don't care what Sian says. She has to blame herself too, and she knows it. The repugnance I can see in her face is not solely aimed at me.

I start, pull myself back, glance down at my glass of Coke, back up at my date, who looks almost frightened now, and I worry how I must be coming across. I'm aware that my face is slick with sweat, although it's not even hot in here. I have no idea who I am any more, or what I want. The feelings are too dark and intolerable, and far from appropriate in this situation. What did she just ask me? For me to go *home* with her? Surely it's impossible. I'm incapable.

I wipe my brow, make a monumental effort to seem normal. To deal with this situation. 'Er, d'you want to get something to eat?' I say.

Carla seems even more unnerved by my suggestion.

'First?' I add, desperately, as if I'm fishing for the right words in a pond full of scrabbled letters.

Carla looks relieved, as though she thinks maybe I'm not odd after all. 'Er, if you like,' she says. 'I'm a bit broke, though.'

'It's OK, it's on me.'

Carla tosses her head and her smooth blonde fringe moves in a single sheeny sweep, and yet still the gesture is a hesitant one. When she stands up to go to the bathroom, her legs are slim and bowed slightly in the tight black jeans she's wearing, and her heels are so high she's nearly as tall as me. Her nose is ever so slightly too big for her face and it makes her more sexy somehow. I try to imagine taking her clothes off slowly, item by item, unfettered by alcohol, unmoved by feelings. While she's in the bathroom I guess what kind of underwear she's wearing, and I think it might be lacy and alluring. Possibly brand new. I try to imagine how she smells, deep in the centre of herself. Would she throw herself at me – or is she as placid and timid in bed as she is in real life? What do these kinds of girls do in these kinds of circumstances? How would I cope with my impulses? Do I still *have* any impulses? All is a mystery, waiting to reveal itself.

When Carla comes back, the awkward silences resume, and she disconcerts me all over again. And then out of the corner of my eye I see two dark heads – and at first I assume I'm mistaken, but soon I realise I'm not.

Shit.

I stand up more abruptly than I'd intended, and the chair legs scrape across the polished stone floor. 'I'm sorry, Carla,' I say. 'You're a lovely girl, but . . .' What *can* I say? 'Look, I'm not . . .' I try again. 'Honestly, it's nothing to do with you. I just need to go.'

And with that I pay the bill and leave, and when I reach my blacked-out Tesla I'm shaking so hard I have to lie down in the back, where no one can see me, until I'm composed enough to drive home.

Chapter 29

LAYLA

Although Charles had tried to play down the circumstances surrounding Henry's disappearance, Layla had been furious. She'd *told* Charles that she'd had a headache and was going for a lie-down, but what in hell had he been doing? Had he, as Henry had claimed, been holed up in his office as usual, doing God knows what, having told his son, who'd just woken up from a tantrum-induced nap, to go away? Or was *Charles's* version of events true – that Henry had snuck straight out of the house in search of his stupid drone, without even letting his father know he was awake? It was so hard to get to the truth, know who to believe, and that was sad enough in itself. You expected little children to lie, but not grown men. She didn't expect to have to doubt her own *husband*.

Layla sat up in bed, scowled at the memory of the weekend's traumas. Charles had managed to absolve himself of all responsibility, of course, saying that he'd expressly told her he'd had some work to do, and that it wasn't his fault she'd needed to sleep off her headache – and the way he'd said it he might as well have put inverted fingers around the word, mid-air. And yet the truth was she'd only had a couple of glasses of wine at lunch. Her headache had been brought on by distress at Henry's distress, not by a bloody hangover, but she hadn't bothered to argue. And so now Henry's disappearance was officially Her Fault, which seemed to be how Charles liked it.

Layla groaned, got out of bed, her limbs feeling both jumpy and leaden, her brain on go-slow, and she wasn't sure how much wine she'd drunk last night. (It was definitely more than on Saturday lunchtime, though, and Charles could simply get lost.) It was Monday morning: Henry was back at school and her husband was about to head off to work, and Layla would be left here. Alone. Trapped. What was the expression? In a gilded cage.

Layla walked to the wardrobe, surveyed her clothes, searched for something to wear. She knew she was pissed off, but she wasn't quite sure what about, just how far the extent of her malaise spread. She started to wonder whether Charles had been this dogmatic with his other wives, his other children, and if so how his older son and daughter had turned out. Layla, of course, didn't have a clue, and it was astonishing, now she came to think of it, that she'd never even met them. Although they'd moved abroad with their mother after the divorce, and rarely came back to the UK, it was still a strange set-up, and it only made Layla yet more anxious. She dreaded the prospect of Henry drifting away from *her* for any reason, and she prayed that boarding school wouldn't prove to be the catalyst – wouldn't give rise to the whole shebang of fucked-upness his father seemed to be blessed with. She even wondered whether Charles would care if Henry *did* separate from them, seeing as he didn't seem bothered about being virtually estranged from his two adult children. In fact, since Henry had gone, she'd realised that her husband was a veritable emotional island. How had she never noticed before?

Layla sighed, picked out an old pair of jeans and a mustard jumper that had seen better days. At least Henry himself had seemed unscathed by Saturday's incident. In truth, he'd appeared to positively relish the drama he'd created, as well as having been apparently quite taken with the new neighbour. He'd even asked whether he could go back to see this Andy Meyer the next time he was home from school, but Layla had said no. She couldn't let her son impose and, more importantly, she didn't know anything about the man. He'd seemed decidedly misanthropic at best, full-on weird at worst. It was inappropriate on so many levels.

It was only once Layla had heard Charles's Mercedes growling its way off the driveway and down the lane that she finally went downstairs. He hadn't come up to say goodbye. She hadn't gone down. One-all. It felt as if her entire skin was itching, inside out, in the concealed part where it met flesh, and the sensation was becoming so intolerable she knew that that was it: she'd reached her limit for now. It seemed she couldn't be contained within the elegant confines of this house for a single moment longer.

Layla threw on some old trainers, grabbed her coat and bag, and left Hope Close on foot. She marched past Joan's joyless borders, oblivious to Ted's unsightly van, uncaring who was spying on her, almost tempted to flick the V's, just in case someone was watching. She found herself walking down the lane towards the village, being forced to step off the road and take cover on the verge whenever cars passed by, inevitably far too fast. She even took the shortcut she'd normally avoid, cutting off the edge of the Common, passing through the spooky woods where someone had been murdered once – a friend of Nicole's, apparently. On exiting the woods (safe, in one piece!) Layla stalked past the church and the pub and the little primary school that would have been perfect for Henry, and as she saw the other mothers dropping off their children she was tempted to go over, interrupt them and tell them that she too had an eight-year-old son but that he was *incarcerated*, thanks to her robot of a husband, although of course they would have thought her insane. She'd walked the two and a half miles to the train station in the next village before she'd acknowledged that that was where she'd been heading all along, and it was only once she'd physically stepped on to the platform that she decided what she would do, her deep-seated need to get away from Hope Close trumping any rational thought. She didn't care where. She just needed to go somewhere.

The London train was slow, packed with commuters whose manner was distinctly Monday-morningish: stiffly reserved, perhaps a trifle depressed, apathetically accepting of terrible service, Stockholm syndrome-style. Layla sat quietly, her eyes shut, pretending to be asleep. It was only when she looked out of the window at last, to see that the train was pulling into Clapham Junction, that she had an epiphany. Clapham was where she used to live, where she'd been happy once . . .

Layla jumped up from her seat and pushed her way off the train. Almost on autopilot, she made her way towards her old patch, started wandering down the Northcote Road in that way that you do when you have nothing to do, nowhere to be, are just killing time. There was an inexplicable murkiness in her brain, and she felt the urge to transform it into a spectacular, unwieldy rage. But at what? At whom? At Charles, for instigating this? At herself, for allowing it? Or at someone else altogether?

Layla had rarely been back to Clapham since she'd moved out to Surrey, and being here on the fashionable shopping street made her feel even more alien somehow, as though she didn't belong anywhere any more. The market was in the process of setting up, but it wasn't how markets used to be, where men with loud gruff Cockney voices would be laying out geometrically perfect displays of apples and oranges, or great slabs of meat, or household cleaning products and toilet rolls at knockdown prices. This market was populated by elegant-looking women with cut-glass accents, selling high-end kitchen equipment and wooden barrelfuls of stuffed olives and loaves of artisan bread. Layla found herself remembering all the times she'd walked this street in her past life, with a newborn, when she'd been almost as desperate as she felt now. She would never know if she would have struggled anyway, or how much the news story that had broken when Henry had been so young had affected her. She supposed it didn't matter. It was what it was. There was nothing she could do about it now.

Layla was drifting in and out of shops that were just opening, idly perusing overpriced cushions and picture frames, being gobsmacked at the prices in an Italian deli where she'd picked up – and promptly put down again – a packet of squid ink spaghetti that cost £6.75. Even though she tried not to think about it, she could still recall every single headline that had surfaced, as the horror had unravelled, and then tightened, holding her and her husband in thrall to the whims of the media, to what other people would say. Henry had been only *eight days old*. How could her brain have been exposed to such wicked things when her baby had been so tiny? So innocent. When her baby had had *Charlie Dolphin* for a father. She didn't care how many times Charlie, or her mother, or her friends, had insisted it was just a name – it was her *husband's* name, and her child was a Dolphin, too.

The Dolphin Murders, they'd called them. They'd been the most notorious and vile child killings in decades. They'd stretched right into Layla's consciousness, through her tablet, out of her TV and radio, and they'd sucked the mother sap right out of her. The horror had dried her up, and maybe she would have got postpartum depression anyway, but the circumstances most certainly hadn't helped. And so, regardless of the exact reason, she'd been left with a screaming hungry baby, and a silent impenetrable husband, and a mind smashed to pieces by horror and hormones. How had she and Charlie ever been expected to come back from that? *Had* they ever come back from that? Is that what the real problem was?

And how had she allowed her son to be sent away from her, to be possibly bullied by his classmates, purely for who he was, what he was called? Boarding school was difficult enough at that age, but in Henry's case it was potentially ruinous.

As Layla came out of the shop, deep in thoughts she'd never let herself have before, the woman she almost walked into was a facsimile of the wife she might have been, perhaps could yet become one day. She was wearing a soft jersey blue-and-white striped jumper, pristine white skinny jeans, brand-new Tod's shoes. Her hair was shiny, semi-curled up at the ends of a long, professionally blow-dried bob. Her lips were dusk pink and glossy. Next to her stood a smartly uniformed little boy, Henry's age.

'God, sorry,' Layla said. And then she did a double-take. Did they know each other?

'Layla?' The woman seemed as flustered as Layla for a second. 'Goodness, how *are* you?' As she leant into Layla, air-kissed her, she smelt of flowers and expensive soap. Layla couldn't remember her name. Annie, Tanya, Janey? What on earth was she called?

'How's Henry?' the woman said, clearly blessed with better instant recall than Layla.

'Oh, he's good, thanks.' Layla couldn't reciprocate the question, seeing as she had absolutely no idea of the boy's name. In fact, how many kids did this woman even have? Layla's brain appeared to have been scrambled by how overwrought she felt. 'And how are your brood?' she managed at last, riskily, potentially erroneously.

Layla's gamble paid off. 'Oh, they're all fine,' the other woman breezed. She nodded towards the boy with her. 'Although I've just had to take Max to the doctor's for his allergies. How's Henry getting on at boarding school?'

Pippa. That was her name. She'd been one of their old neighbours, from a few doors down. Pippa had about a hundred kids.

How had Layla forgotten? Pippa was staring at her quite oddly now, and as Layla put her hand to her cheek, she realised it was wet.

'Henry's doing OK, thank you,' Layla said, and the words came out slowly, as if she were speaking a foreign language. 'Although he's not a boarder. He's a day boy.'

'But aren't you living all the way out in Surrey now?' Pippa persisted. 'You must have dropped him off early this morning?'

'Yes,' said Layla, firmly. 'I did.' She smiled determinedly.

'Well . . .' Pippa said, and it was clear that she too was feeling more than a little awkward now. 'That's good. Er, anyway, must get Max to school. Lovely to see you . . .' And with that Pippa almost imperceptibly shrugged her shoulders, swung her honeyed hair and walked away – leaving Layla wondering just what she'd been thinking, and what on earth she'd become.

Chapter 30

NICOLE

Nicole hadn't hesitated when she'd received the call from Layla. She'd been in the spare room, in a cerise Lycra bra-top and black cycling shorts, tackling a particularly brutal hill on her home exercise bike, listening to a true-crime book about a serial killer, when the phone had cut through the narration. Nicole had never heard Layla like that, but she was glad that her neighbour had trusted her enough to ask to be picked up from the station. It felt like their friendship was moving on somehow, and that was fine in Nicole's book. It gave her a secret glow, helped assuage her own loneliness. Plus she knew how Layla must be feeling, having lost Henry – and it was as if she sensed some kind of primal connection between herself and the younger woman.

Nicole had hopped off the bike and swiftly changed into clean designer leggings and a hoodie, pulled on her nearest trainers. She'd even foregone putting on any make-up, and instead had grabbed her bag and jumped straight in the car. But then, just as she was pulling out of Hope Close, Layla had texted to say that the train was delayed and that she'd get a cab instead. She didn't want to mess Nicole around, the message had said. Nicole had hesitated, pulled over in the lane for a second . . . before deciding to pretend she'd not seen the text in time. After all, she was on her way now, plus she had nothing better to do – and it sounded like Layla could do with a bit of moral support.

When Nicole arrived at the station, she was inevitably early, so she thought she might as well park up, go inside, meet Layla off the train. It would help pass the time. Plus Nicole was keen, too keen in truth, to know what was going on. Where had Layla even been? And why had she sounded so upset?

As Nicole waited, the air was whipping along the platform in cold thin belts, and people were hunching into their coats, the mood morose, a twelve-minute delay in the train's arrival seemingly the end of the world. The seconds limped by, as they are wont to do when you really, really want them to pass. And then, when the train finally trundled in, it was one of those miserable provincial ones that stopped at every station, and were always freezing cold.

Layla was the last person to disembark. As Nicole watched her step down on to the platform from the very rear of the train, she was decidedly dishevelled-looking, as if she'd merely thrown on her clothes this morning, rather than having got consciously dressed. Nicole started walking towards her, smiling, but Layla was shuffling along, eyes cast to the ground, seemingly oblivious to everyone.

'Layla!' Nicole said, once she was near enough, making Layla start – and then look noticeably displeased to see her.

'Oh. What are you doing here? Didn't you get my message?' Layla's face was flushed, and her eyes were bright, the pupils disappearing into pinpricks.

'Yes, but only once I'd got here,' Nicole lied. 'So I thought I might as well wait for you. Really, it's no bother.' She looked at her Rolex, and it was just gone half-past one. 'Are you OK?'

'Yes.'

'Have you eaten?'

'No.'

'Look, shall we go and grab a late lunch? I've got nothing much on this afternoon.'

Layla appeared to visibly cheer up at this suggestion, which was endearing for Nicole to see, vindicated her decision to come. Layla was so hard to read. Sometimes she verged on seeming rude, and then at others, like now, she gave off an air of real vulnerability, and it almost made Nicole feel as if she wanted to mother her. And yet it was clear that Layla could give as good as she got, too. Maybe that was what Nicole liked about her – she was one of those people it was hard to put into a box. She had a rich husband, albeit with an unfortunate name; a fancy house, and yet she was by no means a snob. She was clearly besotted with her son, but she wasn't one of those earth mother types either. She was evidently well educated, had once had a good job, and yet didn't seem particularly career-driven – in fact she'd given it all up to raise Henry. She was definitely not part of the gym-and-Botox brigade. And she liked a drink – had perhaps been drinking already today. That was the main thing that Nicole had noticed about Layla. She liked a drink. Nicole might not be conventionally smart, but she was far from stupid. Layla clearly wasn't happy, and it wasn't just about her son being shipped off to boarding school. Nicole wondered what it was that Layla was running from.

'Shall we pop over the road to the wine bar?' she said now. 'I've not been for ages, but I think it's all right.'

'OK, why not?' Layla said. 'I guess I could do with a glass of wine.' As she laughed her voice sounded wistful, or full of bravado, or both, and yet it had an edge to it that frightened Nicole. How many glasses of wine had she already had?

Layla tossed her head now, and grinned sardonically. 'And besides,' she continued, 'I might as well do something to pass the time, now I don't have a son to look after.'

The wine bar was under new ownership and the exterior had been painted in an egg-yolk shade of yellow, with gold and black writing that announced it was now called Bertie's. Nicole had no idea who Bertie was, as the only staff visible through the windows were two young girls, but the place seemed charming enough, with oversized lanterns and a mutely coloured Moroccan-tiled bar lined with bentwood stools. Already inside was a group of animated women having lunch, a pair of young office workers in cheap suits and a single man in the corner, his back to the room. Nicole sat Layla down and ordered two large glasses of Chablis and some food to share. She could always pick up the car tomorrow if needed – although she didn't mention that potential plan to Layla.

'Are you sure everything's all right, Layla?' Nicole said, once they were settled. 'I'm worried about you.'

Layla was staring at her hands, the rings that adorned them, as if they were foreign objects. 'I don't actually know,' she said. She started twisting her wedding ring with the forefinger and thumb of her right hand, as though she were trying to get it off.

'It's OK,' Nicole said. 'You can tell me.' She smiled encouragingly. Some people needed prodding, even when they were desperate to unload. Maybe that's what Layla was like.

Layla raised her gaze and stared straight at Nicole. 'I think I've made a mistake.'

'What d'you mean?'

'Living here. Having this life.' Layla's expression was contorted now, and she had the kind of face that showed how she felt, morphed into whatever mood she was in. With her chin in her hands and her dark hair falling across one eye, as now, she reminded Nicole of a chastised, stroppy teenager. 'What have I done?' Layla added, perhaps to herself.

'But I thought you were happy here?' Nicole said. 'I know you're sad about Henry, of course, but I thought you liked it here other than that.'

'Well, I don't. But there again, that's no one's fault but my own.' Layla took a huge gulp of wine. 'By the way,' she added, 'our new neighbour's in the corner.'

'*What*? Are you sure?'

'Yes.'

'I know I had a go at him,' Nicole whispered, 'but I actually think he's quite dishy.'

'He's a wanker,' Layla said. 'If he'd answered the door to us when Henry first lost his drone, none of the crap that followed would have happened. It broke Henry's little heart.'

Nicole made no comment on the cause of Henry's mental anguish or otherwise, and besides, he'd seemed fine when Nicole had seen him getting in the car to go back to school on the Sunday.

'Well, how do you know he was even in?' she asked.

'His car was there. I could see it through a crack in the gates. And I'm sure you or Joan would have alerted me if he'd gone out for a walk.'

Ouch, Nicole thought. Layla might not be in a good way today, but there was no need to be bitchy.

'Sorry,' Layla said.

'That's OK.'

The door tinkled and a pretty girl with long legs and blonde hair entered. Nicole tried not to ogle as she headed over to their neighbour, where she proceeded to have a brief conversation with him before she sat down.

'I think that's a blind date,' Nicole said. 'Probably Tinder.'

'How d'you know?'

'I can tell.' Nicole tapped her nose knowingly.

Layla turned her head and peered at the couple in the corner. 'So what?' she said. 'It's a free country.'

'I never said it wasn't.'

The waitress appeared at their table with the shared platter they'd ordered. The sourdough bread was a little stale, and the cheeses and jamon, although nice enough, were minuscule portion-wise. They were still only midway through eating when their neighbour passed by their table, swiftly followed by the girl he'd been with, both looking distinctly stony-faced. *Well, that was a quick date*, Nicole thought, *even by Tinder standards*. She felt inordinately curious to know what had happened, why they'd appeared so miserable.

'Shall we get another glass of Chablis?' said Layla, clearly more intent on ordering wine than remotely caring what their neighbour was up to.

'We-ell, I suppose I could leave the car here,' Nicole said at last, as if she'd only just thought if it. She patted her recently reinflated lips with her napkin, all thoughts of Andy Meyer forgotten for now. 'Go on then. Why not?'

PART TWO

OCTOBER

Chapter 31

LAYLA

The six o'clock news was just starting when Charles phoned, saying an urgent client meeting had come up and that he wouldn't be home for dinner after all. Layla tried to ignore the voice that whispered that that seemed like a very late client meeting, and that Charles wasn't to be trusted anyway – that he had used those exact ruses when *she'd* been the other woman, although she hadn't even known it at the time. It, whatever 'it' was, had been going on for months, but somehow Layla hadn't noticed before Henry went away to school, five weeks and three days ago. Now the house roared in her ears, trumpeting its emptiness. The only thing that stopped it was the wine.

Layla took her glass and went into the front room and gazed out at the neighbour's gates for the umpteenth time. They were black and solid and impenetrable – and there was something about the fact that she couldn't see anything of his existence that made her more curious than she might otherwise have been. He was young, about her age probably. He was rude. He had eyes that reeked of mystery. *He'd been alone with her son.* She'd barely seen him since.

Layla returned to the kitchen, opened the double-doored larder fridge, stared at the tuna steaks she'd marinated for dinner and which she now had no intention of cooking. She debated whether to throw them away or leave them there for days to go off, make her point through the stench of rotting fish. In the end she lost interest in the dilemma, and instead took out the wine bottle from the fridge door and topped up her glass. Feeling warm and dreamy inside, she drifted into the living room, sat down on the still-plumped cushions of the enormous truffle-coloured sofa. The imprint she made was evidence of her existence, proof of her family's absence. She couldn't be bothered to turn on the TV. She drank the wine. She got up. She looked out of the window again, noticed Ted's van wasn't there. She thought about calling Nicole to ask her over to share a bottle of Shab-lee (as Nicole would insist on calling it, in a mock-posh accent). They'd got together a few times since their impromptu, ultimately boozy lunch the other week, but Layla wasn't sure she was in the mood for Nicole tonight. In the end she decided against it. She sat down again, wondered if Charles had remembered that it was her birthday next week. He hadn't mentioned anything, and so neither had she, although normally she would have, so that Henry could get her something. She banged her knees together repeatedly, so they thudded dully, the faint echo in sync with her frustration. She jumped up once more and went upstairs, looked out of her bedroom window this time. The elegance of the Georgian panes was lost on her as she stared blankly out, wondering yet again who her new neighbour was, what nasty little secret he was hiding. He had one, she was sure of it. Why else would he be holed up here, with no friends, no family, no job even – or at least from what she could tell?

Just then, as if magically, as if purely for her delectation, the forbidding gates started to open. The staid black car creeping out on to the close was an unknown model to her, and she wondered what it was, where he was going. After the car had swept slowly away, the gates began smoothly sliding back towards each other

. . . and then they stopped, presumably not intentionally, leaving a person-sized gap in the middle.

Layla watched, fascinated at first, but after a minute or so of further gate inaction, she shrugged and returned, inevitably, to the fridge to top up her glass. And yet somehow there was only a drop left, and so she placed her lips around the bottle's neck and tipped. She thought of Henry then, and she was a pathetic mother, away from her child, and drunk to boot. She was a pathetic, frigid wife. No wonder her husband didn't ever want to come home. The need grew in her, to do something that would make her feel relevant, alive again. She thought about calling her mother, or even Nicole, to discuss her idea, but she knew they would only try to dissuade her.

Layla's decision, when she finally made it, was not a rational one. She snuck out through the utility room so that Joan Taylor wouldn't spot her front door opening. As she scooted around the edge of her garden, she stumbled against a rose bush and it scratched her hand, made her bleed. She swore softly and continued along the side of her house, glancing around her as she went. The curtains were firmly drawn in the Taylors' house. The lights were off at Nicole's. Ted's blue van was still absent. Nicole would probably be in her TV room at the back of the house, curled up with Stanley, watching Netflix. No one would see.

In one swift movement Layla came out from the undergrowth, dived across to the neighbour's drive and slipped through the gap in his gates. And as she did so something must have happened to the sensor, because no sooner had she passed through, the gates resumed their retarded trajectory to close silently behind her, and they were tall, with spikes on the top . . . and try as she might, Layla could not make them open again.

Chapter 32

I've grown to quite like Tinder. Hooking up, as it's euphemistically called, feels as commitment-free as hiring a prostitute, and yet more real somehow. Our momentary responses are genuine, or so I believe, and frankly that's what counts. And even if my dates do sometimes want more from me afterwards, it's always unclear, always unspoken, and a quick DM does the job of sorting out any misunderstandings. After all, it's not like either party ever makes any promises, and it's amazing how different it feels from all the girls that went before, who somehow imagined their lives with me, thought they knew me, felt like I owed them something. They were crazy. It was crazy. Perhaps it's no wonder I lost it.

But now, here in my new existence, over the course of just a few weeks a pattern has formed: one of mindless fucks with no regrets, at least on my part. I even know the profiles to go for now – the ones whose photos are posed and scantily clad, with very little in the way of written descriptions. These are the ones that if they swipe you back you can pretty much be guaranteed they'll put out. It usually starts out in a bar, which makes it safer for both of us – in my case to ensure I'm sufficiently attracted to them, as you can't ever rely on the pictures; in theirs to check I'm not a murderer – and I always, every single time, wonder how they would feel if they knew the truth. It makes me feel guilty, if I'm honest, that

I'm deceiving them, but what else can I do? I have chosen a new life, with a new name. It was the only way I could even begin to contemplate re-entering the world. Shame precluded anything else.

As always, I travel to meet my date in my brand-new Tesla. As I sweep through the headlight-lit, high-banked lanes, they briefly remind me of tunnels leading into or out of a prison, and even though the image no longer makes me shudder I shift my brain away from it. Instead I try to concentrate on purely biological thoughts, of strangers' bodies, and what I will do to them, and what they will do to me, and sometimes I can't help but hear the monologue in my head, and wonder at just how much of a robot I've become. It makes me think of how things used to be with Sian, when we were friends still, and life was fun and innocent . . . and yet again I wonder whether it's her fault, or mine. I can pinpoint the exact moment of my betrayal, of course. You can probably watch it on YouTube. The thought makes me feel sick.

The pub my latest date has suggested is modern, sharp, soulless. She is attractive enough in that soft, plump way that suggests mild gluttony, a welcome contrast to the hard angles of our surroundings. Her skin is fresh and glowing, not thick with make-up like some of the girls, and her rare, shy smile is astonishing in its brightness. When I suggest after one drink that we go back to hers, she looks surprised, then pleased, then worried, in that order. She even suggests going to mine, but I politely refuse. She can't come to my house. No one is allowed to breach my defences. No one but me is allowed to control the aftermath. This way I can get up wordlessly, dress and head home, and I won't have to explain myself, and it suits me. We will have had a brief, albeit meaningless connection. No one is getting hurt. At least that's what I tell myself.

I follow behind the girl's Suzuki Swift, which she drives with laudable assuredness and precision, and we end up parking in a small square car park outside a block of bland, purpose-built apartments. She shows me into a flat that is painted cream with accents of red and lilac, and is drowning in bolsters and scatter cushions and matching accessories. It's a home that has clearly never been subjected to a man's influence. And in the bedroom she is perfectly compliant, and it is nice enough, and it makes me relaxed, and warm, and on the precipice of deliciously dozing sleep . . .

I jolt, and jump out of the girl's bed just as I feel her stretch towards me, but she is too late. I am free of her. I glance back briefly, which is a mistake. Her eyes are wide and sorrowful now, her full mouth turned down – and as I move away sharply, I feel a pulse of pity, mixed with a kind of disgust. It's a strange thing, sleeping with someone by appointment, there being no pretence that our date is anything other than for sex. It's not dissimilar to my old life, in a way.

And yet looking down at this girl, it's clear I've become careless, and it pulls at me. The fact that I'm sober makes it harder to disengage myself from her plight. Her room is so carefully constructed, so smacking of her lack of a partner – from the twee picture above the fireplace (split into three separate canvases), the plush throw on the end of the bed, the mauve shaggy rug. It is nice, feminine, inoffensive – as is she. The situation is uncomfortable, makes me question myself. I bend to pick up my clothes from the padded chest I've laid them over, and then I walk casually out of the room and along the hallway. I've never liked being watched as I get dressed. It feels too personal somehow. Just as I reach the bathroom, a little boy of six or seven comes out of the room next door to it. His eyes are thick with sleep, his hair in cute disarray, his pyjamas too small for him. The boy stops dead, as do I, and I quickly move my clothes in front of my genitalia, but not before the boy's eyes have grown dark and horrified. As have mine.

What the fuck? I almost can't bear it, that he's here, taunting me. That he's alive, when Bobby is dead. It's the unexpectedness of it I can't cope with, like that time with the boy and the drone.

'Jesus,' I say, and dive into the bathroom, lock the door. What the hell. I'd seen the toys and the other child-related paraphernalia, of course, but I'd assumed that any actual children were elsewhere. Who'd been looking after the boy while his mother had been out? Or having sex with me? Might the father even be here? What the fuck have I got myself into?

I dress quickly, and when I come out of the bathroom, the boy is still standing there, and it is like looking back into my past, at what I have done, and I so badly need to leave I almost shove him out of the way.

'Who are you?' the boy says.

What do I say? I feel a dread strike somewhere, just above my groin. I have to get out of here. I have to hotfoot it back to my house, get behind my gates, where no one can reach me.

'I'm Toby,' says the boy, as I still fail to answer. 'Will you play trains with me?'

'Uh, it's past your bedtime, kid. I'll see you later.' I ruffle the boy's head and turn. I'm confused and unprepared for this situation, and there's something inside me in danger of fracturing all over again.

Footsteps pad down the corridor. The girl, Sarah, has light brown hair, and it is tumbling over her shoulders. She is wearing an oversized T-shirt and fluffy pink slippers, and she looks about nineteen now, but I'm sure she must be older than that. Her eyes are wide and doe-like, and they terrify me.

'Oh, you've met Toby,' she says. She smiles at me, and then at him. 'Toby, darling, this is Mummy's friend, Andy.'

Chapter 33

Layla

She had no coat. The evening was freezing. She had no phone either. She tried pulling at the gates, but they were shut fast. She thought about shouting out, but who would hear her? Only the Taylors, and she certainly didn't want them knowing her business – before she knew it she'd be on the front page of the local paper. The only vaguely positive aspect to her plight was that at least the alcohol she'd drunk should keep her warm, stop her dying of exposure.

Layla stumbled around the perimeter of the garden, wondering which cameras she was tripping, looking for an opening, but there was none. Next she circled around the property itself, partly out of curiosity, to see what work the neighbour had had done, partly to try to find a route into the house, where she could get warm, find a phone – and who cared if she was trespassing? But the whole place was dark, and all the doors and windows were locked, which was probably just as well. Layla had always disliked the house anyway, had thought it had an odd atmosphere, and she still didn't know why a young single man, who picked up young girls in bars and had no apparent friends, family, job or even personal history – at least if Joan were to be believed – would move into it. Something wasn't right. She knew it wasn't.

Layla was beginning to feel frightened now, and she wished Charles could rescue her, but he wouldn't be home for hours. She could already feel the cold creeping through her bones, causing her nerve endings to shake and her teeth to chatter, the first step towards her body eventually shutting down, admitting defeat. *Don't be mad*, she told herself – Charles would be home long before that happened.

Officially trapped, Layla wondered how she would explain it to her new neighbour. What might he even do? She had breached his considerable defences. He'd be surprised, wrong-footed, might react badly . . . Perhaps the best option was to stand at the gate and shout after all. It was embarrassing, but surely not as bad as being here when he arrived home . . .

Decision made, Layla started yelling. Sadly, though, as well as affording complete visual privacy, the gates appeared to have admirable noise-absorbing properties – and so, when after ten minutes or so no one had come and her throat was sore, she gave up. The night sky was cloudless and huge, its great expanse of black air growing more bitter by the minute. Drastic measures were called for. She did another lap of the house, found the bin area and retrieved from the recycling a large flattened cardboard box. This would have to do. She hauled the box out and dragged it over to the porch where, after some effort, she managed to rip off one of the lid flaps. She sat down on the smaller piece of cardboard and pulled what remained of the box over her, put her head between her knees and blew on her hands. And then she waited, for her neighbour to come back.

Chapter 34

Joan

'You know, there's definitely something not right about that man,' Joan said to Lionel. She was in the kitchen, boiling Lionel's handkerchiefs, and the rank smell of dried germs, washing powder and warm soup was permeating the kitchen. She gave the contents of the pan an occasional prod with a pair of metal tongs, and each time she felt a surge of satisfaction as she pushed the bubbling fabric down, subsumed it in the witch's brew. Sometimes she wished she could do that to people, boil down their bones.

'Why?' Lionel said now, wiping soup off his chin with his napkin. 'Which man?' He glanced up at her then and, not for the first time, she acknowledged that although he might have been reasonable-looking once, now he seemed caved in, as if his personality had leached away, disappeared entirely. His once-blond hair was lank and thinning, a trifle too long. His rosacea was as bad as it had ever been. She hated the pathetic jumbo cords he always wore. He didn't have an ounce of style, never had had, in truth.

'The new neighbour!' said Joan. 'There's nothing about him on the Internet.'

'And?'

'Well, don't you think that's peculiar?'

'No, not really.'

'I've been searching for ages and there's nothing at all. Not a single thing. No pictures that look anything like him. Usually there's *something* online about people these days. Especially someone his age.'

As she saw Lionel suppress a sigh, Joan bristled. It had always irked her that Lionel didn't enjoy a good gossip, like her sister had. Men were so annoying in that respect. It was a shame Joan didn't have any female friends that she knew well enough to share her latest theories with. She'd tried to nab Layla the other day when she'd been getting in her car, but Layla hadn't seemed remotely interested in Andy Meyer's lack of a digital footprint. Instead she'd said that she had to dash, as she was off to watch Henry play football. *How ridiculous*, Joan thought now. Driving twenty miles each way to watch a bunch of eight-year-olds kick a ball about! Layla clearly didn't have a clue how to mother that child. Henry should be home, where he belonged, so he could play football in the garden; not have to make do with seeing his mother for half an hour a week, if he was lucky, and in the middle of a muddy field at that.

Joan felt tears mounting suddenly, and she swiped at them, put them down to her sister's untimely death. It had been terrible for Anne, clearly, but it had affected her, too. It had made her feel lonelier than ever – and had compounded her grief about her nephew. After all, Peter had once been the son Joan had never had, and she still felt distraught that his life had gone so off the rails, had ended the way it had. Joan was sure that that was what had ultimately killed off his mother too. Poor Anne had never got over it. Joan closed her eyes tightly, did her best to steer her mind away from her anguish, channel it back towards her ever-increasing curiosity about Andy Meyer.

'I'm telling you, Lionel,' she said now, 'there's something off about him. And he looks familiar to me, too. As if I know him, somehow.'

'Well, have you asked any of the neighbours what they think?' Lionel said.

'Well, I tried with Layla . . .'

'What about Nicole?'

Joan could hear the snarl in her voice. 'Are you joking? I will never talk to her or her revolting husband ever again, after what they've done to me. To say that I came at him with a weapon! That Nicole witnessed it, when she was nowhere near. Good grief.'

'Hmm,' said Lionel.

'And what's *that* supposed to mean?'

'Nothing, dear,' Lionel said hastily. 'I just think the whole situation is unfortunate, that's all. Have you heard any more from the police?'

'No, I have not! I'm telling you, Lionel, it was *him* who pushed *me*. Don't *you* believe me either?'

'Yes, of course I do, dear,' Lionel said, but Joan could tell he was lying. She almost wanted to smash his stupid, weak-chinned face in, break his long, girly fingers.

'Well, why don't you ask Layla again about the new chap?' Lionel said now. 'She might know more. Maybe she's gone round and spoken to him, tried to find out exactly what he was doing with Henry that day.'

Joan paused, amazed that she hadn't seriously considered that option. Perhaps Lionel was right, praise the Lord. She decided she would find a way to ask Layla what she knew. After all, Layla was the only one in the close who appeared to still be speaking to her, and Layla was the one who needed to know who the new neighbour was more than anyone. Just in case.

Chapter 35

LAYLA

The motion of the gate made Layla jump. Panic and relief fought for precedence, but it was relief that won. It seemed she wasn't going to die tonight after all – or not from the cold at least. The car headlights illuminated her before she'd had a chance to lurch her cold-addled bones fully upright. She staggered out from the porch into the driveway, and spread her arms wide, hopefully in a symbol of peace, of expansive forgiveness at what he'd put her through. And then she remembered that he was the one who needed to forgive *her*. She was the trespasser. Her arms continued to move upwards, as if independent of her brain, until they were above her head in a position of surrender – and if she'd had a white hanky, she would surely be waving it.

Layla watched as her neighbour braked suddenly and, almost before stopping, jumped out of the driver's seat. As he moved towards her his gait was aggressive, animal-like, and the look in his eyes was menacing, as though he might strangle her.

'Oh my *God*,' he said, as he got closer. 'It's *you*! What the fuck are you doing here?'

'I'm so sorry,' Layla said. 'The gates weren't closed properly, and so I, I, er, tried to close them, and then they shut behind me.'

'You're trespassing. Get off my drive.'

'Yes, yes, I will. Please will you unlock the gate again.' Layla could barely speak. Her lips felt rigid and her jaw was clicking.

'I will – when you tell me why you've been snooping on me.'

Layla didn't know what to say. How could she explain it? He was angry enough as it was. She needed to be careful.

'I, I was just having a quick look.'

Wrong answer. Layla's neighbour appeared so incensed now it was as if he were a cartoon character rendered briefly immobile, steam pouring out of his ears, as he debated which way to spring. Fight or flight – which would he choose? She prayed it would be the latter, that he would simply press the button to reopen the gates, leaving her free to escape, and then storm off into his house. He wasn't wearing any shoes or socks, which was weird, and she didn't know what had enraged him so, but she could tell it was more than simply finding one of his neighbours camped out on his doorstep.

As Layla watched her apparent adversary stalk past her, unlock his front door, she still wasn't sure what was going on. She regretted now that she hadn't made a run for it when he'd first returned home, legged it through the gates before they'd had time to shut again, instead of hanging around trying to explain herself. What was there to say? It was clear they were never going to become friends – and who knew what was going to happen now?

'Come with me,' he said.

The mood was incendiary, yet fragile at the same time, as if one of them might break. It seemed Layla had no choice. As he ushered her inside, switched on the lights, directed her along the hallway, down into the living room, her mouth felt dry and her knees were trembling, but from full-blown terror now rather than cold. She imagined him producing a skein of rope, tying her up, putting a gag over her mouth.

'D'you want a blanket?' he said, and she was so surprised at the question she couldn't work out where this was heading, what he wanted, whether perhaps he was even being kind.

'Er, no thanks, I'm OK. I'd just prefer to get going, if that's all right?'

'Yes, it is – once you've told me what you were doing.'

'Nothing. I'm so sorry.' As Layla stared at him, at his angry face and his expensive jeans and his naked feet, she felt a terrible pull of sympathy for him, which almost overrode the trepidation, but not quite. There was something fucked-up about all this, but she didn't know what it was.

'Are you OK?' she said, instinctively, the urge to mother strong inside of her, outweighing her doubts.

'What d'you mean?'

She gazed down at the floor, glanced up at his eyes, which were dark, remote, filled with an emotion that was deep-seated, unknowable. Dangerous?

'Sorry, nothing,' she said. 'Look, I'm so sorry you found me on your doorstep like that. There was no malice intended, I promise.'

'Well, what were you doing then?'

'I guess it's just that . . .' Layla paused. How to explain it? How would he react? She looked about the room, as if for the first time, stunned at its transformation. It had that art museum feel to it now, so empty and white it was as if no one lived there. Gone was the family paraphernalia that the Warners had cluttered the place with, the aubergine walls and tacky leopard-skin throws, the faux-fur cushions, the dolled-up studio portraits of Marion, the old hussy, adorning the walls. Now there was hardly any furniture, and it made her feel sorry for him again, that he lived alone, and in such austere surroundings.

'It's just that what?' he persisted.

Layla stopped daydreaming, stared at him, trying to work out who he was, what the best thing to say would be. Finally, she decided on the truth. Twist or bust.

'Well,' she said, at last. 'If you will insist on going around erecting go-fuck-yourself gates, it just makes people want to look behind them.'

Her neighbour's face softened, and she thought he might even be about to laugh, but he didn't.

'What's your name again?' he said now.

'Layla.'

'Layla what?'

'Layla Montague. My husband's Charles Dolphin.' She watched closely, for a flicker of recognition, the telltale look of disgust, but there was nothing, as if he'd been prepared for it. 'You already know Henry, of course,' she said.

He looked awkward now. 'Yes . . . I'm sorry about that.'

'About what?'

'My outburst the other week.' He looked straight at her then, and she could see pain in his eyes. 'You do know I didn't hurt him?'

'It's OK,' she said. Henry had seemed perfectly fine afterwards, so perhaps it was time to give the guy a break – plus she still needed to make sure she got out of there in one piece, of course. 'Anyway,' she added, emboldened suddenly. 'You're Andy, aren't you?'

He looked shocked, as if a state secret had been leaked. 'How d'you know that?'

Layla stared at him. 'I don't know. I think one of the neighbours told me.' His level of discomfort was sky-high again, and it seemed abnormal. She'd only asked him to confirm his name. 'What's your surname?' she said.

'Why?'

'I don't know. I was only asking.'

Again, she watched him hesitate, thought he was going to refuse to answer.

'Meyer,' he said, eventually.

Layla knew she needed to brazen this out while she had the upper hand.

'Well, pleased to meet you, Andy Meyer,' she said. She jutted out her chin, stuck out her hand.

Although Andy appeared uncertain, he complied, and when his skin touched hers something happened, and she knew he'd felt it, too. It was a judder of connection, underlying and volatile, almost as if they already knew each other.

'Can I go now?' she said, taking her hand away.

'Yes, of course.'

'Well, see you around,' she said.

'Sure,' he replied.

Layla turned and walked steadily up the three or four stairs to the hallway and left the white, blank house without looking back, praying he wouldn't follow her. She waited for the gates to open just enough for her to get through – and then she ran, not even caring if they were shutting again behind her, simply relieved she was out of there. When she got home Charles still wasn't back, and when she checked her phone there weren't even any missed calls from him, the tosser, so she went to the sideboard and poured herself a couple of fingers of whisky, just to warm herself up. Just to get over the shock.

Chapter 36

NICOLE

As time continued to pass and the world edged towards winter, it wasn't even her children that Nicole missed any more. It was the stuff that came with them. The piles of coats. The raided fridge. The sneaked shots of spirits. The loud music. The constant selfies. The revolting bedrooms. Nicole missed it all. Solitariness was closing in on her, and even her husband felt like a stranger now. In fact, Ted seemed so completely oblivious to her these days – how she looked, even to her presence in the marital bed – she'd stopped bothering trying to look nice for him. The main reason she exercised at all now was to give her something to do, somewhere to go. Maybe she should simply get obese, like some of the women in Sainsbury's, and see if Ted noticed. She was already putting on weight, what with the amount of wine she was drinking with Layla these days, but at least that was one diversion, and frankly, it was a godsend.

Nicole sighed, put her arms behind her head, almost ready to pull out her own hair with boredom. Life stretched before her, punctuated by Christmas and birthdays and the odd non-specific visit from her adult children, the seasons relentlessly passing. It was the inevitability that depressed her. Spin classes, hot yoga, home gym, Ted going about his business, Joan Taylor going about everybody else's, Layla seeming perpetually sad about Henry, Stanley getting older and older . . . *Another year gone. Another year of not knowing.*

Nicole put her hands back on the handlebars, pushed harder, pedalled faster, the Italian Alps passing majestically by her, ripe with summer flowers and snow-capped mountain tops, the sun high and happy . . . until finally she acknowledged that what she was doing was a lie. The whole scene was a lie. She wasn't cycling in the Alps at all. She was cooped up in a back bedroom in Surrey, on her state-of-the-art exercise bike, complete with surround-vision video screen. She wasn't remotely on her way to the Great St Bernard Pass. She was on her way to absolutely nowhere.

Aaaargh. Nicole flung herself off the bike and lay down on the carpet, sobbing. *Everything* she thought or said these days was a lie. Yes, she missed her kids. Yes, she missed their noise and mess. But that wasn't the half of it. Maybe it was Tasha having gone, plus the fact that her daughter reminded her so much of herself at that age. Perhaps that was what it was. She'd tried so hard to be strong. But now she didn't have anyone to be strong for, so what was the point?

The sound of the dog barking madly was what finally roused her, reminded her that she still had Stanley, of course; that he still needed her. Yet even the doorbell ringing, as it just had, was a Potential Event around here – a prospective baddie, a possible intruder (at least in Stanley's eyes) – and that was how little happened in Hope Close these days. Nicole sat up, rubbed her eyes, sniffed, wondered who it could be. And then she jumped to her feet and legged it down the stairs, so as not to risk missing them.

As Nicole shut the door, brown-paper-wrapped parcel in hand, she already felt a little better. She liked the postman. He was one of those cheery types who called everyone 'love' and seemed immune to political correctness, and he'd handed over her package just now with great bonhomie, although she wondered if he would have acted in quite the same way if he'd known what was inside it. Nicole had no idea what Ted would make of the contents of the package either, although it was definitely worth a try. Events at the Warners' house had given her ideas, if the truth be told. Twenty-seven years was a long time to be married to the same person, after all.

As Nicole took the package upstairs and hid it under the bed in the guest room, she found herself wondering if Charles and Layla ever got up to that sort of stuff. She'd be surprised, but there again it was hard to tell from the outside – as the Warners had so spectacularly proved. Maybe she could ask Layla when she went over there next – once they'd had a few drinks, of course. But she definitely needed to do something to try to distract Ted. He'd seemed obsessed lately, set on a mission to destroy Joan Taylor – and although it might well be true that he'd ended up with a pair of secateurs in his face, his determination to take Joan down seemed an overreaction to Nicole. His injury hadn't been that bad, was almost completely healed now, and although he kept insisting that Joan could have taken his eye out, she hadn't. And besides, Nicole thought, Joan was just an old woman, albeit an unpleasant one. Would someone like her deliberately try to *stab* someone? And at least since the fight Joan had stopped moaning about the van and the weeds and the bins, for the first time in years. Why couldn't they all just leave it there and try to live in peace?

Nicole sighed as she put on her coat, readied herself to take out Stanley (who was shadowing her, having picked up on the minuscule clues that his mistress was done with her strange bike-that-never-went-anywhere, and that it must be time for a walk). Nicole regretted now that she'd made a statement to the police saying she'd seen what had happened in the fight, could corroborate Ted's version of events – when she hadn't and couldn't. Why had she ever let Ted persuade her to do that? She should have left him to wage his own wars.

As Nicole put on Stanley's lead, patted his silky head and led him towards the front door, she finally acknowledged what was also worrying her. It wasn't purely that she'd lied to the police, which was bad enough. It was what the consequences of her collusion might be – especially seeing as, if her husband's temper was anything to go by, Nicole was far more inclined to believe Joan Taylor's version of events than Ted's.

Chapter 37

LAYLA

Wine o'clock, Nicole called it. Although it was still only early evening the air was pitchy, and it made Layla feel better in a way, that they operated under cover of darkness. She was still surprised at how she and Nicole had developed their little ritual. They seemed to get together at least one night a week these days, usually when Ted was working late – and Charles never got home much before eight anyway. Nicole would always turn up with just the one bottle, but then invariably they'd end up opening another. Layla was finding hanging out with her neighbour – especially now it didn't involve hot yoga – more fun than she'd expected. It was infinitely preferable to whiling away the hours alone, and she and Nicole got on well, despite the age difference, despite their different backgrounds and interests; despite the fact that, before Henry had left, they'd sometimes gone weeks without even setting eyes on each other. But it was funny what loneliness did to people. Layla nurtured Nicole. Nicole nurtured Layla. They both missed their children. They both got drunk. Charles came home early sometimes, and Layla would hide the bottles (yes, plural) in the back of the larder, and yet she was sure he knew. He never complained, though, and Layla had no idea what he was thinking. Seventeen years seemed an ever-increasing age gap, as if she were regressing and he was steadily outgrowing her somehow. Being Wife Number Three was an odd role to fill. It was weird how Charles had had a whole other existence that she would never be a part of and couldn't possibly understand. She found it freaky that he'd married his first wife and become a father when she'd been just a toddler, and that she still knew virtually nothing of his life at that time. Never mind, she'd tell herself. Charles was a good enough husband. They made a good enough team. Or else they had done.

This particular evening, Nicole had arrived at Layla's dressed in what might be called posh loungewear – aubergine cashmere leggings, a navy roll-neck jumper, Ugg boots – and she had on far less make-up than usual. Layla thought it made her look softer somehow. Nicer. The two women had long given up all pretence of discussing Nicole's kitchen extension, and Layla even wondered whether Nicole had ever been serious about the project – especially seeing as Ted, the supposed instigator, hadn't seemed to know anything about it when Layla had mentioned it to him in passing. Odd, Layla had thought, but she hadn't really minded.

For some reason Nicole was clearly in the mood for drinking tonight, and they'd nearly finished the first bottle of wine already, even though they hadn't got much beyond discussing each other's days (sorting out bills, food shopping, descaling the dishwasher for Layla; the inevitable spin class and an online shop for Nicole) and how much they loved *Fleabag*. Layla could tell that Nicole was revving up to something.

'So, how's Henry, Layla?' Nicole said now, as she lolled over the counter, wine glass in hand, her perfectly toned rear perched on one of Layla's kitchen bar stools.

'OK, I think. I'm going to watch him play football tomorrow.'

'Oh, that's great, Lay. And when's half-term?'

'The week after next. I swear he doesn't even miss us now, but I still count the days, obviously.'

'Well, thank God it's that way round,' Nicole said. She tipped up her glass and when she brought it down her eyes were brittle-looking and shiny. It seemed as though she were about to say something, and then she stopped. No matter how drunk they got, both women danced around the subject. It felt too dangerous for either of them to say what they really thought about Henry, as if there was no clue which way the conversation might go, what danger zones or dead ends it might lead to.

'And how are your kids?' Layla said, by way of diversion.

'Oh, they're sound. Tasha seems to be having a whale of a time up in London. Jason's totally loved up – which won't last, of course, now that they're living together.' Nicole laughed. 'Sean's still working in a call centre, trying to get his break into TV.' She took another sip of her wine and then tossed her head, as if to get her hair out of her eyes. It looked almost auburn in this light, and Layla wondered what its natural colour was. 'My problem's with Ted.'

'Oh,' said Layla. Nicole had intimated it enough times, but Layla had deliberately not picked up on the hints. She didn't want to know. 'I'm sorry to hear that.'

'It's the same thing that's been going on for years,' Nicole said, as if Layla had actually asked her what the problem was. She looked directly at Layla, and it was part-challenge, part-plea. 'I've tried everything, Layla, but he never ever wants to have sex with me.'

Layla studied her nails, which needed trimming. Nicole had dragged her along to get them done once, and although the parlour had primped and painted them beautifully, Layla had found the visit boring, and hadn't bothered again. Plus she'd started taking an interest in gardening lately, partly because Joan had turned up unannounced on her doorstep with some wallflowers – to say thank you for Layla's help after 'The Incident', as Joan had called it – but also because Layla had read that nurturing plants could be a potential alternative to raising small boys. And having nice nails seemed to be incompatible with gardening, at least if Joan's gnarled hands and dirt-striped fingernails were anything to go by.

'D'you know why he's not keen?' Layla said, at last.

'Oh, he keeps telling me not to worry, that he's tired or stressed. But he would, wouldn't he?' Layla could definitely hear the bitterness in the older woman's voice now. And then Nicole put her head in her arms on the kitchen counter and started bawling, lustily, like a rankled child.

Layla was unsure what to do. Was it that time already, she wondered. The time for Nicole to go a little bit crazy? Layla worried about it sometimes, that perhaps the two of them were drinking too much, becoming a bad influence on each other – but then she'd tell herself that all they were doing was helping each other through this period of adjustment. And besides, what else were you meant to do on cold wintry nights in the middle of nowhere?

Nicole stopped crying as suddenly as she'd started. She sat up straight, filled up both their glasses and merrily started regaling Layla with the latest episode of Vangate, as if she'd never spoken about her problems with Ted at all. It was almost as if she had a tap for each of her emotions that she could switch on and off at will. Layla envied the skill.

'Ted's definitely decided he's taking the old boot to court,' Nicole said.

'Really? What for?'

'Actual bodily harm.'

'Gosh, isn't that serious?' Layla said. She hesitated, unsure whether to ask. 'Wasn't it six of one, half a dozen of the other?'

'No.'

'How d'you know?'

'I saw.'

171

Layla paused. She was sure Nicole had told her at the time that she'd been upstairs when it happened.

'Really?'

'Yes. Joan went for him,' Nicole said.

'*Really?*'

'Yes . . .' Nicole's tone was resolute now, and Layla took the hint not to ask anything else. She found the entire situation depressing. It was never worth falling out with the neighbours, in Layla's opinion, but each to their own, she supposed. It seemed to her that some people wasted so much time and energy on hatred – as if there were a giant, hopeless lack in them somehow. But this was a different situation now. If Nicole really was prepared to lie in court about it, purely to stitch Joan up, that was inexcusable: a new level of awfulness altogether. But maybe Layla had got it wrong. She'd need to ask Nicole about it when they were both sober.

'Have you ever seen the new guy again?' Nicole said, clearly off on her next chosen topic of conversation.

'Well, actually, yes, I have.' Despite herself, Layla enjoyed the look on Nicole's face.

'*You what?*' said Nicole. 'When? How? Do tell.'

'Last week. He'd left his gates partly open.' Layla declined to mention that he'd found her camped out, pissed, on his porch. It would have made for a pretty funny story, but now that it came to it, she still wasn't quite willing to share it.

'For Christ's sake, Layla, why didn't you tell me? This is a *major* development in Hope Close. Was he as much of a dick as when Henry went to get his drone back?'

'Pretty much.'

'What does he do for a job?'

'I didn't ask, funnily enough.' She crossed her fingers. 'I only went over to tell him about his gates.'

'And is he single?'

Layla cocked her head at Nicole, as if to say, *Seriously?* She found she almost wanted him to be, though, and it was an unwelcome revelation to her, made her feel guilty. Confused. She determined to breeze it out.

'How the hell would I know!' she said. 'He's rude. That's all I know about him.'

'It's weird,' Nicole said. 'I still can't understand why someone his age would want to live somewhere like here, like a hermit. He never seems to have anyone round. Apart from—' She stopped.

'What were you going to say?'

'Nothing.' Nicole took a comb out of the side of her hair and used it to pin back her fringe, exposing her forehead. Her face looked immediately younger, despite the newly exposed wrinkles.

'You think something odd went on with him and Henry, don't you?' Layla said.

'No! I didn't say that.'

'I know you didn't say that,' Layla said, her tone slow and measured. 'It's what you meant, though.'

Nicole looked like she might start crying again. 'I don't know, Layla. I just don't trust that man. There's something not right about him.'

'Well, Henry's perfectly OK, thank you very much,' Layla said, but even as she said it, she thought, how would she even know? She had no idea how her son was. Not really.

'What did he say when you told him about his gates?' Nicole said.

'Nothing. I told you.' Layla took a nervous slug of wine as Nicole drained her own glass, got down from her bar stool, went over to the fridge. She was visibly swaying as she returned, brand-new bottle in hand, and her cheeks were tinted pink, high up near the temples, and her eyes were glittering.

'So what should I *do*, Layla?' Nicole said. She unscrewed the bottle and sloshed wine extravagantly, causing a mini tidal wave that was just about contained by Layla's glass, and then filled her own to the brim.

'About what?' Layla said. It could have been about any number of things, but Layla was used to Nicole's non-sequiturs now, and it made spending time with her more interesting in a way. You never knew what subject she would tackle next, be it the neighbours, or her children, or her latest anti-aging treatments, or her views on the American president . . . or anything else besides. Layla liked it.

'About Ted, of course!'

'Oh.' *Here we go*, thought Layla. She thought she'd managed to dodge that topic. 'Honestly, Nicole, I don't know.'

'Well, do *you* have that problem with Chazzer?'

Layla threw back her head and laughed. Maybe she should take to calling her husband Chazzer too. Perhaps that might help.

'No, not really,' she said. She didn't volunteer that she was glad when Charles left her alone these days, which, now she came to think of it, had been more and more frequently of late.

'Well, you're lucky. Sometimes I feel like this can't be it. This can't be the rest of my life.'

'Have you tried talking to Ted about it?'

'Are you kidding me? I can't talk to him about anything. He's a fella – he doesn't *do* talking. We don't discuss anything. Never have. Jesus, look what happened when I brought up the Warners.'

Oh my God, Layla thought. Surely Nicole and Ted weren't swingers on top of everything else. That would be too much. 'What about the Warners?' she said tentatively, her curiosity getting the better of her.

'Oh, nothing,' Nicole said. She looked wrong-footed for a second. Her voice started slurring. 'It's not about *them*.'

'Well, what is it about then?'

Nicole stopped, hiccoughed, dabbed at her eyes with her fingers, and then slung back yet more wine.

'It's OK, Nicole,' Layla said gently, more sober suddenly as she recognised the need in Nicole. The desperate need to offload. 'I won't say anything to anyone. I promise.'

Nicole looked exhausted, haggard almost. 'I just hadn't thought about him for so long,' she said. 'But now that the kids have gone . . .'

'Thought about who, Nicole?'

Nicole took a deep, ragged breath and it sounded as if she were struggling to compose the sentence, make sure the words came out of her mouth in the right order.

'I had another baby,' she said. 'Before Jason.'

Chapter 38

JOAN

Joan was in the snug, which was anything but, huddled over her ancient computer, almost ashamed that she was still trying to find out who the mysterious Andy Meyer was. Lionel kept telling her it was a waste of time, and that she should leave it all alone and mind her own business, but she didn't see why she should take heed of her husband's advice. It had never got her anywhere before.

Joan felt as alone this evening as she ever had, perhaps because the evidence of her social standing in Hope Close, or lack of it, was mounting. The new neighbour might as well not exist for all the interaction Joan had with him. Layla clearly didn't like her. (When Joan had taken some wallflowers round, albeit with the ulterior motive of quizzing the younger woman on what she knew about Andy Meyer, Layla had merely taken the plants and said thank you, and then politely but firmly shut the door.) And now there was full-on, all-guns-blazing war with Ted, seeing as he'd seen through his threat and had now brought formal charges against her for aggravated assault. It was ridiculous. It hadn't been her fault that Ted had been so aggressive, nor that she'd happened to have a pair of secateurs in her hand. She'd been gardening, for heaven's sake. *Of course* she hadn't meant to injure him. She'd merely been trying to protect herself from the brute. And besides, the wound was nowhere near as bad as Ted had made out, and she was sure he hadn't needed to wear such a massive plaster on his face for weeks on end. He'd probably just been making a point.

But still, Joan was scared. Ted might be an animal of a man, but he was a rich one, who could afford the best lawyers, and she was worried how it would go in court, if it ever got that far. Lionel had said repeatedly that she should go over and apologise to Ted, try to persuade him to drop the charges, let bygones be bygones, but why should she apologise for other people's failings? She'd done that too many times in the past.

Joan shifted in her seat, rolled her bony shoulders, continued her fruitless scrolling. At least trying to find out about her new neighbour, get to the truth behind his sudden invasion of Hope Close – why he looked so familiar, what the untold story was – felt like it offered some way forward, would perhaps lead her out of the misery that was threatening to engulf her. She clicked on to yet another Andrew Meyer, only to find he lived in London, Ontario, and was clearly at least three decades older than his Hope Close namesake.

Joan sighed, navigated off the page and instead searched the TV listings to find out what time *The X Factor* was on tonight. Trash TV was her secret guilty pleasure – and almost certainly the only thing she had in common with Ted and Nicole. Joan had been an early adopter of the genre, and right from the start she'd been hooked – astounded at the self-delusion of so many of the guests, entertained by the car-crash performances, enthralled by the sob-inducing back stories – and even though she'd known full well that her emotions were being played, she'd enjoyed it. Reality TV and real-life crime documentaries had long been her outlet, had helped with the years and years of self-denial and sadness that had been backing up in her, causing a clog, a potentially fatal blockage – until her sister's untimely death appeared to have finally sealed up her heart. All that was left now were bad feelings. Hatred of Ted. Disgust at the Warners and their wicked perverted ways. Hostility towards Layla's cantankerous, defecating cat. Resentment of Layla and Nicole's burgeoning friendship. Loathing of gates and vans and bindweed and attempted tree-lopping. Suspicion and distrust of Andy Meyer, who quite possibly had done nothing wrong at all, had simply chosen a quiet life in the country. Eternal contempt for her own husband. Revulsion of her nephew's actions, uneasily coupled with deep grief at his death. The list was endless.

Joan's epiphany, when it finally came, was sensational. It set her senses alight, unveiled her to herself, allowed her to view how others saw her. *She was nothing more than a horrible old witch.* Hardened and wizened and barren. No wonder nobody liked her. No wonder she was never invited to any of the neighbourhood gatherings, and never had been. Perhaps there was nothing wrong with everyone else after all. Maybe it was *her* that was the problem. Why couldn't she simply let others get on with their own lives and not get involved? Not pass judgement? Be more like Anne had been?

Joan flopped her head on to the computer's keyboard, feeling dizzy. It was easy to despise the world. Self-disgust was so much harder to bear. Everything she did was a waste of time and energy, and nosy and nasty to boot. She needed to stop snooping out of the window, trying to see how many times a week Nicole slipped over to Layla's, bottle of wine in hand; or what time Charles came home from his mistress, imagined or otherwise; or how often the mysterious Andy Meyer came out from behind his unlovely gates to get up to God knows what. Instead Joan needed to leave them all alone to get on with their lives, and hopefully Ted would eventually forget about pressing charges, and her knee would slowly get better . . . and in the meantime she would lie low, stay off the computer, pass the time watching her favourite TV shows while knitting baby clothes for the local hospital. Joan lifted up her head, tossed her shock of hair, tried to shake out the bad thoughts. Enough was enough. She'd keep herself to herself from now on, and be done with the lot of them.

Chapter 39

NICOLE

'Oh, Nicole,' Layla said, reaching over and taking her hand, and even in her state of distress Nicole noticed how soft it felt, how old it made her own hand look, despite the special algae-based hand cream she used twice a day. 'You poor, poor thing.'

'*I'm* not the poor thing,' said Nicole. 'My baby's the poor thing. I gave him away. I *abandoned* him.' She started crying again, but this weeping was different, with great gusting tears that felt as if they'd started somewhere low in her gut, had maybe never made it out into the world before. And then she stopped, wiped her eyes, feeling panicked suddenly. Why had she blurted it out, to someone she'd only recently become friendly with, after years and years of keeping her counsel? What on earth had she done?

'Layla, please promise not to tell anyone,' she said. 'Ted doesn't know. The kids don't know. It was so long ago, years before I met Ted.'

'Gosh, how old were you?' Layla said, looking confused, as if she were mentally trying to do the maths.

'Seventeen, by the time I actually had him.'

'Oh, sweetheart,' Layla said. 'That's so young.'

'Yes, and completely shameful for a good little Irish Catholic girl.' Nicole slumped on her stool, rested her arms on the marble worktop, turned her head towards Layla. She'd said it now. She might as well tell Layla the whole story. 'I was sent off to have the baby with my auntie in London. And, look, I know how much you miss Henry, but I gave my son up at six days old. Can you imagine that?'

'No,' said Layla, gently. 'I can't. But I'm sure he knows you did the best you could.'

Nicole sat up straight again. She'd never thought of that. 'D'you think so?'

'Of course you did.'

Nicole smiled, drained her wine glass. 'Thank you, Layla.'

'It's OK,' Layla said, squeezing her hand again. 'Honestly, everything will be OK.'

Nicole wasn't sure. How could it be OK, when she didn't know who her son was, how he was, whether he had made a success of his life, or was lying dead in a ditch somewhere? She looked around Layla's uber-modern kitchen, her head spinning, trying to convince herself that her son was all right, perhaps looking for proof somewhere. She certainly wasn't going to find it in here. The giant island had one of those induction hobs that was mind-bogglingly complicated, and an extractor fan that came up out of the work surface on hydraulics, and she had no idea how Layla ever managed to cook anything on it. In fact, now she came to think of it, she could see why Layla always said she bloody hated this kitchen. Perhaps the only thing it was good for was drinking wine in. And telling long-buried secrets. *In for a penny and all that*, Nicole thought now, her eyes welling again. She might as well get everything out while she was at it.

'I've been thinking lately about trying to track him down,' she said. 'I just miss him so much. Every birthday. Every Christmas. I've tried to forget him, but it always feels like I should have four children, not three. And now Tasha's gone too, it's brought it all back somehow. I keep wondering what he looks like, what he does, where he is.'

'Well,' Layla said. 'Why don't you try to find out?'

Nicole sniffed. 'I'm too scared to. What would I do if I actually found him? I'd need to tell Ted and the kids first.'

'Well, you don't need to think about that now,' Layla said. 'At least you've told someone at last. Hopefully that helps a bit.'

'Yes,' Nicole said. 'It does. It really does.' She leant over and wrapped her arms around Layla, kissed her on the cheek, full of gratitude to her neighbour. And then she let her go, and they opened a third bottle of wine, in a sort-of-celebration of her having shared her secret, at long last. Layla turned the music up as loud as it would go now, and Nicole started singing along to 'You've Got A Friend', the second empty wine bottle her microphone, her voice a soaring, and (at least according to Ted) remarkably accurate parody of Carole King's.

Nicole was just reaching her final crescendo when the kitchen door opened. She turned and looked blankly at Charles, then at Layla, whose eyebrows were raised in semi-quizzicalness, as if she didn't even recognise her own husband. Nicole thought about carrying on singing, and then decided against it, instead ground to a halt like a record player in a power cut.

'Oh, *hello*, darling!' Layla said. 'You're home early – and with your stern face on too!' And then she winked at Nicole, who even in her drunken state could see that Charles was fuming.

'It's nearly eleven o'clock, Layla. Why didn't you answer my calls?'

'I'm sho shorry,' Layla said. 'I've been bizzshy. As have you, I'm sure – although I'm not sure who with thish time, of courshe.' Nicole gasped, but Layla just giggled, blew her husband a kiss . . . and then she put her head to the cool, mottled marble, and passed out.

Chapter 40

Joan

Although Joan had kept her promise and had managed to keep herself to herself of late, it didn't appear to have helped. She still couldn't work out what was wrong with her. She kept veering from abject apathy to irrational rage, about everything and nothing, and then back again. Both states of mind were normal in the bereaved, according to an article she'd read in the *Daily Mail*, and so maybe she wasn't a complete harridan after all. Perhaps she was simply human.

Joan found it strange how Anne's death seemed to have hit her so much harder than any of her previous losses. It still hurt just as much now as when it had first happened. Although she and her sister hadn't always seen eye to eye, Anne had been her very best friend in the world. She'd been the only person Joan had ever been able to talk to about her deepest, most private feelings, at her times of greatest despair. And now? Now all Joan had was Lionel, and there was no way she could confide in him – and if she'd ever thought once, a trillion heartbeats ago, that she and her husband might have been right for each other, she certainly didn't any more.

Joan looked up from her knitting, blinked her eyes, gazed out into the garden, at the beautiful maple tree that she'd planted when she'd still had hope in her heart, and that Ted hated so much. It seemed that whatever she did, she couldn't stop reliving the trauma of her sister's death. The pain of sitting holding Anne's hand as the breath had slowly shuddered out of her shrunken body had been hard for Joan to bear. It had affected her. Even when she'd arrived back in Hope Close, the house had had that desolate, unlived-in feel, as if the heating had been off and the plaster had cooled down, so that the cold had crept into Joan's bones too, despite it having been May, and a warm one at that. The memory was unnerving Joan now all over again, making her feel as if unknown, unknowable ghosts were alongside her, taunting her, prodding her . . .

Joan flung down her knitting (losing a few stitches in the process), grabbed the remote and flicked off the TV, snuffing out *The Voice* – which wasn't nearly as good as *The X Factor* anyway. As she stood up from the chair, she felt a hot stab of pain in her knee. She left the room and limped up the stairs. Even entering the little back bedroom felt agonising, and yet she forced herself to do it. The birds were chirping outside in the garden, but it wasn't a joyful sound – it was discordant, as though there was something wrong with the cadence of the earth, and it reminded her of the time she'd visited a concentration camp once, many years before. It was the quiet that had struck her. No birds sang there, her guide had told them, and Joan wondered now whether nature somehow knew the difference between good and evil, whether depraved deeds permeated into the trees and the branches, the rottenness seeping into the dank dull earth for the animals and the birds to become aware of, and ultimately turn their backs on. But what was going on in Hope Close? Why were the birds squawking instead of singing here? Why did the atmosphere feel so unnatural, nefarious even? Was it simply her frame of mind? Or was it something to do with one or other of the neighbours?

As Joan pushed a grizzled strand of her hair out of her eyes, she was alarmed to discover that they felt damp. She hadn't cried when Peter had died, even though she'd loved him like a son once – but he hadn't deserved any tears. And yet she hadn't managed to cry at her sister's funeral either, even though she knew people had been looking, judging her for it. She hadn't cried for years, in fact. What was the matter with her? She didn't need to voice the answer. Grief took many and varied forms.

Joan took off her slippers now and lay down on the single, untouched bed and sobbed for her losses, for perhaps the very first time: warm salty tears pouring out in a great deluge of pent-up, long-denied loss . . . She sobbed for the nephew she'd once adored, and for the babies she'd never had, and for the chances she'd never taken, before she'd become old and ugly, both inside and out. She wept alone for hours and hours, and she'd never known there were so many tears in the world to be cried . . . and afterwards, even though (or perhaps because) Lionel hadn't come looking for her, at last she felt a little better.

Chapter 41

LAYLA

These days when the doorbell rang Layla no longer bothered to run for it in the vain hope it was the postman with something from Henry. She'd long ago acknowledged that any missive from her son would be slim enough to slide through the letterbox – and the letter would be written on thick blue paper and would be childish and brave and utterly heartbreaking. Layla cried when she got them, and she cried when she didn't. The little grain of hatred for Charles was continuing to grow in her brain, and it was invasive and pervasive, and when she couldn't fight it Layla found that the only thing that would help was another glass of wine – and so she did her best not to think about Henry until the afternoon, when it was time to start cooking.

Today, before Layla even had a chance to answer the door, the bell rang again, the gap between the two attempts to get her attention impolitely short. She sighed. It was probably Nicole, who was nothing if not persistent, but Layla wasn't in the mood for her neighbour today. In fact, Nicole was beginning to scare her a little now, as if she were a peep into her own future – a reminder that if Layla stayed here long enough, then that was how she might become, too. From board director to bored housewife. It was almost funny.

This caller, though, was indeed the postman. He thrust a package at her. 'Oh, you are there, love,' he said. 'Can you take this in for your neighbour?'

Layla looked at the name and address and blanched. She didn't want to have to see Andy Meyer again, at least not any time soon. Not after their last encounter.

'Well?' the postman said.

'Uh, OK,' Layla replied.

'Thanks, darling.' The postman filled out something on his hand-held machine and shoved it at her. Layla tried to sign on the little electronic fascia, but the markings she made were completely illegible, although the postman didn't seem to care. 'Ta, love,' he said. 'I'll put a card through and let him know.'

'OK, thanks.' Layla stared at the package. She had no idea what was inside it, but it was large and squishy and made her feel uncomfortable somehow. She sniffed at it, but that gave her no clues. The handwriting was lopsided and loopy. It intrigued her . . . as well as made her wonder what had happened to her, that she was wasting time pondering what was inside a parcel meant for one of her neighbours . . . and what on earth she was going to do with the rest of her life.

Aristotle came in through his cat flap, but instead of being proud and purry, arched of back, he slunk in in a sick, slack-boned manner and went and hid under the table.

'You OK, Ari?' Layla said. 'Are you missing Henry too?' She bent down to him then, but his eyes were cloudy, and his tail swished angrily. When she tried to pick him up, he made as if to scratch her – and so instead Layla chucked him under the chin, and left him there.

Chapter 42

The loneliness is pressing in on me, to the point that I can no longer stand my own company. Perhaps it was having the neighbour in my house that time. She broke through my boundaries, quite literally, and it seems it has affected me.

In desperation I've come out for a drive. It's something I've started doing lately, purely for the sake of it, mainly when I want to escape from my own head. For some reason it makes my bad leg ache, but I don't care. The pain is worth it. I find the process of driving slowly around country lanes, as carefully as if I were taking my driving test, uses inordinate amounts of brain power. Allows me to focus on something other than the past.

And yet. It seems I still can't shake off the memories, and maybe that's just the way it's meant to be. I can try to change every last thing about myself – my name, my appearance, even my very thought processes – but true escape comes only with death. Maybe death would have been the better option after all. That was certainly what Sian would have wanted. But hey, it's never too late. Perhaps I should give myself a time limit to get my life back on track, and then, if I miss my deadline, I can simply give up, find an obliging tree in a tranquil verdant hollow to swing from. After all, there are enough of those around here. I had no idea just how beguiling the area is.

Or . . . maybe I can try to find a route through all this inside my own mind. The Internet helps. Driving helps. Music doesn't, funnily enough. Tinder used to help, before I came up against a fruitcake, and lost a perfectly good pair of shoes in my rush to get away from her, her son and, I kid you not, her babysitting mother! And yet I can't live in isolation forever. It will kill me. But could I ever tell anyone the truth? Could I even, one day, tell the only person who might care, who lives here in Hope Close? Would they ever forgive me? I don't think so.

And so the sad fact is that, for now, I'm too scared to confide in anyone, even my therapist. Instead his best suggestion is that I should join a club – one other than Tinder, I presume – make some friends . . . The thought makes me snort, makes me feel as if I were five again. I can't remember the last time I had friends, real friends. Sian was possibly my first and last one, and I miss her, in a funny sort of way. We grew up together. We are bound together, albeit through tragedy and crime and death . . .

As I take a slow sweep past the woods at the edge of the village, feeling suspicious and anxious, I keep telling myself that my last Tinder date was clearly oblivious as to who I was, what I've done, but still I can't help worrying that maybe she and her over-friendly little son were a double bluff, a honeytrap . . . And now it's happening again, and my mind is careering around blind corners, trying to navigate potentially fatal switchbacks, even if I manage to keep the car itself steady. *I am imagining things.*

At last I turn into the lane that leads to Hope Close and the trees are shaking off their leaves, exposing the sky, which today is barge-blue and bright. As I drive through my ghastly black gates, I check the post box, and inside there's a red delivery card, which makes me uneasy on a number of levels. A package has been left for me with a neighbour – with my bewitching intruder, no less. That means I have to go and call at her house, talk to her again, at least make some kind of perfunctory contact, to collect it. Furthermore, and more pertinently, I wasn't expecting a package, and it's freaking me out. Only Ocado and Deliveroo know where I live. Who would be sending me something here? In my new name? *Maybe it's my shoes,* I think. *Perhaps my date has tracked me down, is going to come after me.* I try to remind myself that I have an official diagnosis of paranoia. My logic is flawed. I'm being insane.

I park up, get out of the car, head into my blank, ascetic house and decide that I really do need to find something to do. It strikes me that this place could do with some pictures on the walls, but I don't possess any, and even if I did I wouldn't know how to hang them. I don't own a toolkit. I went to prison way too young to learn things like that. I can't cook. I am inept at the basics.

Stress is gathering in me, like clouds. I'm still worrying about the package. Who sent it. Who knows I'm here. I feel tempted to simply not go over and collect it, but that would be worse somehow, as I know that eventually either she or the husband will come calling, try to give it to me themselves. Even the *threat* of an intrusion is an intrusion, and a constant, ever-looming one at that. I can't escape it. I groan, crack my knuckles, decide I may as well go now, get it over with – plus my curiosity has been piqued, rendered rampant in fact, by what the package might be. It was too big for the post box, according to the notice, so it won't be a credit card or anything else official. I'm stumped.

I go outside, click the buzzer, and as I pass through my partially opened gates I realise it's only the second time I've been out in the close on foot – and look how the first time ended. It feels as if I'm being watched, and I glance around, search for the twitching curtains. What a cliché. What the fuck have I done, moving here? It was an act of futility, especially now that I've seen her. A total waste of time. It's clear there's absolutely no chance of us skipping off into the sunset, Morecambe and Wise-style. It was pure fantasy.

As I march to the house in the corner, I realise I've never looked at it properly before. It has a handsome symmetry and a pared-back elegance. The front garden has a formal, topiaried look about it, suggesting a paid gardener. It's that kind of place, those kind of people, and it almost makes me laugh that I found the wife pissed, under a cardboard box, like a tramp. I wonder if she told her husband.

I take a breath and then I ring the bell, and I can hear the *ding-dong* noise echoing across the hallway inside, and its timbre carries a sense of hollow isolation that I'm all too familiar with. Finally, the door is opened, by her, and she startles me all over again. She looks so young, not much older than me, and she has on skinny jeans and a chunky red roll-neck jumper that dwarfs her. Her glossy dark hair is piled on top of her head, and *she* most certainly doesn't have dead eyes. They are large and wideset, and alive with a mixture of sadness and mischief and a strange vulnerability that I recognise, in myself. When she smiles she has dimples. Once again, I'm overwhelmed by my response to her.

'Er, hello again,' I say. 'I think you've got a package for me?'

'Oh, yes. Hang on, I think the cleaner might have moved it.' She looks at me as though she's daring me. 'Come in for a second.'

I stiffen. 'It's OK,' I say. 'I can wait here.'

'Oh. All right. Give me a minute.'

As I wait a cat saunters around the half-closed front door and turns its big yellow gaze on me. I put my hand down to stroke it, and it immediately scratches me before staggering off, as if it were drunk. An angry parallel stripe raises itself on the back of my left hand. I swear quietly and hide it in my jacket pocket.

Eventually, Layla comes back with the package, and it's the size of a briefcase and squashy. I'm forced to use both hands to take it from her.

'Goodness,' she says now, noticing the scratch, which has begun to bleed a little. 'Did Ari do that? I'm so sorry. I don't know what's the matter with him at the moment.'

I don't answer her. I can't. I've already seen the handwriting, and I can't believe it. I'm so shocked I just grab the package and stalk off, without even saying thank you, boiling with outrage and panic that it's true – but how can it be? How can it possibly be true that, after everything I've done, all the precautions I've taken, it seems I've been found?

Chapter 43

LAYLA

Well, what a rude tosser, Layla thought, as she shut the door to her new neighbour. Next time the postman asked her to take something in for Mr Andy Meyer she would simply refuse. What was it with some people? Why was *everyone* around here odd? There was Nicole, who despite being a good laugh, especially when drinking was involved, had some serious skeletons in her closet – and a neediness that Layla was beginning to find uncomfortable. Joan Taylor was just a nosy old cow, and the husband had an air about him that Layla didn't like either. And now there was this new guy, who couldn't even be civil enough to say thank you when she'd just given him his bloody parcel.

Layla stomped over to the window and glared out at the close. It struck her, for not the first time, how the houses were a mismatched lot – but there again, so were their occupants. It was as if they'd all been flung together . . . and that was what was so weird about where people live, the randomness of who your neighbours might be. It mattered, Layla realised now; and surely that was why she'd always been unhappy here. She was living amongst strangers. Why hadn't she just insisted the family stay in London, and that

Henry went to the local school? Why had she been in such thrall to her husband and his wishes?

Layla stalked through the house into the kitchen, yanked open the warehouse-sized glass doors and marched down to the very bottom of the garden. The ground was squelching and slippery and Layla was wearing only socks, but she liked it, the slithery feel of the earth as she paced the length of the fence, up and down, up and down, like a prisoner. She felt so *trapped*, and what was the point of having an enormous garden, and a wooden fort, and a rope swing in the tree and a real football goal if the person they were all for *didn't even live here*. The emptiness pressed in on her, and no matter how hard she tried to imagine Henry enthusiastically shooting up his hand in English, or leaping grinning over the vault in PE, or tucking into his lunch, instead she kept picturing him sobbing quietly under the covers in bed, the circles under his eyes dark and purple, the bruising of his soul beginning to show on the outside. She was his *mother*. Her job was to protect him.

My baby, Layla kept repeating, over and over, as she paced the fence. Beyond were the fields, the mare and last summer's foal rugged up already, grazing aimlessly in the middle distance. Aristotle came out and watched her, and even his yellow eyes looked sickly, and suspicious, and he was mewing at her, loudly, lustily, and that was *enough*.

'Just shut *up*, Ari,' she yelled, and then she turned around and ran back to the house, feeling, for the first time since Henry had left, as if she really couldn't cope any more. And so, even though it was only four in the afternoon and not even dark yet, she gave up on trying to restrain herself, and headed straight to the fridge.

Chapter 44

I think it's safe to say that I've got off to a pretty appalling start in Hope Close. Worse, I'm now convinced that there's someone spying on me, and I need to decide what to do about it. I've rung my solicitor to try to find out how he's managed to fuck it all up, and yet he swears that there's no way anyone could possibly have discovered who I am. But I don't believe him. He even sent me a package, the buffoon. It turned out to be a throw for the couch of all things, a belated house-warming present, but what a fucking idiot. His secretary had written the label, and I swear to God when I first saw her handwriting it had looked *identical* to Sian's. Now, of course, I can see that it's not my former partner-in-crime's writing at all, but it had panicked me. The package itself had panicked me. Layla had panicked me, when she'd shoved the parcel at me. I'd been up to my eyes in panic. It seems Sian haunts me still.

It is a bright autumnal day and the whip-crack wind is wreaking havoc with the leaves, which are tumbling gaily from the sky on their way to imminent death and decay, eventual resurrection. That is the thing about nature. There is a purpose to everything that happens. A rhythm, a set procedure, a grand plan – as sure and clearly defined as the seasons, which come and go and will do so forever. We humans have no such set structure. We have way too much freedom, to choose what tortured path we take to our eventual, inevitable, paltry, pointless deaths. Oh, to be a tree, with no option but to be stuck in one place forever and ever, no choice to flee or shelter, but just to take whatever God and nature throw at you and accept the consequences.

Jesus. I can hear my own thoughts, and I'm beginning to wonder if I'll need a top-up back at the cottage-asylum, or even a return trip to Spain. It's an option, I guess. And any mental relapse would hardly be surprising under the circumstances. My plan to slip into Hope Close quietly, lie low, get my bearings before I even think of approaching her, consider revealing myself, has gone horribly, almost comically, wrong.

I walk to the bottom of my enormous rear garden and gaze back in the direction of my carbuncle-house, and from here I can see into next door too. Peeking into the backs of properties feels intrusive, like opening up a doll's house and staring in, and I wonder if the neighbours have ever tried to do that with my house. I still don't know why the previous owners had mirrored glass put in at the back, but I'm not complaining. It's my good fortune that the house has one-way windows, just like my Tesla. The only way I can be seen by anyone in Hope Close is in the brief moments when I exit my gates in my car, or when I come down to the far boundary – and this is the first time I've done that. It occurs to me now that I'll need to get a gardener next summer, to mow the lawn, keep the weeds under control, and in my current state the thought of having someone on my property is almost intolerable. And besides, I might not be here by then, and I'm not even sure what the literal meaning of that sentence is. I'm almost past caring.

I continue staring through my reinforced fencing into next door's garden, but there's nothing to be seen. Just a plethora of kids' play equipment not visible from my house, for a seemingly phantom kid. I've only ever seen Henry once, and that was enough to do my head in. I'll be glad to never see him again . . .

. . . And then I spot Layla, peeping from behind an upstairs curtain, and I was right. *She's on to me.*

I try to reel my words back in, like I've been taught. I have to remember I'm Officially Paranoid. It is my medical diagnosis. I've been instructed to ensure I interrogate any such thoughts, challenge them as appropriate or not. OK, then, I'll do as I'm told. I'll review the evidence. Let's go . . .

First, I'm certain that it was Layla I saw that time at hot yoga. Then a drone miraculously manages to drop into the exact middle of my garden, and her cute little son is sent to retrieve it, alone. Next, there she was again, mysteriously in the wine bar when I was on my first ever Tinder date. Extraordinarily, I then proceed to find her trespassing, actually trespassing, on my fucking doorstep! And *now* there's the parcel incident . . . but, I try to remind myself, that was all it was. A parcel, from my solicitor, containing a cashmere throw. All Layla did was take it in. How can she possibly have controlled that? How can that be part of any conspiracy? And what on earth would she want from me anyway?

So then. What is the truth? Is it simply my paranoia rampaging, mob-like, through Hope Close, or am I right about Layla? That she's some kind of spy? Perhaps I need to do some research, talk to the other neighbours, as soon as I can summon up the courage. And if it turns out that Layla does know who I am, who I *really* am, I'll just have to work out what to do about that. What to do about her.

Chapter 45

Layla

Layla woke up in her bed and it was light. Too light. She shut her eyes quickly, and then forced herself to open them again. Charles wasn't with her. Had he even been home? She vaguely remembered someone helping her get undressed last night. She reached over and the sheets were still warm. Someone must have been here, in her bed, until just a moment ago. *Of course* it had been Charles. Who else would it have been?

Layla felt thick-headed and paranoid, which was how she always felt after she'd been drinking and had had The Dream. One or other on their own she could cope with, but the two together was a knockout blow, and she could feel the undiluted dismay rising and falling, in time with her breath. Vivid images were swirling around inside her head again now, always the same ones, but reaching the forefront as randomly as in a mixed-up slide projector. She saw little Charlie Dolphin, huddled against the cold, his face contorted with hunger and poverty, sitting on a bare mattress in a room with patterned wallpaper hanging off the walls, his three older brothers hunched around him, his mother with a fag in her hand, a hardened look on her face . . . And now Charlie was out in the rubbish-strewn street, and he had holes in his shoes and hatred in his eyes. Next she saw the gun going off, and the head of a rabbit flying into the air, more gruesome and less cartoon-like every time she imagined it. And now it was *her* Charlie, fully grown up, in a grey jumpsuit, and he was in a police mugshot and he had a perfect quiff and eyes made of dead matter. Suddenly the victim wasn't a bleeding rabbit, it was a screaming child, and Charlie had his hand over the child's mouth, and first the child was her, and next it was Henry, and now it was Layla herself who was screaming, and she didn't know if the noise was merely wailing its way through her internal system or being let out into the world, and her head was detonating, blowing up into a mushroom cloud of fragments of body parts and broken dreams.

Layla crawled under the covers, curled into the foetal position, waited for the panic to pass. It always did in the end, if only she could get enough air into her lungs. She heard the bedroom door open and the sound of china on wood, and a firm hand on her arm through the duvet.

'Layla,' Charles said. 'Are you all right?' He pulled back the covers, and Layla didn't even try to stop him. His eyes had that concerned look they got sometimes, almost as if he were a kindly parent, but there was disapproval there, too. What had she done last night? What had she said? And just how much wine had she drunk? It hadn't helped that she'd started so early, of course. No wonder she felt so wretched.

'God, sorry,' she said. 'Did I scream?'

'Just a bit. Was it the . . . the same thing?'

Layla could see the fear in her husband's eyes, and she didn't want to have to tell him. 'No,' she said, but they both knew she was lying. And yet what else could she do? It might not be Charles's fault, but it wasn't hers either.

Layla kept staring at Charles, and his expression said it all. It would never be how it was before. It was such a brutal thing, to have your name despoiled like that, and Layla could only imagine how Charles had felt. She'd seen it in people's faces when it first happened. *Surely not?* Charlie Dolphin was in prison, wasn't he? But there were only three years between the two Charlie Dolphins, and they even looked quite similar. Charles had always said that she was being melodramatic, but it felt to Layla as if her husband had had his very identity stolen from him. The person he'd always been, forever linked to perniciousness and rape and murder. And although now that he was known as Charles it was a little bit better, things would never be quite the same for him again. It was always there, lurking at his shoulder.

'There's tea there for you,' Charles said now. He bent down and kissed her nose. 'I'm leaving for work in a minute. I'll see you later.'

'Bye,' said Layla. Her hands were still shaking, and she waited until Charles had left the room before picking up the mug so he wouldn't have to see the state she was in. She'd hoped the nightmares would have passed by now, but if anything they'd been getting worse again lately. Perhaps it was because Henry was away, and she was worried that he might become a murder victim, too. Surely that was why she'd freaked out when he'd gone missing, albeit briefly, that time. Or maybe it was because she didn't trust Charles, was well aware his sins could take many forms, was ashamed she could even think such things. And, of course, she'd been drinking way too much lately, and alcohol only added to her depression and fear, was no substitute for her son.

Layla sat up in bed, her head thumping a rackety, painful remonstrance that she knew she fully deserved. She'd been a fool. She might have been having a hard time, but she was a mother, whether Henry was here or not. She needed to act like one. She shook her head, forced her mind to clear. It was as she heard the sound of Charles's car leaving that at last she realised what she needed to do. She needed to stop drinking. She needed to sort herself out.

Chapter 46

NICOLE

There had been such an extraordinary development in Hope Close relations that Nicole could still scarcely believe it. It had started with an unexpected knock at the door, and when Nicole had answered it, Andy Meyer, of all people, had been standing there, right there, on her front doorstep. He'd even been smiling, although seemingly not without some effort. But still, Nicole had thought, progress was progress.

'Hi,' he'd said. 'I just, er, wanted to come over and say sorry that we got off on the wrong foot that time – you know, er, over Henry.'

'Oh,' she'd said, genuinely gobsmacked. Andy had stuck out his hand then, and she'd taken it – and it had given her such a strange physical thrill she'd found herself going red. *Good God*, she'd thought. She had to do something about her sex life. She couldn't go around getting fluttery with all and sundry, especially not the oddball neighbours. She'd be coming on to Lionel next.

'Anyway, I'm Andy,' he'd said.

'And I'm Nicole,' she'd replied, lifting her hand to her neck, rubbing at a nerve that had started throbbing. 'But I'm the one who should be apologising to you, yelling at you like that as if you were some kind of child-snatcher.'

Andy had looked pissed off at that point, and she'd clearly said the wrong thing.

'Sorry,' she'd said. 'It's just that I was out of my mind with worry for Henry.'

'That's OK.' Andy had proceeded to bend down, clearly embarrassed, and make a fuss of the dog, who, as ever, was busy checking out who might be crossing his threshold, or otherwise. 'And who's this?'

'Oh, that's Stanley.'

'He's gorgeous . . . Maybe I could take him for a walk sometime?'

Nicole had been shocked enough, but Andy himself had looked *astounded* at what he'd just said. And yet Stanley had clearly liked Andy – and he didn't wag his tail for any old Tom, Dick or Harry. It was Stanley's opinion that counted round here.

And so it had begun . . .

This morning Nicole was in a reflective mood. Andy and Stanley were out on their latest jaunt and she was emptying the dishwasher (which she'd run even though it was barely half full, a fact that made her feel sad in itself), pondering recent events in the close. There'd been a swinging scandal. Vangate. Dronegate. Even Gategate. The last of her children had left home. A little kid had been prematurely packed off to boarding school, whether he liked it or not. There'd been a full-on fight involving her husband and the resident old boot that seemed destined to end up in court. A mysterious new neighbour had developed an apparent love of walking her elderly dog, and yet always took him through her back garden to the fields beyond, presumably to save being seen by the neighbours. She didn't know what to make of any of it.

Nicole was still lost in thought when there was a tap on the side door.

'Sorry, Nicole,' Andy said, as Stanley slunk in, bedraggled and seemingly knackered. 'He's pretty muddy.'

'That's OK. Come on in out of the cold.' She smiled up at Andy as she grabbed Stanley's collar, tried to avoid the inevitable muddy paw prints, and felt ludicrously shy suddenly.

'No, it's all right, thanks,' Andy said. 'I'm going out shortly, and my boots are filthy. I'll just head straight off.'

'Oh, OK.' She struggled to hide the disappointment in her voice, and she didn't know what it was about him. There was a vulnerability there, certainly, but something else, too. A cocksureness, hidden but apparent to her. A sense of entitlement, even. It was jarring.

'Where are you off to?' she said.

Andy looked appalled, and she realised she was being nosy. He was just her neighbour, who walked her dog occasionally. She had no right to ask him anything.

'Oh, er, I've got a meeting.'

'OK. Well . . . thanks for walking Stanley.'

'That's all right.'

As Andy turned and sauntered away, Nicole wondered why she hadn't told Ted about his visits. She was sure that old bag next door would have clocked it, but now that the two households never spoke any more (or at least only through their respective lawyers), it was unlikely that Ted would ever find it out from Joan Taylor. And unless Henry got a new drone, Layla wouldn't have a clue what went on in Nicole's back garden – and therefore wouldn't be able to tell Ted either.

As Nicole towelled down Stanley, wiped his paws, gave him a Schmacko, she had no idea why she hadn't told Layla what was going on. It would be a great topic of gossip between the two of them. What was she trying to hide? What did she even want from Andy? And, more to the point, what did he want from her? As Nicole stroked Stanley's ears, kissed the top of his furry, greying head, gazed into his lovestruck eyes, she decided that there was something, on both counts. She was sure of it.

Chapter 47

Layla

Half-term had come and gone, and although it had been lovely for Layla to have her son home for a whole week, especially as she'd managed to cut down considerably on her wine consumption, it had only made her more uncertain about how Henry truly was. He clearly wasn't the same wide-eyed little boy she and Charles had dropped off on that dreary September day eight weeks earlier, and although on the surface he seemed more mature and polished, more worldly now, there was something about his demeanour that hadn't felt quite right to Layla. Maybe all boarders were like that after half a term away, and she'd been told to expect such changes, but this new level of maturity seemed unnatural to her somehow. A charade. A mask. Furthermore, when they'd picked him up, Henry had still seemed a little isolated from the other boys, and Layla continued to worry that he might be being bullied – although he insisted, perhaps too vociferously, that he was fine, and that there was nothing wrong *at all*. Layla had no idea how an eight-year-old boy was meant to cope with being emotionally resilient twenty-four hours a day, without having his mummy to run to – Christ, she could barely manage it at thirty-six! But whatever the truth of the situation, and despite Charles's constant pleas for her not to worry, Layla wasn't convinced.

It was Monday morning, the day after Henry had been taken back to school, and Layla had got up at the same time as Charles for once, made herself some tea, gone into his study and opened her laptop. She'd been determined not to mope, but her latest endeavour was proving a more difficult task than she might have imagined. As she scanned through positions such as trainee driving instructor, or trainee personal trainer, or Deliveroo driver, or domestic cleaner, or roaming door fundraiser (whatever roaming doors were) she was amazed at how hard it was to find a job locally. There were zero roles for trained architects. It didn't help that Charles appeared so out of touch with how she felt that he seemed to assume she was satisfied with being a housewife. Layla might have been happy to stay at home to look after Henry when he'd been little, but it certainly wasn't the case now he wasn't even bloody well here.

Layla sighed, took a sip of her tea, which had grown cold, developed a sallow slack skin. Maybe it would have been different if she'd had another baby, but it had simply never happened, and while she'd done her best to be phlegmatic about the situation, Charles hadn't ever seemed remotely keen to have any more children anyway. Perhaps he hadn't wanted to risk Layla having postnatal depression again, and all the misery that had entailed – or maybe it was simply that he already had three children, and that was more than enough for him. Looking back, Layla just wished he'd been more honest about it, but then that was Charles through and through. His was a deceit conducted through the medium of omission.

Charles popped his head around the door, briefcase in hand, tie smartly tied, the epitome of a successful businessman.

'Oh, there you are,' he said. He seemed annoyed, although he was trying to contain it. 'What are you doing in here?'

'Just some research,' she replied, smiling cutely, giving her dimples an outing. 'On my laptop.'

'Oh.' Charles appeared uncertain still.

'I take it I am allowed to use your office?' she said, trying to hit just the right pitch of passive-aggressiveness without being overtly rude.

'Of course you are.' He came over, bent down and kissed her on the cheek. 'See you this evening.'

As Layla heard the front door close, it occurred to her that her and Charles's relationship was becoming more and more stilted – as if the absence of Henry was breaking the bonds that had once existed between them, leaving their marriage potentially unsalvageable. It was a shocking possibility, one she wasn't willing to confront just yet. Now wasn't the right time, not for any of them. Her immediate priorities needed to lie elsewhere.

Layla stretched, got up from Charles's desk, went over to the window, watched his car purr away. From here, looking down on the scene, it felt unreal, as if the close were merely a movie set and Charles's car was a decoy, driven by a stunt double, someone she might not even know. She gripped both sides of the crown of her head, beneath her slip-shiny hair, squeezed her scalp, let out a low deep groan. Then she went back over to the desk, stared at her laptop. The answers to almost every last question in the world were inside it, able to be channelled through it in some incomprehensible act of electronic wizardry, but it was identifying the specific questions she needed to ask that confounded her. The need to connect was stronger than ever. Who with, though? Her friends and family were too far away. Drinking wine with Nicole had been a diversion for a while, but they were in danger of turning each other into alcoholic maniacs. Joan was just Joan. And finally there was Andy, the rudest man in the history of the universe. Good God. Layla needed something else to think about.

When the idea came to Layla, she was amazed it had only just occurred to her. Perhaps she'd simply become too wrapped up in her life in Hope Close to realise that there was a whole other world out there still. When she typed in 'architect jobs in London', a plethora of results surged on to her screen, like a last-minute lifeline – and there was her solution, and it made her feel better. If by Christmas it was clear that Henry was thriving at school, was surely going to *stay* thriving, then there was no way she was going to continue sitting around Hope Close doing nothing. She'd get a job in London, become another Home Counties commuter. Charles wouldn't like it, but Layla didn't care. She was an adult. She could do whatever she liked.

Chapter 48

I love dogs. And so when I first went over to see Nicole, under the guise of apologising to her, I immediately took to Stanley – and not merely as a distraction technique. I've even thought about getting a dog myself, but the responsibility still terrifies me, as if I can't be trusted, and the logical continuation of that sentence is too bleak to contemplate. Yet offering to walk Stanley was a genius spur-of-the-moment idea on a number of levels. It's a way to get close, but not too close. A way to get information. But, best of all, a way to get *love*.

So, here I am, after all that I used to be, all that I have put people through, walking an ageing cocker spaniel across open muddy fields, along puddle-strewn country lanes, through damp sagging woods. I am wearing a Barbour jacket and wellington boots. I might as well be wearing a flat cap. My appearance is so removed from how I used to look, who I used to be, I almost forget that one day, any day, I might yet be outed. It seems I am now on speaking terms with two of my neighbours, and although they both seem perfectly pleasant, I find that I still don't trust Layla. She's too beautiful for a start, as if beauty itself is not to be trusted. But who is she? What does she know? My therapist insists I'm entirely wrong about her being a spy. He has told me that all the evidence I have against her is ridiculous, circumstantial at best, and that how I feel is surely simply part of my Disorder with a capital D. I want to believe him. I like Layla. She's fun and unconventional, hard to unpick. I like the boy, too, and even saying that makes my heart hurt. I don't know what to do about either of them.

Nicole, at least, is easier to deal with. She's brassy, wears her heart on her sleeve. And yet. There is something about her, too, that suggests that all is not as it seems. But maybe that's what everyone is like. Surely everyone harbours secrets of one kind or another, and it's just that before I went to prison I was too young and stupid to realise.

I'm finding it so weird repatriating myself into society. It is such a gradual thing. At first even conversation felt beyond me, and that's why my time in Spain was so important. It helped give me my backstory, my strategies, practice for the various facets of my new existence, amongst people who seemed to have almost as many problems as me. It helped me reinvent my past life, into one that doesn't sound as insane as the truth.

Stanley has disappeared into the undergrowth, chasing a squirrel, and this wood is quiet, so quiet, lonely and dark . . . I turn my head upwards, shut my eyes to the sky, direct my mind away from the past, and the present, towards the future . . . and it is a beautiful, brief moment of respite, and I savour it . . .

And then the wind gusts, shakes the rain prettily off the branches, and there is air on my face, spray in my eyes, and I am mad with lust, for life, for everlasting happiness, for that single, pure, euphoric moment of ecstasy to never ever end. *That laughter.*

No. Please no.

And now I see Sian screaming at me, like an evil demented ghoul, yelling that it's all my fucking fault that Bobby's dead – and I wish the wood would close in on me, hug me to death, put me out of my misery. The truth is unequivocal, and it renders everything else pointless. I feel in my pocket for Stanley's lead, look up at the tree branches, and I don't care about the poor person who might find me. I don't even care about Stanley, how he'll get home. I'm done.

As I start sussing out which tree to pick, Stanley appears, whimpering, as if he can feel the unholiness of my thoughts, and he nudges my knee, wags his tail mournfully – and I know I won't do it. Not now. Not to him.

I stoop down, put the dog on the lead, commence my tortured walk home. I try everything to calm down my thoughts, remember what I've been taught. My footsteps are a therapeutic drumbeat. *It will pass. It will pass. It will pass.* But it won't. It can't.

At last, as Hope Close beckons, I force myself to remember the reason I moved here. I wonder what the neighbours would do if they knew my real identity. And maybe the pure, simple truth is that's why I can't ever tell them. It seems that is the real dilemma. Between me and the rest of the world is a dirty little secret that I cannot share, because it will out me, and the world will despise me. *Bobby, I'm so sorry.*

I try to huff the air out, relinquish the memories, forget my attempts at mental disambiguation. The walk home is blank, depleted, unconscious even . . . and far too soon I find myself back, at Nicole's side door, and she's there in a flash, and for the very first time it appears I've agreed to come in for a coffee, and I have no idea how that happened. Perhaps I need her. Perhaps she needs me. Maybe I simply miss my mum. I don't know. It's just what's happening.

Nicole leads me into her kitchen, and it has that reek of money over style, with its high-gloss coffee-coloured units and gold-leafed tiles, its bespoke mud-hued glass splashback, an enormous flat-screen TV looming at me like a black hole. As I stand next to the smoked glass dining table, the uniformly mocha chairs, I can almost smell butterscotch, and that's how brown and sickly the overall effect is. My own kitchen is pretty grim and needs ripping out, but at least it's been painted plain white. The tall wide windows on to the garden and the hills beyond provide the only colour – nature as life, the outdoors as art – and that's how I like it.

'Milk and sugar?' Nicole is saying now. It's almost painful to look at her, at the taut pull of her skin, as though she has screws on either side of her face, just above her ears, beyond the hairline, that she periodically tightens to keep her face crease-free. Her features bear that lack of symmetry that either makes you beautiful, or ugly, or else – as in her case – artificially doll-like and scary. Yet even though it might be hard to tell what Nicole's facial expression is, there's no mistaking the pheromones radiating off her, and although it appals me, there's something strangely appealing about her. She's guileless, and she makes it easy for me to let my guard down. I like her faint Scouse accent, her big personality, her openness. It almost feels as if I know her off the telly, like she's someone off *Gogglebox*, or an ex-*Brookside* cast member. She's familiar. Maybe that's what it is. Or maybe it's simply that she's nice.

'Just black, thanks,' I answer. Stanley lies flopped in the corner, worn out and muddy, and I want to go over and pat his silky ears, make his tail wag, thank him for saving me. He is panting a little, and it doesn't sound quite right to me, but I don't like to say anything. Nicole might think it's my fault.

'Biscuit?' she says, thrusting a canister at me.

'No, thanks.'

'So where did you say you're from, Andy?' she says now.

I'm pretty sure I've never told her. 'Er, well, we moved around,' I say. This is a pre-planned answer. I need to deliver it more assertively. 'London, mainly.'

'Oh,' says Nicole. She hesitates, as though she can't think of anything to say to that. There is a frisson of something, as though I'm peering into a darkened cellar, and I've seen a flash of movement, like a scarf fluttering perhaps. Or a flag. I move the conversation on to Hope Close matters, and this is where Nicole perks up, and she proceeds to tell me all sorts of things that confuse me, even shock me – and I wonder if she is just a massive gossip, a storyteller, playing for laughs, or whether it's all true. I'd bet the latter, if I had to put money on it.

'So anyway,' she says, after a brief lull in the conversation, during which I've been trying to digest her account of the apparently chequered history of my house. She has clearly plucked up the courage to interrogate me now. 'What is it that you do, Andy?'

I give my other pre-prepared answer. 'I'm a tech developer,' I say.

'Ohhh,' she says. She looks relieved, as if *that* explains it. 'There's good money in that, isn't there?'

'Well, it's not bad,' I say, modestly.

'And you work from home?' she persists.

'Yes. That's the thing with tech. You can do it anywhere.'

Again she nods, visibly satisfied with this answer, too. When at last I stand up, I feel relieved.

'Well, thanks for the coffee,' I say.

'Any time,' she replies.

I stare at her, at her long dark hair, which would look better on someone younger, and I feel another tug of something. Pity? Sympathy? Revulsion? Desire? An Oedipal pull? I need to get out of here.

'Bye,' I say.

'Ta ra,' Nicole says. 'See you soon.'

'Will do.'

As soon as I get outside, I walk away as fast as I can without breaking into a run. But once I'm safely back behind my gates I do run, around the front garden, into my house, down to the sunken living room, and I circle it, over and over, like a madman, trying to flee from something that chases me, and which it seems I can never ever escape.

Chapter 49

Joan

The past week's rain had been relentless, rendering the garden so boggy that Joan still hadn't ventured out there, and not just because of the injury to her knee. Even Layla's dreadful cat seemed to have given up coming over to defecate in her borders, and Hope Close felt closed up, battened down – as if all it were focused on was weathering the storm.

Right now, Joan was holed up in the snug, busy with her knitting. She was finding something soothing about the rain pelting the windows as she watched old recordings of her favourite TV shows, all the while knitting one, purling one, turning soft pink yarn into even softer mittens. It felt as if there was a steadiness returning to her breathing at last, for the first time since Anne had died. It wasn't that all the pain had disappeared, but it was transmuting, away from the vitriolic towards a quiet acceptance. Even her grief about her nephew's unedifying death, the children she'd never been able to have, felt less now. It was all too late. They were all gone.

Unfortunately, though, any resolution of historic traumas didn't compensate for the fact that now Joan had a new weight bearing down on her. These days she had a dread of the post arriving, in case there was yet another verbose, barely comprehensible, utterly arrogant missive from Ted's solicitors. She wished that Ted would simply stop haranguing her and leave her alone. Even Nicole had got in on the act now, making outrageous, untrue statements about what she'd witnessed. Joan had always known Nicole was a liar, the type of person who would do or say whatever suited her. It was par for the course with Nicole. And it was a disgrace that Ted had swanned around for weeks with a whopping big plaster on his face, but that the damage to her knee had rendered her effectively housebound. Ted and Nicole were both liars, in fact. Nothing better than common criminals.

Joan stopped knitting, took out her hanky, blew her nose. When she picked up the needles again, she felt a little better, soothed by the movement of her hands, the TV show, the cup of tea and plate of ginger biscuits by her side, the flame-effect fire, the rolling raindrops . . .

And then her peace was interrupted by a horrible shrieking, wailing sound, one that she remembered all too well from the past.

Joan looked up sharply from her knitting, peered over her glasses at the TV . . . and suddenly there he was, looming on her screen – and it was like a jab in her gut, a stark, sickening reminder of a distant, horrible crime. The camera cut away almost immediately, but Joan grabbed the remote control, pressed rewind, paused it on the close-up. *Surely not?* It wasn't possible to tell from his face alone. He'd been so much younger, for a start. She re-ran the tape. Perhaps her curiosity was making it into something that it wasn't, her overall conclusions greater than the sum of the parts. And yet there was definitely something about the way he moved. Something familiar.

Joan stared and stared at the pictures, thoughts coursing through her sharp, busy brain about what it might mean. Eventually she lumbered to her feet, limped through the house to the front room, ignoring Lionel as he sat mutely in his chair, watching football. She stationed herself at her erstwhile familiar snooping position, peered past the curtains, gazed through the driving rain and the late-autumnal gloom towards the murky house opposite . . . and the longer she stayed there, gazing at the gates, the more the throb in her knee intensified . . . and the more certain she became that she was right.

Chapter 50

LAYLA

The rain had finally stopped when she found him, lying on his side in the middle of the lawn. At first Layla didn't even realise he was dead, as she'd always thought that cats slunk away to die, but now here he was, imprinted forever on her image of this otherwise delightful garden, his fur blue-tinged and dull, his yellow eyes open and startled and disgusted. Layla had crept so close to him that by the time she'd realised he was dead she'd already touched him, had felt the cold soddenness of his fur, the alien stiffness of his bones. When she screamed it was blood-curdling, and it went on and on, and although she was sure someone must have heard her, no one came. She longed to be able to help Aristotle, but she dimly knew that there was nothing that could be done. Death was death was death. Irreversible. The finality of it had never meant anything to her before.

Layla ran inside and her hands were shaking as she called Charles at the office, and for a change he answered his mobile at once, and when she told him that the cat was dead he sounded shocked, and said he'd get home as soon as he could. 'But what about your meeting?' Layla sobbed, and he said it didn't matter, as he could bring all the papers home – and unconsciously her dial notched up from perhaps a five back to a six for her husband. She didn't dare go near the rear of the house now, couldn't risk looking out into the garden again, seeing poor Aristotle, who had once fitted inside her palm, who she'd raised before she'd even had Henry, who'd been the most beautiful bundle of silver fur and saffron eyes and the tiniest, pinkest tongue. Who knew you could feel so much grief for a *cat*?

Layla went to the fridge, poured herself a large glass of wine. The thump in her head was shocking in its intensity, and she wanted it to stop. But how on earth had the cat died? she wondered bleakly. He wasn't old. He'd never been ill. He wasn't fat. He hadn't been off his food . . .

And then Layla remembered Aristotle coming to her as she'd been pacing the fence, and her yelling at him . . . and maybe he'd been trying to tell her something, been trying to get her to help him – and the despair she felt at that possibility was quite extraordinary in its depth. The guilt flung itself at her, and stuck. Poor, poor Aristotle, and even in death she couldn't say his name without that sardonic lilt. Her Ari. Her baby.

Layla felt her fear spiralling now, and although she knew she was being entirely irrational, she thought of Henry next, found herself imagining him dead, too, and she wanted to ring the school, check he was there, in his lessons, hadn't been snatched by a murderer, and she even found herself pulling up the number on her phone and pressing dial – and it was only once it had rung five times and they'd answered with that smoothly efficient 'Arundel College, how may I help you?' that she'd hung up, having realised that *of course* Henry was fine, as otherwise the receptionist wouldn't have been so calm. Not if a child had been abducted, possibly murdered. And besides which, calling the school for no apparent reason would have made her, Henry Dolphin's mother, come across as quite unhinged, and that wouldn't have been good for anyone . . .

Layla put down her phone, tried to regain some rationality, and at first it seemed to be working. And then she remembered all over again that Aristotle was inexplicably dead, and she even wondered if he'd been poisoned . . . and she tried to work out, if indeed that was true, which of her neighbours had done it.

PART THREE

NOVEMBER

Chapter 51

NICOLE

The weather had taken a turn for the worse. The nights were dark and windy, the rain seemingly never-ending, and Nicole missed her kids more than ever. She missed their comings and goings. She missed their friends roaring up in their mothers' cars, emptying the fridge, sneaking her and Ted's booze when they thought no one had noticed. And she missed, properly missed, the child she hadn't seen since he was a newborn.

Nicole still didn't know why she was feeling like this, and she had no idea what to do about it. Telling Ted felt impossible, especially as it seemed they barely spoke about anything without Ted flying off the handle these days, and she wasn't sure whether that was his fault or hers. She was fully aware she was driving him away with her need for love, for sex, for reassurance that she was still sexy – and it felt so unfair that her desire to be desired had merely made her less so. How could she possibly tell Ted about her secret son the way things were? Her husband could be unpredictable. He might go mad. It might even be the end of them.

And yet that wasn't the only thing bothering Nicole. Hope Close had become so insular of late, so lonely, it was almost as if it were cut off from the entire world. It didn't help that she was from

Liverpool, where people were friendly, and even in this day and age would be in and out of each other's houses every five minutes, and she hated the fact that no one socialised here any more. The close used to be so much fun once – perhaps too much fun at times, granted – but these days she hardly saw anyone. Her and Layla's teatime wine sessions were a thing of the past. In fact, since her cat had died, Layla seemed to have lost all interest in socialising full stop. Nicole was worried about her.

My God, this place needs a bloody reboot, Nicole thought, as Stanley towed her out of Hope Close and along the lane, although perhaps not quite as determinedly as he might once have done. (Joan had told Nicole once, before they'd fallen out, that *she* was meant to walk the dog, not have the dog walk *her*, but Joan Taylor could just fuck the fuck off.) Even Andy seemed to have stopped coming round to walk Stanley for some reason, which Nicole felt slighted by – and the dearth of friendly neighbours made her *almost* miss the Warners, but not quite. It was sad in a way that they'd left, yet Nicole supposed that that was what happened when people got divorced. She hadn't remotely expected it, though. The Warners had always seemed happy to her, and for years she and Ted used to joke about their pampas grass – which just proves, Nicole thought now, that you never really knew what was going on behind closed doors. Or closed gates for that matter.

Nicole was so lost in thought that she'd walked further than she'd realised, and was already on the Common. She'd need to head back soon if she wanted to make the lunchtime spin class. She'd tried to persuade Layla to come with her once, but Layla had point-blank refused. *Why on earth would I pay someone to shout abuse at me,* she'd said. *What kind of masochist would I have to be? Why wouldn't I just go for a nice bike ride in the countryside?* Nicole wasn't even sure if Layla had been joking, and it had offended her a little, in truth, although she hadn't said so. She hadn't wanted them to fall out. But now it seemed that they had anyway, for all sorts of unspoken reasons. Nicole was pretty sure Ted deciding to take Joan to court hadn't helped. She knew she should never have said she'd witnessed the fight. Not only was she scared about having to say it under oath, she could tell that Layla hadn't remotely believed her. She missed Layla, but what could she do? Whenever she asked her to do anything now, Layla always said she was busy, but really – busy doing what? It seemed that Layla had pushed Nicole away, and it upset her. She'd thought they were friends. What made it even more painful was that Layla was the one person Nicole had confided in, had shared her very deepest secret with, after years and years of keeping her counsel. She still wasn't sure why she'd done it – whether her grief over Tasha leaving had been the catalyst, or if it had been something else entirely. It had clearly been a mistake, though. Nicole was worried that Layla might even tell someone, and that Ted and the kids would find out. The fact that she, Nicole, had been drunk would be no excuse. She should have told her family first, not risk them finding out via village gossip. She was a fool.

Nicole's head was reeling as she paced through the sodden woods, the supple squelch of the earth, the sway of the trees the only sounds that resonated through the dank, sullen air. She felt so lonely, and yet it was as if there was someone else there too, in the woods with her, and she wondered all over again what had happened to her lost child, where he might be. And then she remembered that this was the place where her would-be friend had been murdered a decade or so earlier, and she shivered, decided that she needed to get the hell out of here, and not just because she had a spin class to get to.

Nicole took the path that would lead her directly back to the lane, upped her pace . . . but the voice in her head that told her she'd been stupid, an idiot, grew louder, as if the trees themselves were saying it, as if nature had outed her. When she reached a fork in the path, presided over by a ghostly, hollowed-out tree trunk that somehow reminded her of Joan Taylor, she didn't recognise it, and she knew she must have taken a wrong turn.

'Stanley!' she called, but the dog seemed to have disappeared. The more she called, the more she could feel the stress building in her, making her breath flutter, her voice waver . . . and no matter how many times she shouted for him, all she could hear in return were forest sounds: sappy, soft twigs and tumbling leaves, the occasional squawking bird . . . and still Stanley, her Stanley, didn't come back.

Chapter 52

JOAN

Her trusty Google had failed her. Joan might have managed to convince herself that her new neighbour was in fact Jono Grey, convicted child killer, but it seemed impossible to verify. There was no recent information about Jono Grey whatsoever, which seemed unbelievable to Joan. As far as she could find out, he hadn't even been released from jail, and although she'd tried calling the prison he'd last been in (at least according to the *Daily Express* in 2012), the prison switchboard had categorically refused to hand out information about individual inmates. She'd even tried calling the local Surrey police, to see if he was on their watch list, with equal lack of success, and she wasn't sure how else to check. Jono Grey hadn't been in the news for years. It was almost as if everyone had entirely forgotten about him, despite the insanely high profile of the original story, and maybe that was just what happened when people were banged up for long enough. After a few years you only ever really heard about such criminals if they were due for parole, like Mary Bell; or if they'd been attacked by another inmate, like Ian Huntley; or if they'd hanged themselves, like Fred West. Or, of course, if they had a stupid name, like Charlie Dolphin.

Joan was nothing if not dogged. Despite her earlier vow to be done with snooping on the neighbours, this was a different situation entirely. This was a matter of potential public safety, as there was Henry to think of. Joan found herself becoming so desperate to get another look at her neighbour, check whether her hypothesis was correct, that now she'd had the inkling she found it hard to let it go. In the end, she decided to go ahead and execute her plan straight away. Today, in fact. It was perfectly plausible, and it had worked with Layla. Hopefully it would work with this so-called Andy Meyer, too.

Joan put on her brown anorak and ventured out into the garden, still limping slightly, and every step she took made her hate Ted more, for doing this to her. She crossed the puddled patio and walked down the still-damp path to the greenhouse. She chose the best cyclamen plants she had available and potted them out neatly. Then she ran her soily fingers through her unruly hair in a vain attempt to tame it, and reminded herself of her mother's favourite expression. *There's no time like the present.*

Joan didn't really know what she was hoping to achieve, but there was a compulsion now, pushing her to find out the truth – if only to distract herself from her useless, impotent husband, and the prospect of the potentially ruinous court case that still hung over her, like the death penalty. She was fairly sure that just one look at him, up close, would give her the answer. Perhaps that was all she was after, for now at least. There was no need for her to reveal to anyone what she suspected.

Joan exited her plastic porch and made her way across the close, feeling far more nervous than she'd expected – yet still unable to stop the familiar feeling of ire rising in her. Those gates were *disgraceful*. If Andy Meyer really was Jono Grey, he was truly a philistine, as well as a disgusting criminal.

Joan pushed the square silver button and a light flashed at her, yet it made no sound and Joan didn't know if a buzzer had rung in the house. It was impossible to tell, but either way there was no reply. Joan peered through the crack and could see that the car was there. Was he in, or not? She felt even more anxious now – terrified, in fact. She'd seen his reaction the night he'd brought Henry out from behind his gates, from whatever he'd been doing with the boy. He'd acted like a cornered beast, ready to attack. Perhaps this wasn't wise. Maybe she should give up for now, try to do some more research, think about how she would handle things, if it turned out her theory was indeed correct.

Joan could feel the pain in her knee, throbbing its way up her veiny leg, through her groin, towards her unrequited heart. Really, when all things were considered, what did she have? Everything she'd ever cared about was gone. What did she have to lose any more? *Nothing*. She shoved her hair from her eyes, pressed the buzzer again with her forefinger, for a long, long time. And then she stood back, and waited.

Chapter 53

NICOLE

Nicole had been searching alone in the woods in the pouring rain for a good half an hour when at last she saw him, a dark eerie shadow, and at first he'd scared her, until she'd realised it was definitely him, bombing towards her as if he were a puppy again, through the trees, kicking up the leaves, leaping into her outstretched arms, covering her best coat with mud, whimpering with excited relief.

'Oh Stanley, you silly mutt,' Nicole said, and promptly burst into noisy tears that ricocheted their way around the trees, got swallowed up in the jungle drench. She'd kept it in, and now she couldn't. The relief was too great. She fell to the ground, buried her face in Stanley's wet-dog fur – and never had it smelled so good.

'I'm so sorry, baby,' she sobbed, over and over again. Stanley wagged his tail, but he was panting now, and his tongue was hanging so far out of his mouth it was fly-paperish, cartoon-like. Nicole had no idea where he'd been, how far he'd run. When she eventually stood up, she was soaked through and muddy, but it didn't matter. She couldn't care less what she looked like, as long as Stanley was safe. She bent down and put him on the lead, and there was no way she was letting him off again today. Or possibly ever.

Unfortunately, Nicole's relief was short-lived. Her and Stanley's return through the woods was slow and full of dread, and she didn't even know where she was going. Somehow they'd ended up in a part of the Common she'd never been to before, and it was as if no one else had been there, either. The paths were overgrown and hard to follow, and she had no phone reception, and even the dog didn't seem to know where he was, although usually his sense of direction was second to none. But it was clear that Stanley wasn't himself, and it was almost as if his last sprint towards her, his ecstatic leap into her arms, had exhausted him. Nicole kept looking around her, hearing the stray rustles and cracks of squirrels and birds . . . and imagining wolves and wild boars and murderers. She kept thinking of the dead cake-sale woman, how she'd pretended to Layla that she'd known her, and how obscene that seemed now, and she kept wondering where exactly it had happened, and whether it was about to happen to her, and how that would be divine retribution – was that the term? Her nerves were pulling themselves out of her arteries, or wherever they went, and although she'd never been much good at biology, the one thing she was sure of was that the pain was like knife strikes. She thought she'd never get over the sheer panic and terror she'd felt at the prospect of Stanley running out on to the lane and getting run over, or of her never ever finding him, never seeing him again, never knowing what had happened to him. It had been the worst feeling in the entire world: that she had brought him up from a tiny puppy, nurtured him . . . and had then, in his mind at least, abandoned him. Even Nicole could see that it was triggering all sorts of trauma in her brain. Fear was slipping and sliding through her mind, gathering pace, although their actual, physical speed was getting ever slower, until she was almost dragging Stanley for once, instead of it being the other way round.

At last Nicole reached a road where nice smart cars occasionally shot past, proving civilisation still existed, but it wasn't the lane that led her home. In fact, she still had no idea where she was, and she started to cry again. My God, what was wrong with her? Stanley was puffing now, his breathing definitely not right, and he was shivering, and Nicole knew she needed to get him home as quickly as possible. She took out her phone again and *at last* she had reception, so she didn't even think before she called him. She just prayed he would answer.

Chapter 54

Layla

Despite it still only being eight o'clock in the morning, Layla was on her fourth coffee already. She'd got up early and was meant to be doing job applications, but she found she couldn't concentrate. Instead she kept being distracted by thoughts of her new neighbour, of all people. After the less-than-ideal start, involving a lost boy and a mangled drone, cordial relations between her and Andy Meyer had finally commenced during half-term week – entirely initiated by another drone, of all things. Without even consulting Layla, Charles had bought Henry a replacement, as a reward for him surviving half a term (and yes, that had been the exact expression Charles had used), before promptly buggering off up to his office, claiming he had work to do. He'd said that Henry knew what he was doing with the drone now, and that Layla would be perfectly capable of supervising him – and although Layla had felt sad for Henry, that Charles apparently hadn't wanted to hang out with his own son, Henry had been far too excited to care. And so Layla had been left in charge of a piece of flying plastic and a small boy's somewhat kamikaze piloting techniques, which admittedly had been mildly amusing – until Henry had managed to fly the bloody thing into next door's garden again (almost certainly on purpose), just as the battery had died. Layla had been fuming, and when she'd categorically banned Henry from going to get it, he'd kicked off with a fury that was almost worse than the last time. It had made her wonder where these rages had come from, and they frightened her, made her secretly question what kind of a man her son was set to become.

Layla's predicament had only been solved when Andy Meyer had quite unexpectedly turned up on their doorstep, with the missing, fortunately fully intact, drone in his hand, rendering Henry so delighted he'd immediately stopped screaming. He'd even asked Andy in, in that weirdly overly formal manner he seemed to have adopted since he'd been away at school, and Andy had accepted, and so Layla had found herself making him a cup of peppermint tea. And that, Layla supposed, had been the start of it.

The start of what?

Layla wasn't quite sure why Henry had been so taken with Andy Meyer. Perhaps it was because he was young and trendy-looking, certainly compared to Charles, plus he had James Bond gates and a shiny blacked-out car. But whatever the reason, Henry had begged Andy to come round to visit again, and in fact Andy had obliged a couple more times over that half-term week – ostensibly to help Henry download his drone footage, but also to play PlayStation, which Charles never did, probably didn't even know how to. Layla always made sure she stayed in the room with them, just in case. She wasn't naive, and sometimes she worried about how interested Andy seemed in her son – although she hadn't dared say that to Charles, who tended to be at work when Andy visited anyway. Layla knew she needed to be careful, though, as there was definitely something odd about the situation. After all, Henry was dark, with dimples. He was uncommonly beautiful. Everyone could see that.

Layla screwed up her eyes, pressed her palms into them, forced herself to acknowledge that there was also another issue, one she'd done her very best to ignore. It wasn't only Andy's response to Henry that felt slightly off. It was how he was with her, too. Neither of them had ever discussed it, but after Henry had gone back to school Andy had carried on coming round, for no obvious reason other than to drink peppermint tea. But that wasn't a crime, and it wasn't as if she didn't have the time, especially as she did her best to steer clear of Nicole these days. So she supposed it made sense that she hadn't told Nicole about Andy's visits – but why hadn't she told Charles? She'd been perfectly open with him about Nicole coming round, and what difference did it make what gender someone was? She and Andy simply got on well. She liked the fact that he didn't drink, that therefore she didn't drink when she was around him . . .

Layla tossed her head, like a stroppy pony. Who was she kidding? The situation was infinitely more complex than that. She knew full well that Andy was dark and dangerous and utterly mystifying, quite possibly far more interested in her son than he was in her, but despite that she found that she couldn't get him out of her head, as though he were a drumbeat, an anthem, a death knell. He had got to her, although she didn't know why, what hold he had on her. And yet, despite all her doubts and confusion, Layla was pretty sure of one thing. Andy Meyer had a secret – a nasty, unpleasant one at that – and she wanted to know what it was.

Chapter 55

NICOLE

Stanley didn't make it much beyond the end of the lane these days, and even though Nicole had taken him to the vet, the vet had said that it was just old age, and that Stanley was simply slowing down at last. 'He's old,' the vet had said, in such a way that she might as well have said, 'He's going to die soon,' and Nicole couldn't stand the thought. It didn't help one bit that Stanley had never been quite the same since the day she'd lost him in the woods, and so she kept blaming herself, despite Ted repeatedly telling her not to. She still didn't know what had happened to Stanley during the half hour or so he'd been gone. The vet had said he'd probably just run around in a frenzy of panic and worn himself out, but Nicole was worried that maybe he'd been hit by a car on the road, perhaps had internal bleeding even. Ted had told her, more kindly than was his wont, that that was a crazy theory and, if that was the case, the vet would have spotted it.

Ted, to be fair, had been lovely about the whole situation. He'd left work as soon as Nicole had called him, soaking wet and distraught on the side of the road, and he'd come and rescued her and Stanley in his dirty old van which, for once, Nicole hadn't been appalled to get into. He'd taken them home and helped Nicole give

Stanley a warm bath – before telling his wife that she was shivering, too, and to go off and have a hot shower. Maybe Ted loved her after all, Nicole had thought, and it had made her feel better – or at least until he'd turned her down for sex again that night. Was it her problem or his? She didn't even know any more.

This morning, after another night of Ted-related tossing and turning, Nicole was determined to coax Stanley a little bit further afield on his walk, convinced it would do him good. And although he was so slow now, at least he still liked going for walks, and that was the main thing.

It was a glorious day. The sky was bright and hopeful, as if it had love hearts printed all over it, like in those rainbow-coloured memes that Tasha kept sending her. Nicole came out of her side door, walked round to her front garden – and there was Layla, on her own driveway, about to get into her car. They hadn't seen each other for ages. Nicole stopped still, uncertain for a second . . . and then she composed herself, smiled widely and started walking towards her neighbour, pulling Stanley along gently.

'Hi, Layla,' she called.

'Hi,' Layla called back.

'Long time no see. How are you?'

Layla looked definitely, definitely awkward. 'I'm fine,' she said. 'How are you?'

'OK,' said Nicole. She paused, debated whether to say it. 'Been better.'

'Oh, I'm sorry to hear that . . . but, er, I must dash now, I'm late for an appointment. Look . . . I'll see you soon.' And with that, Layla climbed into her Range Rover and drove off, giving Nicole a quick, faux-friendly wave as she went.

Nicole didn't know what to think. It had seemed so rude – yet perhaps Layla genuinely had been in a hurry. But even if that were the case, Layla had seen Stanley, surely would have clocked how he'd been walking, and yet she hadn't even asked how he was. It seemed Nicole had officially been dumped, although she still wasn't quite sure why, and it almost felt as if she were at school still, and her best friend had gone off with someone else . . . and Nicole wasn't as stupid as Layla seemed to think she was. She could still picture Andy's gates starting to open, and then Layla popping out from the bushes, scooting through the still-tiny gap and disappearing from view. The gates had proceeded to slide shut so fast and smoothly it was almost as if Layla hadn't been there, that Nicole must have imagined it. Layla's dark hair had been piled on top of her head, and she'd been wearing a black puffa jacket and dark jeans, and she'd blended in with the gates, perhaps deliberately. But maybe *that* was why Layla had no time for her any more. Nicole wondered whether Charles knew, had half a mind to tell him, and then decided against it. It was none of her business.

Nicole sighed, started walking Stanley along the lane, but he was definitely reluctant now, and he was panting more than he should be. Eventually she gave up, took him home, settled him into his dog basket, still worried that his breathing didn't seem right. She decided to give her spin class a miss, which was something she would never have dreamt of doing in the past. She didn't want to leave Stanley, of course, not if he was unwell, but it wasn't just that. She simply couldn't be bothered. She went upstairs, half-heartedly sorted out some washing; came down, tidied up the lounge, plumped some cushions; returned to the kitchen, went over to Stanley's favourite cupboard, got out a Schmacko . . . and although Stanley wagged his tail limply, he didn't get up out of his basket, as he once would have done. And even when she gave him the treat, he took it reluctantly – before spitting it out, intact.

That was it, Nicole thought. She was calling the vet again. She bent down and patted Stanley's head gently, stared into his soft dirt eyes, and as she wondered what was wrong with him it made her feel helpless, that he couldn't tell her . . . and he was her Stan, her dear, precious Stan . . . and he wouldn't be here forever, and she couldn't stand it, because she loved him so much . . . and, in this moment at least, it felt like he was all she had left.

PART FOUR

DECEMBER/JANUARY

Chapter 56

Life is a knife-edge. A ridge across two mountain ranges, with deadly ravines to either side. I know that now. But when you're eighteen years old and king of the world, you believe you're invincible. I was sucked into a vortex where I was told I was so fucking great that for a while I truly believed it. All the pain I'd ever felt was gone. It meant nothing. I had it all. And then I had nothing.

I still find it hard to think back to those days, but it seems that I have to now. It's strange how I've been able to reinvent myself on the outside – my name, my appearance, my entire backstory – and yet no matter how often I tell myself I'm Andy Meyer now, my mind won't let me escape the past, forget what I've done. I've tried all sorts of approaches in the years since my old life ended and this new one began, but the more I determine not to think about what has gone before, the more alive and awake the memories become. It encases me in a metaphorical block of ice that no one can melt, in case they see the dark heart of me. Jesus. Prison had been lonely, for sure, but this is something else. In prison, even alone in my cell, I'd still been able to hear the visceral roar and pulse of life lived through my fellow inmates, vibrating through the bars, pounding down the corridors, the abject pain and regret and despair dressed up as macho wiliness. Survival. That was the mantra in prison. And even in rehab, it was shared hurt, plundered pain. We might have been suffering, but hey, at least we were all suffering together. The reasons didn't actually matter. My time in Spain was part therapy, part practice, for freedom.

But now, here in my house, perched on my sofa, I'm completely alone. I only have the TV for company, and it doesn't fill in those silences, replace that beating heart of real, human contact. It seems all the money in the world can't heal loneliness. How to thwart it. How to manufacture emotional ties. Is it even possible? I have to pay my solicitor to be loyal to me. Tinder might have mirrored the mindless fucks of my past, but it delivered nothing more than that. It wasn't enough. And as for the neighbours, it's clear I can't trust them. I can't trust myself. *What if they know?*

No. I need to hold it together. People *don't* know. They *can't* know. I have to tell myself that. I need to be brave, confront the facts, run them through my mind like sifting sand, look for the grains of truth that will make sense of this cesspit of memories. I try to tell myself to look on the bright side, and the phrase reminds me of my mother. She always used to say that, even when we were homeless. I admire how strong she always was. I miss her so much.

And so. One thing I feel certain of now is that I won't be able to keep my counsel forever. I will need to tell someone, one day. Someone other than a Spanish horse, of course – and I only told him because maybe, just maybe, he might have been able to understand, but he could never in a million years have told on me. He couldn't have blackmailed me, like Sian did . . .

And there is that flash once more, that white-hot heat of undiluted rage and regret, that maybe it could all have been different, if it hadn't been for *her* . . . and I don't know what I feel about Sian now, or her role in all this, but what I do know is that hate is too definite a word, too prescriptive, and I am confused and perturbed and sending myself crazy all over again, and I am tearing at my hair and screwing up my eyes and lamenting absolutely everything . . . and so when the relentless buzzing on my door starts, it is unwelcome and infuriating, and I need it to stop.

Chapter 57

NICOLE

Sod it, Nicole had thought, as she'd jumped out of her car, marched purposefully up to Andy's gates and pressed his buzzer. She needed to breathe some life into this place if no one else was going to bother. Her idea, when she'd had it (about five minutes earlier, as she'd driven into the deserted-looking close), had been so simple. She would organise some Christmas drinks with the neighbours. Just early evening. Nothing that would get out of hand. After all, she'd reasoned, she still got on well enough with Andy, and it was time that she and Layla made peace with each other too – although Nicole still didn't know what, if anything, she'd done wrong. She'd even half-wished she could invite the Taylors, seeing as Christmas was meant to be the season of goodwill, but they had an imminent court case to fight. She resolved now to ask Ted to drop it. It didn't feel right, and, anyway, what was the point? What would anyone win or lose, except pride and money? Perhaps it was time to let bygones be bygones. After all, life was too short – and so it had proved.

Nicole's eyes pricked, again, and she couldn't stand it. She had to get herself out of this fug somehow. She pushed Andy's buzzer again. A drinks party was a good idea, she was sure of it, and she knew that Ted wouldn't mind. He was easy-going like that – as long as he didn't have to do any of the work – plus he knew how low she was at the moment. But now Andy wasn't answering, although she knew his car was there. She couldn't just give up at the first hurdle. She pushed the buzzer one more time.

'Hello.' The voice was disembodied, vaguely gravelly, but definitely hostile.

'Oh, er, hi, it's Nicole . . . from next door.'

'Oh.' Andy didn't open the gates, like she'd seen him do several times now for Layla. Nicole clenched her jaw, steeled herself to ask him anyway.

'I was wondering if you wanted to come for drinks . . .' Nicole trailed off. It wasn't easy inviting a blinking light to a party.

'Hang on.' There was a click, and then the gates started to swing apart. Nicole's initial relief that he did still like her, after all, soon gave way to feelings of intense ambivalence. Did his opening of the gates mean he meant her to enter his driveway? Or was he coming out on to the close to talk to her? She'd never actually been inside his property, and she'd not spoken to him for ages. She was grieving, clearly deranged, hadn't thought this through. She hopped from designer trainer to designer trainer, wondering if it was too late to make a run for it. Why did she have to be so bloody impulsive?

After a minute or two Andy appeared at his front door. He had on deepest indigo jeans, those selvedge ones, and he'd shaved off his beard, leaving his facial hair somewhere between a five o'clock shadow and midnight. Nicole felt herself blushing, despite herself.

'Hi,' she said, stepping across the gates' threshold, starting to walk towards him. And then she sensed his mood, which was dark, and stopped tentatively on the driveway.

'Hello.' His lip had a curl to it that Nicole wasn't sure was mocking or not, and his eyes were hard to fathom. It was like the lights in them were dimmed somehow, as if only the pilot light was on, ready to fire up at some unscheduled time, with unknown consequences.

'Yes?' he said, when Nicole didn't speak.

'Er, I'm having some Christmas drinks, for the neighbours,' she said. 'Would you like to come?'

Andy scowled at her. 'What, now?'

Nicole laughed nervously. 'No, on Christmas Eve. Six o'clock?'

Andy said nothing. What was wrong with him? He used to walk her dog. They'd had coffee together. Why was he being like this?

'Oh, well, don't worry then,' she said. She started backing away. This was pointless.

'OK, thanks,' Andy said. He seemed slightly less unfriendly now. 'I'll see. Who's coming?'

'Oh, Layla and Charles . . .' She trailed off. Who else was there?

'What about them?' Andy said, gesturing towards Joan's house.

'Er, no,' Nicole said. Surely Andy must know about Ted and Joan's fight? Who did he think he was all of a sudden? Kofi Annan?

'OK, well, I'll let you know,' he said. She heard the whirr of the gates' mechanism, and it seemed he'd pressed the remote control in his hand, and that it was her cue to leave.

What a prick, Nicole thought. She nearly said, 'Don't bother,' but instead she merely turned and started walking away, making it through the gates in enough, but not plenty, of time.

'Nicole,' Andy called.

She looked over her shoulder at him through the ever-diminishing gap in the gates. 'Yes?'

'I'm so sorry about Stanley,' he said, and then the scene went black, and he was gone.

Chapter 58

Joan

Even though it was a while since she'd called at her neighbour's gates on the pretext of giving him some plants, Joan still hadn't made up her mind whether her hunch about Andy Meyer was correct or not. She'd studied footage and stills of Jono Grey for hours on end. The hair was the wrong colour, but there again it could easily be dyed – or maybe he'd just gone darker as he'd got older, which was normal. He was the right kind of age. And yet the nose was wrong. Definitely. She'd checked. But that meant nothing these days.

Joan was back on her metaphorical horse, her natural curiosity – albeit briefly diminished after her run-in with Ted – returned to full strength. She became obsessed with finding out the truth. She even wondered if she should warn Layla about this so-called Andy Meyer, but there again, what if she was wrong? And seeing as she was already embroiled in one unpleasant situation in Hope Close, it was probably best not to go around stirring up any more trouble, especially as Joan was frightened of her new neighbour, whoever he might be. Their exchange when she'd called at his gates with the plants had been more than merely awkward. It was as if he'd instantly rumbled that she'd rumbled him. A double-rumble, if you like. He'd been offhand at best, full-on aggressive at worst – but more than that, he'd seemed horrified, and that was probably the thing that had sealed it in Joan's opinion, even if she still had no evidence. *It was him.* She'd seen the fear in his eyes. The threat of exposure. And he hadn't wanted her prize cyclamens, either.

Joan went over to the sink, started peeling the potatoes in time for tea. She still didn't know what to do about the situation. She accepted that most people were allowed out of prison at some point, but why did they have to flaming well move in opposite her? Nimbyism, they called it at the council, but surely it was fair enough not to want a potentially dangerous convicted criminal living across the road from you? Perhaps she should go to see her MP – whom she hadn't managed to catch up with for ages, now she came to think about it – and try to get some advice. She would need to tread cautiously, in case she was wrong, but it was worth a try. Knowledge was power, after all.

Joan put the potatoes on to boil and turned her steely focus to the carrots, enjoyed the neat methodical process of stripping them of their outer flesh. Just as she was finishing, her knee started throbbing, less badly than before, but enough to remind her that her and Ted's court case had been scheduled for early January. The stress was set to ruin Christmas – but there again, she'd be spending it with only Lionel this year, so it was as good as ruined already.

Joan sighed, thought back to how different things might have been if she'd taken her doctor's advice to secretly 'be intimate', as he'd put it, with someone other than her husband. It was what lots of women did in her situation, the doctor had said, but it had seemed so wrong, wicked even. And so instead, Joan had carried on as she was, had distracted herself from her childlessness by pouring her love into her garden and into Anne's son Peter – or at least until he'd ended up breaking her heart as well. She still felt so ashamed of him, and it was hard to not feel self-pitying sometimes, when she looked at it like that, but it was what it was.

Joan was a stoical type, and a tenacious one, too. As she put some flaccid-looking lamb steaks under the grill, she decided that if it truly was the case that Hope Close was full of criminals of one kind or another, she wasn't going to take it lying down. Oh no. She would hold her head high and fight Ted in court, even if he did try to use all his money and power to quash her. And she would find out the truth about the new neighbour too, even if it killed her – for the sake of Henry and Layla, if nothing else.

Chapter 59

NICOLE

What the hell just happened? Nicole thought, as she stalked away from Andy's house and up the driveway towards Layla's. She'd liked him once, but not any more. He was a rude, ignorant pig. She prayed that Layla and Charles would agree to come for Christmas drinks, if only to be a foil in the unlikely event that Andy turned up. Henry would be home from school by then, of course, but the drinks would be early evening, so he could always come, too. Nicole would be sure to get some colouring pens, and juice boxes and Twiglets, and hopefully Henry would enjoy himself, despite Stanley not being there for him to play with. But even that thought was enough to set Nicole off again – and it seemed that everything felt raw at the moment, and her actions were becoming increasingly erratic, to the extent that she was never quite sure how she might respond to daily life events, what she would do next.

Despite Layla's car being outside on the driveway, there was no answer at her house, and no response from her mobile either. Nicole even wondered with a lurch whether Layla was at Andy's again. Perhaps that was why Andy had acted so strangely, hadn't invited her in. Maybe he and Layla were having an affair. That would explain everything.

Eventually Nicole gave up on Layla, her enthusiasm for her whole Christmas drink project having waned to such an extent that she was tempted to cancel it. The only person she'd invited so far was Andy, and he was a tosser who wouldn't come anyway, and Layla didn't like her either, so why was she even bothering? As Nicole turned on her heel and skulked away down Layla's drive, she wished she could be done with Hope Close. This was no way to live. Now the kids were gone, and poor Stanley too, perhaps it was time for a change at last. Maybe she and Ted should downsize, try to get their marriage back on track that way. After all, the sexy underwear and toys route hadn't worked (had just led to more humiliation, in fact), and since Stanley's death she'd pretty much lost all interest anyway. So for all sorts of reasons it seemed that now might be the time for her and Ted to move on, one way or the other, physically and metaphorically. They certainly couldn't carry on like this.

Chapter 60

LAYLA

Charles had accepted an invitation to Christmas drinks at Ted and Nicole's, and Layla wasn't happy about it. She deliberately hadn't opened the door to Nicole earlier, or answered her mobile, but clearly Nicole was not to be deterred. When Charles had answered the home phone later that evening, Layla had been able to hear the conversation from the kitchen, Charles's clipped tones responding to Nicole's overly loud Scouse ones – his saying what a lovely idea that was, and how it would be good to see everyone, even hopefully get to know the new neighbour at last. Layla wondered how her husband would have responded if he'd been aware that she already knew Andy Meyer really quite well. She still didn't know why she hadn't told Charles about it. After all, surely it wasn't a crime for her to have friends? And yet it seemed that in these sorts of circles mysterious, abrasive, handsome companions of the opposite sex were strictly off limits. Charles might have been ignorant of her relationship with Andy, but it seemed Nicole wasn't, in fact was almost certainly annoyed about it – although Layla didn't really know why. Surely Nicole didn't fancy Andy Meyer too. She was old enough to be his mother.

Layla pulled herself up. What did she mean: *too*? It was a word that had slipped out so innocently, so unashamedly, that Layla felt forced to acknowledge that it might be true. *Perhaps she fancied Andy Meyer.*

Oh God, no – she sounded like a hormonal teenager. But surely that would explain why her heart leapt every time her phone buzzed these days, in case it was him, and how peppermint tea was suddenly her favourite drink ever. What on earth was she doing, getting herself into this situation? How had she allowed herself to end up here, the bored, neglected, much younger wife – *third* wife, no less – of a man she barely knew any more, with no job (her attempts to kick-start her career having been over almost as soon as they began), her child sent away . . . and now possibly about to embark on an affair with one of the neighbours? *No.* She was worth more than that. She'd taken her vows. She was a mother to Henry. She couldn't allow herself to split the family apart, like her own father had done. She would need to sort out her marriage, her child's schooling, her career, one way or the other, before she even thought about doing anything else, illicit or otherwise. She needed to act like an adult.

'Well?' said Charles now.

'Well, what?'

'Are you happy to go?'

'Go where?'

Charles sighed. 'To Nicole's drinks party.'

'Yes, of course I am. Why?'

Charles stared at Layla then, and his gaze was full-beam, searching her face for clues. She felt uncomfortable, as if she were about to be sent out into the world completely naked, and sometimes that's how he made her feel. Unsure of herself. Frightened, even.

'It's just you don't seem too keen on Nicole these days.'

Wow. Charles had noticed. It was another of those moments, where she assumed her husband was oblivious to the ins and outs of what went on in Hope Close, and yet clearly he wasn't. For not the first time, it occurred to Layla that Charles had hidden depths. But of course he did. He'd had a whole life before he met her. There was no way she could possibly be aware of all there was to know about him. In fact, he was positively, actively surprising her lately, and perhaps it was because Henry was no longer around to provide a foil to their relationship, and now she was noticing. Noticing the things she didn't know. But whatever the reason, when she looked into Charles's face these days she didn't just see a husband who had a passing resemblance to George Clooney. She also saw a man who had once been a boy, who'd been married far too young to a woman she'd never even seen a picture of. She thought again how sad it was that Charles was virtually estranged from his older children, and it made her worry that one day he might become estranged from Henry, too.

'So, what is it with Nicole?' Charles pressed.

'Oh, I don't know.' Layla hesitated. 'I was drinking too much with her, and she started being a bit needy, and telling me personal stuff I really didn't want to know . . .' Layla stopped, chose not to tell Charles any of the secrets Nicole had divulged. It wasn't fair. She'd promised.

Charles was staring at her, waiting for her to continue.

'She's nice,' Layla said lamely, 'but . . . but I just don't think we're that compatible.'

Charles continued his study of Layla, as if she were an exhibit in a museum. He touched her face lightly, and then he squeezed it, and she could feel that her jaw bones were solid, unyielding under her flesh, pressing against the bones of his fingers.

'Well, as long as you're sure, Layla,' Charles said, holding her gaze. 'I'd hate for you to be lonely.' And then he let go of her face, and left the room.

Chapter 61

Joan

An obsessive quest for truth was a strange and strangely fulfilling pastime, Joan thought, as she pored over her computer printouts. A time-filler. Perhaps she'd always been the same. As a little girl she'd been consumed by books, the act of reading her escape route into another world, where no one else mattered apart from the characters in her story, numbing the fact that she loathed the atmosphere at home, fully aware that her mother hated her. It had shaped her, moulded her into the person she was destined to become.

Joan didn't know why, had no idea where she went wrong, but the fact was she'd always found it hard to make and keep friends. She knew that her neighbours called her an ugly old witch, and that they laughed at her shock of Brillo pad hair and the silly red ankle boots she often wore when she went into the village. And yet the one thing Joan had, that no one else seemed to bother with these days, was morals. Good heavens, this place was a veritable breeding ground of iniquity. Nicole was a liar, and the Warners had been perverts, and her new neighbour was almost certainly a criminal who'd changed his identity, and Ted was a vicious thug, and Charles was probably a philanderer . . . and as for that Layla! She was clueless, had everything wrong about everything.

Joan still held a grudge against Layla. She was too beautiful, for one, and then there had been all that trouble with Layla's ridiculously named cat. Joan knew that Layla thought she'd killed the cat somehow, but despite how much she might have despised the creature, there was no way she would have done something like that. If anyone had murdered it, it was probably that Andy Meyer, or whatever his name was.

Joan stared at the article for the umpteenth time – at the pictures of the dead boy, the slaughtered mother – still hardly able to believe it. It seemed almost inconceivable all over again. What Jono Grey had done was wicked, unforgivable. He had deserved every last bit of his comeuppance. Could it really be true that now he was here, masquerading as somebody else?

Joan found her eyes smarting at the image of the little boy with sunshine in his eyes, the dark features, the dimples, caught in a frozen moment of eternal beauty, never to grow old, never to enjoy and endure all that life was to throw at him. He'd looked so like Henry, Joan realised now, and surely that was why 'Andy Meyer' had such a soft spot for the boy.

Joan sighed. Life was tough, and then you died, which was probably just as well. She'd tried so hard to believe in God her entire life, but it seemed now that there was no salvation for anyone. According to Anne there was only forgiveness, but Joan thought that some deeds were too wicked to ever absolve. She wondered if she should have forgiven Peter, like Anne had, but it was too late now. He'd died, and that was the end of it. And anyway, even if there had still been time, it seemed that whatever she did, no matter how hard she tried, Joan simply didn't have forgiveness in her.

Chapter 62

NICOLE

As predicted, Ted had been perfectly affable when Nicole had told him about the drinks party, although he had made a point of double-checking that she wasn't planning on inviting the Taylors. But, Nicole conceded, seeing as he seemed determined to take his vendetta against Joan Taylor to its full and direst conclusion, it would hardly make for polite chit-chat over drinks anyway.

'Well, who's coming then?' Ted had said.

'Charles and Layla,' Nicole had replied, ' . . . and maybe Andy.'

'Who? The freak?'

'He's not a freak. He's quite nice.'

'Hmm,' Ted had said. 'Anyone else?'

'No.'

'Well, it's hardly a party in that case,' he'd said, and he was right. Nicole wished she'd never even instigated it. She felt so uncomfortable with all the neighbours these days, and she wished as fervently as she ever had that the Taylors would just move or die or something. Living next door to someone in an atmosphere of mutual warfare was depressing, debilitating, never-ending. Horrendous, in fact. But the Taylors would never move, more was the pity. They'd surely die in that house, be buried in the back garden. And living opposite people you used to be friends with but who now seemed to do their best to avoid you was almost as dispiriting. Downsizing was becoming an increasingly tempting option, and at least Ted hadn't rejected the suggestion out of hand. She didn't really care where they went, if it meant she'd never have to see this place or these people again.

Nicole's line of thinking wasn't the most apt or constructive, given it was fifteen minutes before people were due to arrive. But at least she was ready on time for once. Tasha, who thankfully was already home for Christmas, had said her mother looked a million dollars, but Nicole certainly didn't feel like it. She was in her tallest heels, her tightest leather trousers, her longest eyelashes. She had downed a restoratively strong gin and tonic. She was feeling ludicrously nervous, as though something very, very bad might be about to happen. She almost imagined Joan turning up with a shotgun – and perhaps Tasha was right to have told her mother to take a chill pill.

Andy was the first to arrive, at six on the dot, ruthlessly punctual, wholly unexpected. The last time Nicole had seen him in here, Stanley had been sitting at his feet, and it was a gut-wrenching memory. There was something so unnerving about Andy. He was good-looking, of course, but it was more than that. He had a way of being that commanded attention, which was ironic as he was hardly ever seen out, lived like a veritable hermit.

'How would you know how he lives?' Tasha had said earlier. She'd been helping her mother prepare the buffet, which involved opening over-promising boxes and packages from Waitrose and putting shrunken sad-looking individual tartlets and mini-sausages out on to plates, plonking great hunks of fancy cheese on a wooden platter with a big bunch of grapes, ripping up French bread. Nicole wasn't one of those hostesses who would spend hours in the kitchen.

She usually preferred to rely on her conviviality – plus plenty of booze, of course.

'Andy might be an Internet billionaire in real life,' Tasha had continued. 'Or perhaps a porn star! You don't know what he gets up to in private.'

'Oh, shush, Tasha,' Nicole had said. 'He's already said he's in tech development.'

And yet, still, an image had flashed into Nicole's head of Andy naked, with a hairy chest and a handlebar moustache, sprawled aggressively open-legged on a sheepskin rug. It had made her giggle at exactly the moment the doorbell rang, and she was unable to look Andy in the eye when she went to let him in. She blushed even further when she ushered him through to the kitchen and Tasha winked at her, openly and shamelessly – but fortunately Andy ignored it, and Ted was upstairs still, and so didn't witness it.

Chapter 63

JOAN

Joan was back in full-scale spying mode, peering out of the living room window with the vim and alertness of an overexcited toddler. She seemed to have developed a sniper-like sixth sense for movement, and seeing as quite unbelievably she'd just seen the Criminal (as she now thought of him) go in to Nicole's already, bottle in hand, she'd been expecting the Dolphins any time soon. And yet it was still a jab in the heart to actually see Layla, in a cinched-in black dress and killer heels, tottering across the close, flanked on either side by two of the men in her life – Charles, on her left, in chinos and a smart blue blazer, and on her right little Henry, who wore defeat in his very bones, and moved with the infinite weariness of an old person. It was painful to see, and Joan wondered what Henry had witnessed these past months at boarding school. It still happened, she told herself, and there was no one there to defend him, and she pursed her mouth with the bitter taste of disapproval. Layla was clearly a fool, and a weak one at that.

Joan rarely missed a trick, and although she knew there was no way that she and Lionel would have been invited, it still vexed her that the neighbours were having a party and that they'd been left out, as usual. It was so rude – bullying by omission, in effect.

Joan almost wished they could call a truce, like those German and British soldiers who'd played football on Christmas Day across the trenches, seeing as it was meant to be the season of goodwill. But, she supposed wryly, that was only a world war. This was a court case about a pair of secateurs. It was ridiculous.

'Are you still spying, Joan?' Lionel said, as he came into the room. He had on his jumbo cords, as ever, and his brown lace-up brogues that he still polished every morning, even though he rarely went out any more.

'I'm not *spying*, Lionel,' she said. She let go of the cream velvet curtain beneath its dated pelmet, and it swung silently back into place. Lionel switched on the light. The room was a veritable study in neutrals, and although such a combination could often look gorgeous, set off by texture and contrast and homely finishing touches, Joan's take on it exuded that cold empty chill of a house that was unloved, of a heart that was unswayed by the lure of the aesthetic. Joan kept the house as spotless and anaesthetised as a hospital.

'Well, come away from the window, dear,' Lionel said. 'Come and watch the news – that'll cheer you up.'

Joan ignored her husband. She retreated into the kitchen, heated up the soup (parsnip, home-made, underseasoned) that she'd made earlier, tutted as she buttered the rolls, which were on the cusp of being stale even though she'd bought them today. She placed the meals on trays and took them into the snug, where she and her husband sat and stared at the TV with that grim acceptance that this was their life now, and sod that the Dolphins had tasteful white fairy lights around the windows, and that Nicole had reindeer on the roof, and Joan didn't care how ironic the latter were meant to be – in her opinion they were the height of vulgarity. And then she remembered that everyone else was at a party that she wasn't invited to.

Joan felt something give in her then. It was all just too much. Grief and rage and long-pent-up disappointment threatened to overwhelm her. She couldn't bear how she felt, really she couldn't. The whole situation was a complete and utter travesty.

Joan stood up, plonked her tray on the table, went to the hall cupboard and pulled out her anorak, found her trusty red ankle boots. She was certain now that Andy Meyer was in fact the infamous Jono Grey. She couldn't let him get away with it. It was time the neighbours knew the truth, too.

Chapter 64

Layla

Poor Nicole looked undernourished in that outfit, Layla thought. Black was too harsh on her, and the leather trousers rendered her body virtually prepubescent-looking, which didn't match her face, of course, no matter how many fillers she'd had. Layla found it alarming how much weight Nicole had lost since her dog had died – in fact, she looked almost ill now. It made Layla feel bad for Nicole, particularly as she knew how distressed she herself had been when Ari had died. But, she thought, at least Stanley had had a peaceful death, of old age. At least he hadn't been poisoned . . .

A shiver of suspicion struck Layla all over again. Charles had said that Aristotle had probably eaten rat poison over at the nearby farm, but Layla still couldn't help wondering whether someone in the close had done it. There was no point surmising, though. It was done. There was nothing she could do to bring Aristotle back.

Layla took a slug of her drink and wished she could go home. There were too many undercurrents, and she felt uncomfortable that she knew such personal things about Nicole, things that Ted had no idea of, especially when she was chatting to him. It didn't feel right to her. And then there was her unease about the upcoming court case, too. Lying on the stand was *illegal*. Did Nicole not realise? Layla knew that everyone was different, that everyone had their own way of justifying their actions – but what if something really bad happened to Joan as a consequence? Layla hadn't wanted to compromise Charles by telling him, and so the secret was sitting there, like a little hand grenade, and she was never quite sure when the pin would get pulled out.

Ugh, Layla thought, this whole situation was too stressful. She'd hated teetering across the close in her heels, knowing that Joan would probably be watching, in the full knowledge that she hadn't been invited. And, on top of all that, Henry was sitting obediently at the end of the dining table with the colouring book Nicole had bought for him, and although Layla would once have been grateful for such good behaviour, tonight it felt wrong. In the past Henry would have kicked off, insisted he'd rather be playing outside with his drone, or on his iPad – but these days he seemed overly compliant. Broken, even.

Layla glanced at the kitchen clock. How much longer did she have to give it before they could politely take their leave? The atmosphere was curling up, expiring slowly, and Nicole seemed to know it. Perhaps in desperation, she appeared to have sought refuge in champagne, and she'd just put on some cheesy Christmas music to boot, giving rise to a distinct danger of her starting to sing along – which, in Layla's opinion, would just about finish everyone off. Even Tasha, Nicole's rather charming daughter, had disappeared off upstairs, and who could blame her.

Just as Layla felt that things couldn't get any worse, she felt herself grow even tenser as she watched Andy wander over to Henry, put an arm on his shoulder.

'How's the drone going, little fella?' he said.

'Yes, rather well, thank you,' Henry said, in his super-polite new manner. 'Would you help me upload the footage on to Daddy's computer again soon?'

'What was that?' Charles said now, turning his head over his shoulder. He'd been having an awkward chat with Ted about football, and his expression was hard to decipher. 'What did you say about my computer?'

'Nothing,' Henry said.

'Have you been on my computer, Henry?' Charles asked, and his voice was preternaturally steady.

Henry shook his head in denial, in that way kids do when they know it will make no difference – when they realise they have been well and truly rumbled, but they don't know what to about it and so continue to deny it anyway.

'Andy's come over once or twice to bring Henry's drone back,' Layla said. She tried to keep the whine of apology out of her tone. 'Henry crash-landed it in his garden again.'

'Oh. I see,' said Charles, clearly not seeing. *Oh fuck*, Layla thought. She needed to get home, sort this out in private.

'How did you even get on my computer, Henry?' The low note of threat was unmistakeable in Charles's tone now, and Layla was astonished. She'd never known him to show any kind of emotion in public. He was usually one of those guarded types, who barely gave anything away at all. Showing any sign of displeasure in polite company was unseemly in Charles's eyes.

'I *said*, how did you get on my computer, Henry?' Charles was not letting this go.

'I found your password,' Henry snivelled, performing an entirely understandable volte-face.

Layla had had enough. There was something that didn't feel right about anything any more. She glanced over at Nicole, who was pissed, and was hanging on to Ted as though he were a piece of furniture. If there really was some kind of secret on Charles's computer, which was the only reason Layla could imagine he would be looking so ashen, she wanted to interrogate him at home, not here. Did Andy know what it was? Maybe that was why she got the sense that he pitied her. Had been pitying her, now she came to think of it, for quite a while.

'I think we need to get Henry home, Charles,' Layla said, at which point Nicole burst into tears and begged them not to go.

'Jesus, love,' Ted said, as his wife lolled all over him, but to give him his due, he stroked her hair gently.

'It's just I miss Stanley so much,' Nicole slurred. 'Everyone's always leaving me these days.'

'It's not that, Nicole,' Layla said, as evenly as she could manage. 'We just need to get Henry to bed.'

'But I miss you, Layla. Why don't you ever come over any more?'

Oh, God, Layla thought. Now really wasn't the time.

But unfortunately, Nicole was not to be deterred. 'I miss Stanley, and my kids,' she droned on, 'and how Hope Close used to be . . .' She stopped then, delivered, considering how drunk she was, a perfect dramatic pause. 'And I miss someone else, too.'

Layla started shooting furious 'don't say it' glances at Nicole, unsure quite what she was about to come out with, praying it wasn't what she thought it might be.

'Teddy,' Nicole carried on, oblivious to Layla's warnings. 'There's something you need to know, and I feel so bad because I've already told Layla, and so anyway—'

'Just *stop it*, Nicole,' said Layla, sharply, as if she were talking to a child who was about to do something extremely naughty. She smiled sweetly at Ted and said, 'Sorry, Ted. Girl talk. Not for little ears,' and she nodded in Henry's direction.

Ted grunted and his cheeks flushed, and Layla knew she'd annoyed him, but surely that was better than letting his wife carry on talking. Nicole needed to tell him whatever she had to say when they were alone, and preferably when she wasn't drunk.

Just as everyone was looking unsure what to say or do next, there was a loud, continuous knocking on the front door, as insistent as if it were a police bust.

'I'll go,' said Layla, rushing to answer it, relieved to get out of the kitchen. When she got to the door, though, she was mortified to see it was Joan. The old woman's hair was wilder than ever, and she had spittle at the corners of her lips, as though she were so enraged she couldn't even contain the words that were about to come out of her mouth. Had Nicole *invited* her? If so, Joan hadn't made much of an effort, wearing as she was an anorak over a pinny, those hideous ankle boots. Seriously, Layla thought, how much more excruciating could this party get? She *knew* she and Charles shouldn't have come. Hope Close was chock-full of basket cases.

'Oh,' Layla said. 'Hello, Joan.'

Joan ignored Layla. Instead she barged straight past her and stormed into the kitchen, as if she'd been ordered to evacuate the place, as if the house might actually be on fire. She marched straight up to Andy, who looked horror-struck at her very approach, and that was before she'd even said anything.

'*You*,' Joan screeched, pointing at Andy, admirably theatrical in her delivery, 'are not called Andy Meyer at all. You are a liar. I know exactly who you are! You are Jono Grey, from Easy Come.'

Chapter 65

Please God, someone help me. That witch has come storming in and she's ranting and raving, spouting all kinds of unbelievable rubbish . . . but why the hell would she think that? What else does she know? How *could* she know?

Jesus Christ. How on earth am I going to explain this? What do I do now? I want to run, but Joan is blocking the door, her ghastly hair like a cobweb lollipop, and I can hardly push an old woman out of the way. I'm not as bad as Ted. And then I remember I'm far, far worse.

They're all glowering at me, their tongues hanging out, either literally or metaphorically, I'm not even sure. Even the daughter has reappeared, presumably to see what the fuss is about. The sear of the spotlight is on me again, and it feels as bright as it ever has. How did I hope to get away with it? Did I really think I would never be found out? (Well, *yes*, in fact, I did. I thought any exposure in Hope Close would have been of my own doing. I'd honestly had no idea that people round here were so fucking nosy.)

But anyway, regardless of how or why, it seems that right now I am standing in Nicole's sickly brown kitchen, in a remote cul-de-sac in Surrey, and my life is reeling madly backwards, like an out-of-control car rolling down a hill to the inevitable collision, and I swear I can't stand it. I don't know how long it takes me to have so many memories. Half a second perhaps? Two minutes? I can see it all, every last moment that got me to that point of devastation, flashing across my mind's eye like the brightest comet in the entire universe . . . and now the images are coming together, transforming into Bobby's face, and his eyes are shining with love, for life, for me, for everything that matters to an excited little kid . . . just before his expression turns to sheer, abject terror. *How could I have done it to him?*

And then the picture fades, and I'm back in Nicole's kitchen, exposed and helpless, unsure what is going to happen next, knowing it won't be good . . . But now it seems my subconscious is taking over again, and the memories start slipping and sliding once more, as if over wet rocks, all the way back to the very beginning. All the way back to Sian.

Chapter 66

LAYLA

Exactly what was on Charles's computer was still an unknown, although Layla was one hundred per cent certain it wasn't good. Perhaps she should ask Andy Meyer if he knew. Or, as Layla reminded herself, Jono Grey, lead singer of manufactured pop band Easy Come, if what Joan Taylor had said was to be believed. The old woman was clearly insane, as well as universally disliked, and it made Layla feel sorry for her.

Layla still didn't know how one innocent little drinks party had descended into such incredible chaos. It was as if Joan's unwelcome arrival had momentarily shocked everyone into stunned inertia – before all sorts of hell had broken loose. After the initial breathless silence, Ted had gone mad and threatened to physically throw Joan out, and then *Charles* of all people had seemed as if he might square up to Ted to stop him attacking Joan. Joan herself had looked terrified at the mayhem she'd caused, and had proceeded to leave as quickly as she'd come.

'Who are Easy Come?' Henry had asked at that point, clearly relieved to have had the focus of suspicion taken away from what he might or might not have seen on his father's computer, which everyone seemed to have forgotten about. And after that unanswered question, Andy Meyer had sworn softly and buggered off too, which almost made Layla think that maybe what Joan had said was actually true, absurd as it sounded.

The quite staggering finale of the drinks party was a paralytic Nicole delivering her drunken revelation about her erstwhile secret son after all – apparently having decided that she wasn't going to be upstaged, by Joan Taylor of all people. She'd announced that she couldn't keep it in a moment longer, especially as Layla already knew and might therefore tell Ted. And at that point Tasha had become as hysterical as her mother, and Ted had gone even more bananas and got Sean and Jason on speakerphone, saying that they might as well hear the whole fucking story while Nicole was at it.

Layla felt exhausted just thinking about the events of earlier this evening – not least because she was still trying to deal with the fact that there was clearly something very damaging on Charles's computer. But there was no way on earth she would turn a blind eye to it, or be palmed off with excuses. She'd told Charles that he could show her every last file on it, even if it took them all night. She'd insisted he give her his phone, too – just in case he could get rid of files that way – and then she'd come up and parked herself in his study, so he wouldn't have a chance to delete anything. She'd ordered him to put their son to bed and said that if he didn't come in to see her by nine o'clock, then that would be it, and she didn't care if it was Christmas Day tomorrow. Layla didn't know where she'd got the strength from. She looked at the clock. Ten to nine. Charles had better get a move on.

About two minutes before his deadline, Charles came into the study, looking shame-faced and exposed, and he reminded Layla of Henry, as if he were a little boy who'd been caught with his hand in the cookie jar. Her resolve instantly tightened again. She wasn't letting him get away with this, whatever 'this' was.

'OK, show me,' she said.

'Show you what?'

'What you have on your computer that is apparently so compromising.'

'And what's that supposed to imply?' Charles said.

'I have no idea.' Layla's face was set, and woe betide him if he tried to fuck with her. 'You tell me.'

Chapter 67

One word. Four letters. *Sian.* My best friend. My nemesis. She was a little firecracker bundle of vitriol that I wish with all my heart and every single other organ in my body that I had never crossed. But cross her I did, and we all paid the price.

I have left the shitshow of a drinks party, in fact have left Hope Close altogether. I've come out in my allegedly ultra-safe car and I'm not sure where I'm driving to, but it doesn't matter. It seems there's nowhere in the world for me to go that's safe, anyway. Any hope I have of redemption is gone. Any hope of family is gone. Obliterated. She will never accept me now and, after her performance tonight, nor would I want her to.

It is nine o'clock on the night before Christmas and I was dreading this time of year as it was, but I wasn't expecting it to be this bad. If I was tense, suspicious, on edge before, I'm a million times worse now. I simply cannot believe it. *My cover has been blown.* It's only a matter of time before the media descends and the entire world will know who I am. Armageddon beckons.

I'm too fuzzy-headed to think straight, so I let my car lead me, and before I know it we're on the A3 heading into London, and it seems that I have to go back there, at last. Back to the scene of my crime. Who knows what I will do when I get there? I think I have an idea.

And now tears are running down my face and the whole world feels busted, utterly futile. I am not worthy of it. It is not worthy of me. In a few hours it will be Christmas Day, and it's just a day, another stupid, good-for-nothing day, eighty-six thousand four hundred lousy seconds that will tick right on by, just like they did yesterday and will do so tomorrow and tomorrow and tomorrow, without Bobby in it, whether I'm in it, or not . . .

As the car eats up the miles, my brain tries to eat up the metaphorical road I have travelled, and it seems clear that I still haven't remotely dealt with it – despite jail, despite Spain, despite twice-weekly therapy sessions, even despite having told the full, dismal story to a magnificent black stallion called Jorge. The truth is, I can't forgive myself, can't stop blaming myself, whether I'm about to be outed to the world or not. Is Sian in any way culpable, too? I've tried to tell myself that she is, but now I'm not so sure. After all, mine was the original sin.

As I reach the outskirts of London and start my journey through the south-west of the city, towards my inevitable, inexorable destination, all I can try to do is analyse what happened, start back at the very beginning, all over again. I even think about calling Sian, but that would be madness. I don't know where she is. I don't have her number. We hate each other. My only other relative left in the world is lost to me. And so instead, the river is beckoning. The truth is beckoning. I'm coming. It's coming. Here goes.

Chapter 68

NICOLE

It was done. She'd done it. She'd finally told Ted. OK, it hadn't been at the right time, or in remotely the right way, but at least he knew at last. It hadn't helped that she'd been so drunk, of course, or that she'd blurted it out immediately after all the other quite incredible drama that had unfolded at her ill-fated drinks party, but perhaps she'd simply wanted some attention herself, for once. She'd been revving up to confess to Ted anyway, had been waiting for the opportunity, and it had felt so cathartic, she was glad the truth was out now. Ted had been marvellous under the circumstances, once he'd stopped ranting and raving, and she'd been taken aback by his attitude. It was fortunate that she'd managed to refrain from making any other confessions about her more recent behaviour, and maybe Layla was right that there were some things she should definitely keep to herself. Tasha had still stormed out, though, yelling she'd had no idea that she had Jono fucking Grey as a neighbour, as well as a secret fucking half-brother. That was more than enough drama for one night, she'd yelled, and she'd better have some good fucking presents waiting for her in the morning. Nicole felt exhausted just thinking about it. It didn't help that her head felt in danger of detonating.

'Great party,' Ted said as he came in the room with a glass of water and some paracetamol.

Nicole groaned.

'I am such an idiot. No one's ever going to talk to me again . . .' She paused, sat up, looked at her husband as if he were an alien species. 'Anyway, why are you being so nice to me?'

'What d'you mean?'

'Bringing me headache pills.'

'I think you need to be looked after.'

'Really?'

'Really.' Ted sat on the bed, put his brawny hand on her leg through the covers.

'Have you spoken to the kids again?' Nicole asked.

'Yes, they're OK. A bit shocked. I told them I was sorry I flew off the handle.'

'Well, it was hardly surprising . . . and it's all my fault anyway.' Nicole groaned again, clasped her hands to her head. 'I'm sorry I'm such a pisshead drama queen.'

Ted laughed. 'Well, it made for an entertaining evening. Shame about the neighbours. Bunch of fuckers, the lot of them.'

'And you don't mind what I told you?'

'How can I mind?' Ted said. 'It was before I ever knew you. And besides, it's bloody Christmas Day in an hour, so you timed it well.' He grinned, then looked serious. 'What made you tell me now?'

'I don't know. I just felt so lonely after the kids had left, and then poor Stanley died, and it made me think, what if *he* died – my son I mean – and I'd never even known him. Or maybe he's already dead. I've got no idea.'

'Well,' Ted said. 'You don't need to worry about that now.' He kissed her, a proper kiss, for the first time in as long as she could remember. 'Maybe I need to give you a bit more attention, too.'

'Good grief, what's got into you?' Nicole laughed.

'Well,' Ted said. 'If it's true I've got an ex-pop star as a neighbour, I need to up my game.'

Nicole blushed. Ted was getting a little too close to the truth for her liking.

'And besides,' he said, reverting to form, but surely not even realising. 'You can't think about any of that now. We need to get some kip. We've got kids to make it up to in the morning, presents to unwrap – and you've got Christmas dinner to cook.'

Chapter 69

The road is unfamiliar to me, but I know that if I keep following the signs I will get there, eventually. It's inevitable. Maybe I'll stop at an off-licence en route. Sobriety sucks anyway – and it doesn't look like I'll be driving back, so I won't need to worry about being over the limit. As I cover the miles, past the twinkly Christmas lights that seem to be everywhere these days, my mind is still twist-tailing, trying to work it out. Soon enough, as I knew I would, I start seeing signs for the river, and eventually I cross one of the bridges, drive along the north bank. I know the exact spot I'm looking for.

I abandon the car a few hundred yards from Tower Bridge, and as I walk along the riverbank towards it, it's lit up and breathtaking, a vibrant cobalt blue – the colour the sky was that day. I stare up at the bridge, down into the river's dark swirling waters, and I imagine the water must be so cold, and it's Christmas, and where do I go from here? What should I do for the best?

I'm nearer now, and the dark shadows of the Tower of London loom at me, make me wish I was locked in there, like the common killer I am, ready to have my head struck off. Maybe that would have been easier. To have the decision taken away from me. I find my memory drifting backwards and it feels as if I'm floating in some kind of pop confection, as if I'm not real, as if Sian's voice on the end of the phone isn't real, and our baby itself isn't real – as if it's all a mirage, and that soon I'll wake up and none of it will have happened. For so long I thought that that was what I would have preferred.

And yet now, years later, the problem is more philosophically complex than you might think – and you can say what you like about the rights and privileges of the incarcerated, but I learnt a lot in prison. It's a question of existentialism in its purest form. My dilemma is this: that without the road I have travelled, without alcohol, without Sian, I would never have had Bobby, and although he was here for only a fleeting moment in the whole history of time, did that make everyone's pain worthwhile? I don't know. I will never know. The sequential nature of life that leads you along the wrong paths and into hopeless dead ends is a torrid thing to debate. Would I prefer never to have taken that road? Did the seven short years of Bobby's life mean everything or nothing to me?

I reach the bridge, try to defeat the fuck-minded flashbacks. I claw at my face, pull it into the shape of *The Scream*. I know it's my fault, I know how it looks, but I honestly never saw it as kidnap. I saw myself as being pushed into it. I saw it as taking my son out for the day. That was how I saw it. But I was wrong, and it was an act of utter stupidity and inexcusable selfishness.

The bridge is colossal, and it takes me longer than you might think to walk to the middle of it, especially as my leg is hurting, like a memory. It is busy, even on Christmas Eve, but no one pays any attention to a lone man with dark hair and fashionable stubble walking along the pavement, gazing out at the city. I can see the Shard sticking up proudly, a big *fuck you* to its opposers, and I like its jagged unfinishedness. Its rawness. Its imperfection. It is me. I am it.

And now clouds are rolling, tears are rolling, the boat is rolling, planing, creating glorious butterfly rainbow spray. The world is so bright and full of colour, so pin-sharp clear and perfect and wonderful. Bobby is screaming with delight. *Don't stop, Daddy*, he says.

Go faster, Daddy. It was only an afternoon out on a speedboat with my mum, for Bobby's belated birthday. After endless wranglings Sian had told us that he could go. Mum and I went to pick him up. And then Sian changed her mind . . .

And so of course, afterwards, Sian said that I'd taken Bobby without her permission. And who was there to explain? I'd killed my own mother as well as my son. There was no one left but me, and who would believe my version of the truth? No one, that's who.

And thus there it was. It was unbelievable. I couldn't believe it. What I did was insane, wicked, unforgivable. I wiped out my family, albeit to the most picturesque backdrop, the tabloids' photos of the mangled speedboat framed exquisitely by the marvellous sight of Tower Bridge at sunset. The juxtaposition is dreadful.

What made everything worse, my guilt intolerable, was my own culpability. My ignorance. I knew about drink-driving, of course, but it honestly, truly, never occurred to me that driving that boat might be illegal. I was twenty-four, a complete idiot. It's no excuse, but Sian had stressed me out that day, and it was only a little pick-me-up. I hardly ever even did it any more. I'd taken enough, though, for the jury to decide that my senses had been impaired, that I hadn't been in control of the boat – and seeing as I'd ignored Bobby when he'd screamed at me at the last minute to stop, when he'd seen what I clearly hadn't, it seems they were right. I can still see my son's immeasurably perfect face, the look in his eyes turning from the utmost joy to the hugest terror, and then . . .

No. I can't go there. Not ever.

I wait for a break in the traffic and then I hop over the barrier, and although my once-busted leg is still stiff, I'm surprised it's not more difficult to do. I stand on the edge of the bridge and I am as alone as I've ever been. The water is oily, evil, eddying. Torrid. I feel Bobby beckoning. My eternally brave mother. I shut my eyes . . . I'm ready.

Chapter 70

LAYLA

As was her wont when she felt trapped in this wretched place, Layla stomped her way down to the very bottom of her garden, past the spot where she'd found her poor cat – and the memory merely confirmed to her that the past few months had been nothing short of crazy, and not remotely in a good way. When she reached the fence, she turned and looked back at the house – noticed how well-proportioned and handsome it was, remembered how much she hated it – and then she screwed up her eyes, took in a long gusty breath of air, and screamed. Charles and Henry weren't here anyway, and she didn't care whether Andy next door heard – in fact, maybe she even wanted him to. She was pretty certain he wasn't there, though, as she hadn't seen a single sign of him since he'd stormed out of Nicole's party a few nights earlier. His car wasn't there either, or at least wasn't visible through the crack in the gates where it was usually parked, and Layla had even considered asking Henry to send up his drone to check. There was something untoward about the whole situation, and Layla was worried about Andy, or whatever his name was. She'd looked up Jono Grey online, of course, had tried to spot the resemblance, work out whether Joan might somehow be right – but it was an extraordinary accusation, and how in hell would *Joan* know, anyway? The whole thing was bewildering, not helped by the fact that Layla had her own crisis to deal with.

Layla put her hands over her face, tried to get her thoughts straight. The last few days had been truly torturous, and she was relieved that she'd booked herself and Henry on a flight to Deauville tomorrow. She was so desperate to get away from Hope Close, she'd even contemplated spending the night at one of the airport hotels, make out to Henry it was just a fun part of the trip to see Granny and Barney while Daddy went back to work. Henry had seemed to cope surprisingly well with everything, and maybe it was true that kids were resilient – or perhaps Layla was simply a better actress than she'd imagined she'd be in such circumstances. But it had been Christmas. Henry still believed in Santa Claus. What else could she have done? Throw Henry's daddy out on Christmas morning? Her son didn't deserve that – even if her husband did.

Layla slid her hands down her face and stared at the house as if it were a place where someone else lived, and she thought about how, soon enough, it might be. She took out her phone from her pocket, contemplated calling Nicole, to ask her to come over for a coffee . . . and then thought better of it. She wasn't ready to confide in anyone just yet, let alone someone as highly strung as Nicole.

Layla turned away from the house now and gazed across at the Surrey Hills, beguiling even in winter, as she tried again to make sense of events on the night before Christmas. She pictured Charles slinking into his office like a naughty schoolboy, yet with skin as grey as his hair, making him look almost dead. She'd been presiding over the computer as if it were her precious newborn and she was not to be messed with. He'd tried to deny it, of course, like the pathetic loser he was.

'Don't lie to me, Charles,' she'd said, in a manner that her husband had chosen not to argue with. In a way she'd been relieved when he'd proceeded to open up the emails between him and the unknown woman with whom he was having an affair. The exchanges had certainly been passionate, and some of the pictures had been unpleasantly racy, but somehow his reaction at the party had meant Layla had imagined far worse.

Layla shivered. She had no coat, even though it was five degrees at best. It was time to go in. She returned to the house, went upstairs, pulled out her suitcase from the top of the wardrobe, started to pack for her and Henry's trip to Normandy. He and Charles would be back from the cinema soon, and she wanted it all to be done before they got home. For there to be as little fuss for her son as possible.

As Layla went into Henry's room and pulled out an assortment of his clothes, she tried to work out where this had all started. Had it partly been her doing, wearing Charles down as she had, until he'd finally agreed to have another child? Looking at it dispassionately, without the presence of either man or boy to cloud her judgement, it was clear now that her husband had preferred it when it had been just the two of them. Layla and Charlie. Charlie and Layla. It had had such a ring to it, he'd said. And besides, forty-five had been quite old for him to become a father again, and he'd only ever done it for her. She'd been grateful, at first.

Layla continued filling up the suitcase, still thinking back to those early days as a newly formed trio. As she remembered her fevered adoration of her baby son, Charles's gentle passivity, her mind was flitting between scenarios, trying to understand, desperate to get to the truth . . .

At last Layla knew she could deny it no longer. It seemed boarding school hadn't only been about tradition after all. Perhaps Charles had never really wanted the burden of a third child, at all. Maybe he just didn't care enough, about either of them. The realisation was bad enough for her, but when she thought about their son it was unbearable.

Layla knew then what she had to do. Charles had cheated on her. He'd been a reluctant co-parent at best. She would tell him she wanted a divorce. Then she'd enrol Henry in a local day school, set about finding some part-time work – and they could all move on with their lives from there. It was time she looked after her son's best interests at last. There was no way he was going back to boarding school. She didn't care what Charles had to say about it. It was non-negotiable.

Chapter 71

It's so strange, I think, as I lie here in the private hospital room my lawyer has arranged for me just off Harley Street, an ancient episode of *Only Fools and Horses* chattering away quite comfortingly in the background, how, if you try hard enough, you can trace almost everything back to the original source. And in my case, that is most definitely true: how my life turned out is all, every last bit of it, because of Sian. I find myself almost fixated on the reliving of my story, perhaps hoping that the ending will be different this time, although of course it can't be. Only how I feel about it can change. The facts themselves are irrefutable.

I still don't know if I'm lucky or unlucky, that I came to my senses that night. I'd been in a world of my own – freezing, terrified, reliving the moment, unsure whether I could jump after all, the water dancing blackly below me, like a spell – when at last I decided that that wasn't the answer. I sobbed as I hauled myself back over the barrier, shame washing over me that I'd killed my family, and yet was too much of a coward to kill myself. Too much of a coward to out myself to the only relative I have left.

One of the nurses comes in now, sits down on the bed and holds my hand. I let her. It feels nice. She has done this several times already. She is from Trinidad and her name is Grace and she is comfortingly, reassuringly overweight, and her eyes are sparkly and as kind as any I have seen.

'How are you doing, Andy?' she says.

'OK,' I answer.

'What's a handsome boy like you doing trying to jump off a bridge?'

I stare at her, beseechingly. I'm mortified that the only person I had to call on to help me was someone I pay for the privilege, and he must have told them the details of my plight, and he's always been a bloody idiot. But it doesn't matter. I like Grace. She's kind. In fact, I think she might even be the one. I think it might be time. I can't do this any longer. I stare into her warm liquid eyes and I want to fall into them, be smothered in motherly love.

Time is crawling, rushing, ambushing, dawdling, as the memories move in now, unfettered at last. I don't want to think about what I did but I have to get the story straight in my own head, if I'm going to be able to tell her. I need to make sure I keep to the facts . . .

I'm not making excuses, but after I ditched her, Sian did my head in, and it kept me on edge and it's a lot to deal with when you're barely seventeen years old and you have endless craziness in your life, and your ex-best friend is blackmailing you, threatening to tell on you, unless you give her some of the money that she believes is her God-given right to take from you. It was exhausting. I remember Sian telling me, spitting with bile over our gorgeous newborn's downy-haired head, that I would have been *nothing* if it hadn't been for her. It's scary how much she changed, what rejection and unrequited love and unplanned teenage pregnancy did to her mind. I grew to hate her in return, dreaded every single contact with her. It was an impossible situation, but I tried to make it possible. In fact, it's how I first found my morally bankrupt hired hand of a lawyer, through whom I arranged to pay Sian, just so I could see my son. It sounds so crass and vulgar and immoral, and I wish with all my heart I hadn't tried to keep Bobby a secret, and it's yet another facet of my shame. Finally, devastatingly, Sian put her foot down, told me that I'd no longer be able to see him, no matter how much I paid her. He was seven . . .

I gaze hopelessly at Grace, squeeze her warm velvety hand. Where to start? With the bald truth, I reckon.

'My name's not Andy,' I say. 'My real name's Jono Grey. I used to be a pop star and I killed my family. You can look me up.'

I don't feel relieved for having said it. I just feel dead. As though the streaming waters of the Thames got me after all.

Grace doesn't react. She just smiles that sweet, compassionate smile. And then I remember that I'm in another psychiatric facility, albeit a posh one, and she doesn't believe me – and *of course* she wouldn't believe something like that. She's probably never even heard of Easy Come. I sigh, turn to the wall, and shut my eyes.

Chapter 72

NICOLE

The courtroom was a paragon of original seventies style, proof if any was needed that the public purse was severely challenged. There were four long wide tables of varnished orange wood, with drab green carpets and pull-down seats in a vaguely clashing minty colour. Along the length of the wall perpendicular to these tables was a mammoth, ugly shelving unit, also orange, mostly bare – although occasionally populated with tired-looking leather-bound books, presumably of a legal nature. A flat-screen TV had, at some unknown stage in the courtroom's history, been attached to the wall in an apparently random position, black shiny wires trailing from it, so high up that people would have to crane their necks to view it. The public gallery looked across at these shelves, down on those tables, and dotted amongst the latter were mainly men, somewhere between their forties and sixties, at varying stages of male-pattern baldness, greyness, or both. All wore dark suits and ties. All looked glum. All were hiding behind great swathes of lever arch files, to occasionally pop to their feet to say something allegedly important. The general air was one of extreme fatigue, especially as the counsel for the defence was boring everyone rigid. Only the judge maintained the utmost professionalism, seated as she was up high like an angel, her clerk and recorder beneath her, looking out to the grey men. The only bit of colour to be seen in the courtroom was in the flushed cheeks of Lionel, sitting next to his ghastly wife with all the confidence of a kicked puppy. *My God, no wonder rumour has it he drowns squirrels for fun*, Nicole thought now, *if he has to be married to her*.

'Can I now ask you,' droned counsel, 'to go to the bundle labelled number two, tab sixty-one, page two hundred and twenty-eight.'

Despite the seemingly ludicrous nature of the proceedings, Nicole felt as agitated as she'd ever felt. She found it hard to believe that all these people were here, in court, at vast expense, all because of an argument over where a stupid van should be parked. It seemed extraordinary that relations between two next-door neighbours had come to this, but no matter how many times she'd begged Ted to drop the case, it was as if he'd become a man possessed, was determined to take down Joan Taylor if it killed him. It seemed Joan's bizarre gatecrashing of their drinks party had been the final proverbial straw, and Ted still maintained that Joan was lucky he hadn't knocked her bloody head off.

Right now, Ted was in the dock, looking uncomfortable at best, shifty if Nicole were being ungenerous. Even she didn't know the truth about what had happened. She so wanted to believe in her husband, but she was trying to determine his trustworthiness from his posture, the way he was holding himself, the tic in his cheek. It was hard to tell. It felt odd to see him in a suit, seeing as it wasn't a funeral or a wedding. When he wasn't in his work clothes, Ted was a pink-Ralph-Lauren-polo-shirt kind of a man.

'And so, Mr Arnold, is it true that Mrs Taylor asked you to move your van on several occasions?'

'Yes, she did.'

'And, pray may I ask, what was your answer?'

'At first I tried to politely explain that I was entitled to park wherever I wanted on my own property.'

'Ahh, *at first*,' said counsel. 'And then after that, you became very aggressive towards Mrs Taylor, didn't you?'

'No, I didn't become aggressive. It's just that she went on about it so much that in the end I told her I could park wherever I wanted, and that she should mind her own business.'

'That's rather discourteous, wouldn't you say?'

'Well, not really. There's only so many times you can be polite about the same issue when it's absolutely none of somebody else's business.'

'Ah, exactly,' said counsel, and his face assumed an even more superior expression than before. 'And so at that point, you decided that there was no need to be polite at all. Instead you simply decided to push an innocent old lady to the ground, didn't you?'

'No. *She* attacked *me* first, with a pair of secateurs.' Ted pointed to his face – somewhat proudly in Nicole's opinion, especially considering how faded the mark was. 'I still have the scar.'

'Yes, well, who attacked who first is open to debate, and indeed forms the crux of this case.' The barrister stopped, touched his nose, drew out the dramatic pause. Nicole wondered where the punch would come next. Upper-body jab or below the belt. It was impossible to tell.

'There's been a history of intimidation between you and Mr and Mrs Taylor, hasn't there?' the barrister said.

'No.'

'Well, pray, let me put it another way then. Would you say that you have taken great delight in parking your van exactly where Mrs Taylor has asked you not to, rather than complying with her wishes at no great inconvenience to yourself?'

Ted looked confused at this point, as if he wasn't sure what the barrister was getting at. He wasn't that good with big words. Nicole could see the flush in his fleshy neck moving up past his shirt collar, invading the lower part of his face. He seemed as though he was very, very close to losing it. *Keep it together, Teddy*, Nicole thought. *This could ruin us.*

'I don't think parking *my* van in *my* driveway constitutes intimidation. Perhaps if I were to drive it straight at Mrs Taylor, that would do it.'

Nicole started, almost wanted to laugh. She audibly gulped. 'Jesus,' she said, under her breath.

The barrister visibly puffed out his cheeks, looked as if he were ready to pounce.

'Did you just say that you would be prepared to drive your vehicle at Mrs Taylor, Mr Arnold?'

'No, that's not what I said at all. It was a joke, and a bad one at that. I retract it.'

'Hmm,' said the barrister. 'And would you say that this kind of ill-judged "joke", as you call it, is what has got you into this trouble in the first place? That it is symptomatic of your conduct when attempting to resolve such disputes?'

Nicole watched as Ted looked fully befuddled now, his brain pedalling, trying to work out the correct response to the question. Was it yes or no? Nicole didn't have a clue either.

'No,' he said. The truculence in his tone was impossible to miss.

'Well, how do you explain the arguments you've had about the tree in Mrs Taylor's garden?'

Ted did a double-take at that, raised his voice a little.

'What tree?'

'The one in Mr and Mrs Taylor's rear garden that apparently blocks your view.'

'We haven't had any arguments,' Ted said. 'When we first moved in, we invited Ted and Joan in for a drink, to be neighbourly.

And then we asked them to consider cutting down the tree. They said no, and that was it as far as I was concerned.'

'Ahh, but that wasn't it, was it, Mr Arnold? You've been very bitter about that tree ever since you moved into Hope Close, haven't you?'

'No.'

'Well,' said the barrister, clearly in his element now, going in for the kill. 'How is it, then, that we have irrefutable evidence that the tree has been poisoned?'

Chapter 73

It is a clear bright morning in mid-January. The frost is melting in my back garden, so gradually that I try to spot it in real time, but I can't. And yet before I know it my vista is green again, silver sucked away by sun, and it vaguely depresses me, that my fairy landscape has gone, and I don't know what's next for anyone. Was it so crazy of me to have hoped for redemption? Am I truly insane?

I have been back in Hope Close for two days now, and I have no idea where I go from here. I'm alive still, though, and I think I might be glad of it. I went straight from the private hospital back to the cottage-asylum, and I told them the truth this time, and it helped. In a way I'm glad that one of my secrets is out at last. There's no point hiding it any more. I am the boy who was persuaded to audition for a stupid reality TV show, and who ended up in the biggest boy band since Take That. I went along purely for a laugh. Nothing more than that. Mistake Number One.

I never really questioned why Sian and I had grown so close. If I'd ever bothered to think about it, I might have assumed it was because we both had messed-up home lives. After all, my father had beaten the shit out of my mother. Sian's mother had died of a drug overdose. It was one hell of a bond. But even so, I honestly thought we were nothing more than best mates. I never had a clue that she loved me.

Sian had entered us in *The X Factor* as a double act, and we were ecstatic when we got through the first round – so much so that we went back to Sian's house that night and raided her dad's gin. Sleeping with her wasn't planned, either. Immediately afterwards I said it probably wasn't a good idea for that to happen again, that I didn't want to spoil our friendship, and she agreed – in fact, jumped down my throat to agree with me. Mistake Number Two.

It seemed the show's producers liked us. A few days later they sent a film crew into school to document our backstory, show the viewers what good mates we were – how we sat next to each other in class, ties askew, how we hung out in the lunchroom. But then, when we were duly called back for the televised auditions, they told us in front of a live studio audience and millions of TV viewers that Sian held me back, and that I should dump her – and so I did, and with all the callousness you might expect of an overwhelmed sixteen-year-old. Mistake Number Three.

Enough. I try to switch my brain from past misdemeanours back to my current situation, here in Hope Close. I attempt to work out if my latest shrink is right, that maybe the answer truly does lie here. Who knows? I'm still so confused by my neighbours. Nicole's drinks party really was something else in terms of drama, and I have no idea where it has left me. I still can't decide whether it was a mistake to go along that night, or whether it was ultimately for the best. It outed me, and yet it didn't out me. Yes, Joan got one part of the story straight, but she completely missed the other. When she rocked up like a devil-woman I thought she'd somehow rumbled my *other* identity. I still don't know what to do about that.

And yet Joan's not the only woman round here to scare the hell out of me. Nicole freaks me out, too. When I saw her profile pop up on Tinder, I was so shocked I didn't know what to think. I even thought at times that she was coming on to me, which was a truly alarming thought, and almost certainly why I stopped walking poor old Stanley. But it's clear that Nicole is a tough nut, all sharp edges and tight orifices, fillers and fake tan . . . and desperate, so desperate. The thought of her disgusts me suddenly. I hope she sorts things out with her husband, for everyone's sake.

And lastly there's Layla. Ahh, Layla. I don't know what it is about her. There's definitely something, though. She's special. Or maybe it's just that she's Henry's mother, and he is a truly awesome kid. Perhaps that's what it is.

The buzzer sounds and it rouses me. I want to ignore it but also I don't. *It might be her.* As I move towards the intercom I try to remind myself that it won't be. She hates me, thinks all kinds of terrible things about me. And yet I make an instant, definitive decision that, even if she won't come to me, I will go out into Hope Close, knock at her house and tell her. Today. *Now.* I don't even care what the repercussions might be. I need to tell the whole, unedited truth at last. It's time.

Chapter 74

LAYLA

Well, what the hell, Layla thought, as she walked back to her own house. She'd only gone over to check on Andy – or Jono, as she should think of him now – because she'd been concerned about him. She hadn't expected to have it confirmed that he genuinely wasn't some run-of-the-mill loner weirdo – that he really was one of the most infamous ex-pop stars of the past two decades. And yet, extraordinarily, that wasn't even the half of it.

Of course, Layla had already been aware of the main thrust of Jono Grey's narrative. You would have had to have lived under a rock not to be. The headlines from over a decade earlier had been truly sensational, had kept the tabloids going for months. It was a pretty compelling story, although Layla hadn't followed it in much detail at the time. She'd found it too sad, the fall from grace too far, the consequences too tragic for all concerned.

As Layla let herself in through her front door, the house felt emptier than ever, but she liked it. Charles had started moving some of his things out now, and she was glad. It seemed odd how, even if you didn't know you were living a lie, somehow it trans-mutes itself into your very psyche, expresses itself through your pores and cells. And so now that Layla knew the truth, it was a relief to her. The reasons for her unhappiness had been twofold and concrete – a cheating husband and an absent son – and not a general malaise after all.

Layla looked at her watch. She only had an hour or so until she had to leave to pick up Henry from school, and she liked that, too. The deadlines. The meaningfulness of her life again. She had a little boy to look after, give tea to, put in the bath, get to bed . . . She needed to get her act together, especially if she was going to start working again sometime soon.

Layla went upstairs, found her laptop by the side of her bed, sat down and began googling. Before long she was able to start filling in the gaps, make sense of the story Jono had just told her – and it was worse than she'd even realised, made her feel sorry for him all over again. After a while she felt herself being drawn to the window, and soon enough she saw Jono appear from behind his gates, as he'd said he would do, and make his way across the street to confront his last living relative. *Good luck with that*, Layla thought. And then she smiled, turned away from the window and left him to it.

Chapter 75

I stand here, as terrified as I once was alongside my childhood best friend on a brightly lit stage, as I prepare to press the button that will cause my gates to open. I pray that when I go over there it will be her, and not the husband, who answers the door. I have no idea what I will say, but Layla has persuaded me into it, and she's right – there's nothing else left to lose. That girl has a heart of gold, and she's far too good for her cheat of a husband, but at least she knows it now.

As the gates commence their steady opening arc, I wonder how it has come to this, how I can be living here, in this very close – and how I can possibly hope to explain it to her. All kinds of thoughts rush through my mind, all over again, and I feel my resolve weaken . . . but the one thing I've learnt over the past few weeks is to confront the very scariest things, and so that's what I intend to do.

When she answers, she's openly unfriendly, but it's hardly surprising. The last time we saw each other was at a truly anarchic drinks party.

I hold out my hand, as if we've never met before. She doesn't take it.

'Yes?' she says. Hostility radiates off her, makes me want to shrink away into the cold afternoon air. I think of Layla pushing me on, try to remind myself that the only way through life is forward.

This is just another task to get through, cut a path through, as we all have to, myself and the billions of other people on this godforsaken planet, all of us, every last one of us, at the vanguard of very existence. Every second that ticks by brings an unknown event, is a God-given miracle. I must remember that.

'Hello,' I say. I think of my grandmother, who I don't remember, of course, but who wrote such lovely letters to me – and who died before I made it out of prison. I think of my mother. And finally I think of Bobby. Always Bobby. My voice is croaky, sticks in my very craw, but I persevere.

'You were right that my real name's not Andy Meyer,' I say. 'It used to be Jonathan Adams, before I became Jono Grey . . . and, well, anyway, the thing is . . .' I swallow hard, take a deep unwieldy breath. 'I'm pretty sure I used to call you Auntie Joan.'

Chapter 76

NICOLE

Things had been very quiet at Layla's house lately, and Nicole wasn't at all sure what was going on between her and her husband. She still had no idea what their argument over the computer had been about, but it was clear that it wouldn't have been pretty. And yet at least Henry seemed perfectly jolly whenever Nicole saw Layla walking him to the village school, and hopefully that was a good sign.

Andy hadn't been seen for ages, either, having apparently been holed up alone for the whole of the festive period, or else quite possibly not at home at all. Nicole had been desperate to find out what Joan had been going on about, where she'd got her extraordinary theory about Jono Grey from, but she hadn't wanted to ask, risk stirring things up again – especially as Joan most definitely seemed to have the upper hand these days. But, Nicole thought, one good thing was that Ted was being polite to the Taylors now, meaning the bickering had stopped at last.

And so now it was mid-January, and the decorations were long down, and the weather was dreary, and the air was full of freezing fog. Nicole was grateful that Tasha at least was still here, even though she'd be going back up to London tomorrow – and soon the house would be empty and silent again . . .

And yet Nicole felt OK. More than OK, in fact. She and Tasha were sitting in the kitchen, on the Internet, scanning through pictures, trying to decide who to go for. Nicole might have abandoned one baby, but she was determined to give this new one a home, a brand-new start in life.

'What d'you think of this one?' Nicole said now.

'Legs too short,' Tasha said.

'Or that one then?'

'Ears too big.'

'Oh, wow, look at him.'

'He's black,' Tasha said. 'No good for Instagram.'

'Bloody hell, Tasha, how did I raise someone so superficial? All you care about is how they look.'

'Well, I wonder,' Tasha said, and winked at her mother.

Nicole smiled to herself, as happy as she'd felt in a long time. She was so pleased that Ted had agreed to it, and it was amazing how onside he seemed these days. She was relieved now that she'd taken Layla's advice, and had decided not to share every last secret with him. And anyway, she told herself, she'd only been on a few Tinder hook-ups, and they'd been dispiriting at best, humiliating at worst, definitely not worth ruining her marriage over – especially now that she and Ted seemed to be finally getting things back on track, including in the bedroom, thank God. Sometimes Nicole wondered whether her husband had always known that she'd been holding something back. Perhaps she should have told him the truth years ago – especially as he'd said he'd support her if she ever wanted to track her son down.

Nicole's thoughts were running away with her, distracting her from her scrolling, and so she stopped both for a moment, gazed out of the window blankly, found herself imagining her boy's face, what he might look like now . . .

When at last Nicole turned back to her screen there he was, staring straight out at her, and she knew he was the one immediately, even if he was nothing like the brief she'd agreed with her husband. He had a black and white face and a huge grinning jaw, and he was from Romania and he was called Chipsy. He'd been found on the streets of Bucharest and there was even a video of him, and he had the kindest eyes, the most knowing face, the waggiest tail. Nicole smiled to herself. Strange name, but in all other respects he was gorgeous. Perfect, in fact. She was determined to give this rag-tag furry orphan a good home. All she had to do now was persuade Ted.

Chapter 77

Wow. There's all kinds of stuff going on in Hope Close, most of which I never thought I would care about. But I do, and that, as much as anything, is a breakthrough.

First to report on is Layla, and who would have foreseen that she would kick her husband into touch like that? I'm impressed at her fearlessness, her whip-snap decision-making, her unwillingness to compromise – but there again, the guy is clearly a prick. Three wives, and he couldn't manage to stay loyal to a single one of them. Not even someone like Layla. I don't know what his problem is.

Another development is that I've installed a home gym – for the sake of my mental well-being and at the suggestion of my therapist – and right now I'm on my running machine, mid-jog-to-nowhere, looking out at nature, searching for some kind of clue as to where I go from here . . . and one of the best things about this place is that the view from my monumental windows is always different. Today the clouds are rolling low, full of threat, and the light is almost violet, as if something dramatic is about to happen. I'm ready. Bring it on, in fact. The sky is so beautiful, so chameleon, someone should film it – little Henry perhaps, with his too-cute dimples and his accident-prone drone. I'm so glad Layla's seen sense and pulled him out of boarding school, released him from his prison, too. I admire her new-found ability to stand up for what she believes in. There's nothing quite like being kicked to the ground to make you get up again. It only makes me like her more.

The other Hope Close-related surprise of significance is that Ted's court case collapsed – in quite spectacular fashion, by all accounts. I only found this out because Nicole brought her new Romanian rescue dog round to meet me, and she told me so. Chipsy is a funny-looking thing, half-wolf, half-lamb, scruffily, randomly monochrome, and he has clearly had one hell of a life, and he reminds me of me, and I adore him already. But Nicole seemed so confused about what had gone on in court I still have no idea what actually happened, and that's fine by me. I don't need to know the details. The one thing I am pretty sure of, though, is who killed Layla's cat, but Nicole begged me not to tell Layla, and so I won't. Funnily enough, despite Nicole's erstwhile aversion to the truth, I do believe that Ted never told his wife that he was slowly poisoning the Taylors' tree (and as I wonder precisely how Joan's lawyers found out, I grudgingly acknowledge that my solicitor is still ruthlessly, silently effective).

Anyway, the upshot is that Joan, or Auntie Joan as I think of her now, got off on all charges, and her knee is almost completely better, and she is free to return to her gardening and her knitting and her shamefully low-brow TV habits. And who really knows who attacked who first, seeing as Nicole finally came clean and admitted she hadn't actually seen what happened. Joan swears Ted started it. Ted swears Joan did. And they each believe their own truth, and that's just the way the world works, because otherwise there wouldn't be wars, would there? They're not possible unless both sides are convinced that they're somehow the honourable ones. No one thinks *they're* the wanker, after all. But Ted apologised to Joan, and now Ted keeps his van tucked around the corner, in penance for what he did to her tree, and Joan agreed to leave it at that, saying that she was done with fighting. And so for now peace reigns in Hope Close. Even Layla and Nicole seem to be friends again.

Lastly, of course, there's my situation. Moving to Hope Close was a strange choice. A romanticised choice. Totally bonkers, in fact. But where else was I going to go? Maybe I could have stayed in Spain, but I had such an urge to come here, to where I still had roots, to the place I'd visited when I was tiny, apparently – even though I can't remember any of it, of course. Anne got in touch with me after my conviction, saying that she'd recognised Cathy – my dead mother, Peter's ex-wife, her erstwhile daughter-in-law – in the wall-to-wall coverage of my speedboat accident, and she'd sounded so lovely in her letters, and it was yet another blow when she died before I made it out of prison. Maybe that was why encountering her sister was such an unpleasant surprise in comparison. My great-aunt Joan is nothing like I had imagined – but, to be fair, I guess life has a way of taking it out of you. And yet I can see now why my grandmother never told her sister who Peter's son had turned out to be. Joan would have gone mad with vitriol. It seems it is hard for her to forgive.

But anyway, there we have it. Joan's my only living relative in the world now, and it's beyond absurd that she was the one who worked out who I was, and yet she had no idea who I *really* was. Against all the odds, despite all my planning, my impeccably disguised appearance, she was the one person who sussed that Andy Meyer, gate-loving, people-hating, lone-wolf tech developer, was in reality Jono Grey, one-fifth of the now-defunct, always dreadful, hugely successful boy band Easy Come – and who would ever have guessed that Joan was an *X Factor* aficionado? An unfortunate consequence of Joan's impressive light-entertainment knowledge was that for some time she'd suspected me – had been convinced that there was a convicted child kidnapper and killer living in their midst. No wonder she seemed so nervous when she turned up at my gates and tried to give me some plants that time. But now I realise they were surely an excuse, a decoy, a chance to study me up close, confirm my identity, get things straight in her beady little mind.

My phone pings and it is Henry. He wants me to come over and play PlayStation, and I send him a smiley face response, along with the words, *Have you asked your mum?* and I can't believe how happy such a simple exchange can make me.

And yet before I go over to Layla's, I need to finish this latest ploughing through of my thoughts, this most recent attempt to join up the twists and turns of events in Hope Close. The most perverse (albeit somewhat hard to get one's head around) thing about the entire scenario is that, despite Joan's admirably astute investigative powers, she found out the real truth about me *from* me – the fact that I was Peter's son, Anne's grandson, and that I'd once been called Jonathan Adams. And then Joan told me in return that I'd actually *been* to Hope Close once before, when I was just a toddler, and maybe it's fanciful of me, but perhaps that was why it felt so familiar here, as if I had somehow connected with the great expanse of green beyond Joan's garden that when you're tiny feels like it stretches to the end of the world. Joan even found a photograph of me and my father, with the very tree that Ted was slowly killing in the background – and it had been newly planted, a mere twig back then. Joan has treasured that album for years, even after Peter was exposed as a nasty-tempered wife-beater. She cried when she showed me.

And so, there's the truth. Joan was the reason I came to Hope Close. Blood is thicker than water, after all. And although I'm not sure she and I will ever be as close as I once had hoped, we're close enough.

I get off my treadmill and put on my jacket. As I open the front door, click the remote to open my oh-so-hated gates, make my way across my front garden towards the ever-widening gap, I realise I'm grateful to Joan now. Her roundabout discovery of me has been a blessing. She has given me the strength to admit who I am, and even though I moved here with the objective of one day revealing the truth, I'm not sure I ever would have had the courage to actually do it, without being rumbled. And the amazing thing is that, now Joan knows who I am and what I've done, she doesn't hate me any more. She loves me, in fact. And even though Nicole and Layla know now too, they don't hate me either, and maybe I have a chance, a real chance, to one day make amends. I don't know quite how, but I have to be patient, wait for the universe to tell me. And it appears that no one else knows my real identity yet, seeing as the media haven't come calling, and that is a true miracle for which I am grateful.

I pass through my gates and step out on to the road, and the trees are coming out in teeny tiny bumps as though they have a hint of the fever, but I know it's simply spring coming, making its presence felt, and I'm so glad that I'm still here in Hope Close to see it. The air smells fresh, and full of rain and renewal, and although I know there is no going back, and that loss is loss is loss, there's also the future, always the future . . . And of course there's love and forgiveness too – and it seems to me that, in the very grandest scheme of things, that's all that really counts, anyway.

ACKNOWLEDGMENTS

I have so many people to thank for this novel that I'm not going to attempt to name them all. I'd like to start with my brilliant publisher, Laura Deacon, and my amazing editors, Emily Ruston, Gill Harvey and Becca Allen, as well as Sammia Hamer, Hannah Hupfer, Bekah Graham Pickering and everyone else at Lake Union who has been so supportive and has helped make this book possible. I'd also like to thank my former agent (who is now a publisher!) Jon Elek for his generosity and spirit, Nicole Johnschwager for reading a very early draft on a train to Amsterdam and convincing a disillusioned me to finish it, Julia East for lending her beautiful rescue dog to grace these pages, Monique and Pieter Totte for giving me the space to write in the most glorious Ibizan surroundings, and my dad for living in a Surrey cul-de-sac not too dissimilar to Hope Close. (Maybe one of these days he might even read one of my books!) The rest of my family, my friends and my loyal readers have given me their usual support, love and unvarnished feedback, and of course I have my husband and son to thank too. Just because. Life is not always easy, but hopefully this book is a triumph of good over evil, and for that I am grateful. X

ABOUT THE AUTHOR

Photo copyright © Layla Hegarty

Tina Seskis is the author of five novels, including the internationally bestselling *One Step Too Far*, which has been translated into eighteen languages. Before starting to write novels, Tina worked in marketing and advertising, with varying degrees of success. She lives in North London with her husband and son.